Reginald Hill writing as
PATRICK RUELL

Dream of Darkness

I had a dream which was not all a dream

Byron: *Darkness*

> *But there were dreams to sell,*
> *   Ill didst thou buy;*
> *Life is a dream, they tell,*
> *   Waking, to die.*
> *Dreaming a dream to prize,*
> *Is wishing ghosts to rise;*
> *And if I had the spell*
> *To call the buried, well,*
> *   Which one would I?*

T. L. Beddoes: *Dream-Pedlary*

GRAFTON BOOKS
A Division of the Collins Publishing Group

LONDON GLASGOW
TORONTO SYDNEY AUCKLAND

Grafton Books
A Division of the Collins Publishing Group
8 Grafton Street, London W1X 3LA

Published by Grafton Books 1990

First published in Great Britain by
Methuen London 1989

Copyright © Patrick Ruell 1989

ISBN 0-586-20701-5

Printed and bound in Great Britain by
Collins, Glasgow

Set in Times/Helvetica

DIPLOMAT'S WIFE MURDERED BY KONDIS

The body found by a burnt-out car in a gully some distance off the Entebbe road has been identified as belonging to Mrs Sarah Ellis, wife of Mr Nigel Ellis of the UK High Commission Office in Kampala.

Mrs Ellis had been missing for two days after failing to meet her sister-in-law at Entebbe airport, from Nairobi. A spokesman for the Public Safety Unit said it looked as if Mrs Ellis had been killed by a blow from a panga. The PSU are working on the theory that a gang of kondis hijacked the car with a view to robbery but abandoned it after Mrs Ellis resisted and received the fatal blow in the struggle.

Assistant Commissioner of Police, Ali Towelli, said that all branches of the Security Forces were treating this outrage with the utmost seriousness. Those who performed acts of violence against Uganda's citizens and friends should expect no mercy.

His Excellency, Al-Hajji Field Marshal Idi Amin Dada VC, DSO, MC, Life President of the Republic, was informed of the tragedy as he chaired a plenary session of the Organization of African Unity Summit Meeting at the International Conference Centre, and immediately sent a personal message of sympathy to Mr Nigel Ellis, his daughter (5), and his sister, Miss Celia Ellis.

1

Sairey Ellis lay awake, or dreamed she lay awake, all the rest of the night, but even the longed-for dawn was the pinched grey of her mother's face as she lay in her coffin.

Is she dead?
I don't know. I don't know what dead is.
What do you do?
I scream out. I struggle.
Is someone holding you?
Yes, it's Daddy. Daddy has me in his arms.
What does he do?
He hands me to Aunt Celia.
And what does Celia do?

In parts, the Dream was almost too vivid for recall, its scenes like flashes of bright light which burn themselves on the retina and leave shards of colour flickering between the eyes and reality.

She presses me to her breast. She carries me out of the room and down the corridor.
What do you see? What do you hear?
There's moonlight flooding through the window and a smell of rotting flowers and the sound of crickets and a dog barking and it's very warm.

It had come upon her with adolescence and almost destroyed her. Still, she never told her Dream, clutching it to her like an incestuous secret. But she had not been able to hide its effects. Her father had sent for Dr Varley, who had reassuringly diagnosed the cause of her sleeplessness as 'girlish nightmares, pretty commonplace actually, all hormonal, don't y' know? She'll grow out of them.' And it had seemed his breezy complacency was justified when, as she reached physical maturity, the Dream had faded to a nightmare memory.

Where does Celia take you?
Up the stairs towards my room. But I break free and she has to let me go and I run back downstairs and Daddy's standing there in the moonlight closing this long box and I won't let him and I look inside again and I can see . . . I can see . . . I can see . . . Mummy! Mummy! Mummy!

At eighteen, life seemed good. School was behind her, and ahead, if her A-levels were good enough, lay Cambridge. She spent the first half of the vacation in Spain with her stepmother. At 28 Masham Square, their London home, they had a relationship of Swiss neutrality. But in Spain, Fanny Ellis proved an ideal companion. With Fanny, you sailed into all the best places and were greeted as a valued friend by head waiters and Castilian grandees alike. Here, her sophisticated elegance was a bunk-up not a put-down, and her emotional withdrawal came across as tolerant non-interference. So, over five sybaritic weeks, Sairey's Cambridge reading list got only gently dented, but her skin took on a rich chestnut tan which made her re-shade her short spikey hair from shocking pink to olive green.

Nigel Ellis remained in London. Since his retirement he had started working on a book of memoirs and he claimed he was far too busy for a holiday. When Sairey suggested he could work just as well in Spain, he laughed and said, 'The only safe place for a star is under a spotlight.'

Being mysterious was a habit of his some people seemed to find endearing.

Towards the end of August, Sairey and Fanny returned to Number 28 to find Nigel in high spirits. His work was going well, it seemed, and Sairey's Cambridge place had just been confirmed by exam results even better than expected. That night they went out for an extravagant celebration dinner which left Sairey feeling more certainly a member of a united family than ever before. As she lay, wine-drowsy, in her bed, the future seemed secure, the present full of pleasures, and the past a melancholy memory, without power to harm. So, contented, she fell asleep.

Then the Dream came with such force that she brought its terror with her as she burst back into waking. The darkness seemed thick and cobwebby; she was stifling in it! Desperate for the world of air, she ran downstairs and out of the front door.

She'd no idea what time it was. Most windows were dark, but a big red <u>BMW</u> moved slowly towards her between the rows of parked vehicles. She shrank back into the doorway as its headlights caressed her bare limbs. Then it was passing and she was in the dark once more. But the bright, animal eyes of the man's face that filled the passenger window seemed to take in the whole of her body, as though darkness were no defence. The face looked familiar. Perhaps he was a neighbour. But the car crawled round the whole Square without stopping and finally disappeared towards the main road.

She didn't want to go back in, but she felt too vulnerable standing there on the step. She took a breath, plunged back into the hall, grabbed a light raincoat, then ran across the road and slipped through the railings of

Hill likes Timms.

the little park at the centre of the Square. Where its gravel walks crossed stood a dilapidated summer-house, and this was where she headed. Already she felt some of her tension easing. Despite its smallness, entering the park was like escaping to the country. Here, the air felt cooler, fresher, and the burr of the distant traffic was eased out by softer, closer sounds, rustlings and scutterings in the grass; wind in the trees; water tinkling over stones.

Except that there was no water course in the park.

She soon found her answer. The gardener's tap by the summer-house had been left running. She stooped to turn it off and noticed a balled-up handkerchief on the ground. She picked it up. It was sodden wet. And under the cool of the water there was something warm and sticky. She let the thing drop in distaste and saw in the dim starlight that her fingers were discoloured. Turning on the tap again, she let the water wash the brown stain away. And somewhere quite close, as if someone had been waiting for a covering noise, she heard a long soft exhalation of breath.

It said much for the horror of the Dream that her sense of refuge was still strong enough to counter this new fear.

'Who's there?' she said sharply.

At the side of the summer-house, the darkness stirred. The new fear took a sudden surge. She might have screamed but before she could, a voice from the road called her name.

'Sairey! Sairey! What the hell are you doing in there?'

It was her father. She doubted if she'd disturbed him, but Fanny, who seemed to need no sleep, had probably noticed her exit.

The sound of his voice gave her courage. Nigel Ellis brought to the active life what his wife brought to the

10

social – the promise of being perfectly equipped to meet any crisis.

'Who are you?' she demanded. 'What do you want?'

The darkness stirred again, a shadow advanced, began to form itself into a shape. I must be mad, thought Sairey. Daddy's well into his fifties, and he's sixty yards away. Even if I scream now, I can still have my throat cut open before he gets anywhere near.

But screaming seemed the best option. She opened her mouth, then let out only a gasp which had as much of pity as terror in it, as a face floated to the surface of the dark. It was a young man's face, fine-featured, with skin as golden as the image of an ikon, but it was a gilt in need of repair. Blood from his nose crusted his upper lip, while from the lower it still flowed fresh. His left eye was closed with a rainbow swelling, while his right cheek bore a contusion shaped like a star. As her sight adjusted she saw that he was dressed in muddied jeans and a tee shirt ripped in half to reveal more of that lovely golden skin whose colour had not been won from the Spanish sun.

'Sairey! Come out of there at once! Please.'

Her father was sounding angry. She glanced in his direction and could glimpse his lanky figure against the light spilling from the open front door of the house. She returned her gaze to the wounded boy and gasped as she saw his hand reach out towards her.

'Sairey,' he murmured, echoing her father. 'Sairey.'

The name seemed to amuse him, or perhaps it was a grimace of pain not an attempt at a smile which curled his lips. Whatever, Sairey didn't want him to touch her. She took a step back and almost stumbled. The raincoat slipped from her shoulders and she felt the night air, chill as frost against her skin. The young man let his reaching hand fall. But he still smiled, like an old friend at an unexpected meeting.

Sairey turned and ran towards her father.

Nigel Ellis was in his pyjamas but Fanny, sitting in the lounge with a cigarette in her hand and a book on her knee, was fully clothed. The little clock with the mechanical bluebirds which had belonged to Sairey's mother sang half past midnight. The Dream must have been waiting for her just around the corner of sleep.

Fanny smiled and said, 'Hello,' as if greeting them on their return from an evening stroll, then let her gaze drop to her book. Twenty-five years younger than her husband, she had that limpid, nerveless English beauty which can last for ever if life isn't allowed to trouble it.

'Darling, what happened? What were you doing out there?' asked her father again, his long narrow face filled with a concern now matched by his tone. Outside, he had sounded merely annoyed.

As Sairey debated her reply, Fanny said, 'Weren't you wearing a raincoat when you went on your little walkabout, dear?'

'Was I? I must have dropped it. I'll get it in the morning. Sorry, Daddy. I just couldn't sleep and wanted some air. Sorry if I disturbed anyone. Goodnight.'

She didn't offer to kiss either of them, but left immediately. In the hall she closed the door firmly behind her, then paused to listen. She had discovered this desperate need to know what people were saying about her at an early age. Eavesdropping made her feel guilty, and she rarely heard anything which made her feel good, but kicking the habit was proving very difficult.

'I hope to God it's not those nightmares again,' said her father uneasily. 'I hope she wasn't working too hard in Spain.'

'Only at getting a tan,' said Fanny lightly.

'You did keep an eye on her, Fan?'

'Yes, I did. We got on rather better there, as a matter of fact. But if you wanted full-scale parental supervision, you really should have come yourself.'

'You know I couldn't. Any trouble and I want it on my own ground.'

'And is there trouble?'

'Nothing that I didn't forecast. Their predictability is almost criminal. So you think that Sairey's OK?'

'I think so. But if you're really worried, don't ask me, ask John Varley.'

'Yes,' said Nigel Ellis. 'I might just do that, if . . . I might just do that.'

Sairey went silently up the stairs and into her room. She didn't switch on the light, but stood by the window and looked down into the park. By daylight it was a rather dusty rectangle of scrubby shrubs and trees designed to give the inhabitants of the tall Victorian terraces a taste of the country in town.

But by night it seemed deep and bosky, a swaying, melodious grove in which a girl could get lost, or worse.

She strained her eyes to glimpse the hurt boy but could see nothing but the swaying of branches.

Why hadn't she mentioned him? Because he was none of their business. Not her father's, not Fanny's. Not even her own. Unless, of course, he were part of her Dream. Perhaps this, too, was still part of her Dream. If so, at least it was a better part than what lay in wait for her behind closed eyelids. She settled down to keep the long vigil to daylight.

And so she lay awake, or dreamed she lay awake, all the rest of the night. But even the longed-for dawn was the pinched grey of her mother's face as she lay in her coffin.

A Dream of Darkness
Emergent Africa and the new colonialism
by
Nigel Ellis MBE

FOREWORD

The Dark Continent, that's what they used to call Africa. We sent missionaries to convert it, soldiers to conquer it, farmers to tame it, merchants to exploit it, and finally, politicians to buy it.

That was the Western dream, to own Africa. But despite all our efforts, it's still the Dark Continent, still up for grabs.

Only, this time it'll take more than a boxful of Bibles, a few glass beads and a Union Jack.

The main difference between the old colonialism and the new, is that *then* we interfered openly and by force, *now* we interfere covertly and by bribery, by treachery, by corruption.

This book is no academic analysis of Western influence and interference in African affairs. It is simply the recollections of an old African hand, telling no more than he knows. And in case that sounds rather disingenuous, perhaps I'd better start by telling you a little about myself.

I'm no saint, no tinpot, holier-than-thou holder of the nation's conscience. Nor am I one of your true blue,

14

cloak-and-dagger boys, grounded at Eton and groomed at Oxbridge. True, I did go to a so-called public school, but not one of the magic inner circle, more a doss-house for the sons of nostalgic ex-pats. And true, I did go on to University, but it was London not Oxbridge, and it only took a year for us to part, by mutual agreement.

That's what I'm not. So to what I am.

I was born on my father's farm near Nyeri, in Kenya. I was the second child, though I understand there had been several unsuccessful attempts to provide my father with a son and heir since my sister's birth fourteen years earlier. Perhaps that's what wore my mother out. Whatever the cause, when I was eighteen months old she died and Celia, my sister, thereafter took on my upbringing and the running of the household.

My childhood was happy. The farm was prosperous so I never wanted for anything, but neither my father nor my sister spoilt me. I led a hard and healthy outdoor life and the only indulgence I obtained was getting my English-based education postponed till I was nearly fifteen. After three not too unhappy school years and the previously mentioned abortive university year, I wasn't yet ready to settle down to farming, so I took a short-term commission in the King's African Rifles. Mau Mau was just beginning and it felt good to have the prospect of some immediate active service. Young men are naturally bloodthirsty and more often than not, it's their own blood they slake their thirst on. I had a more tragic lesson. Our farm was one of the first to be attacked. The farmhouse was torched to the ground and my father savagely assaulted and left for the flames to finish off. Fortunately, my sister, who had been in the barn when the attack started, remained hidden till the terrorists left. Then, with great courage, she pulled our father from the burning house and managed to keep him alive till help came.

15

That experience turned my father into an old man. His hair went white and he was never able to walk again without a stick. But the greater damage was done to his spirit. If it had been a question of keeping the farm going till he recovered, I would, of course, have resigned my commission and returned to Nyeri. But he had lost his trust in Africa and wanted out. Celia, too, seemed eager to go 'home' and, coincidentally, the short lease on which we let the family house in Masham Square in London was coming up for renewal. So it was decided to sell up in Kenya. It was sad, of course, to see the farm sold, and sadder still to wave them off from Mombasa as soon as Father was fit to travel. But I had no desire to be going with them, and I must confess I was not too distressed at the prospect of not having to devote my life to the repetitive slog of running a farm.

After my stint of soldiering, I looked for something else to do. The old colonial service seemed just the ticket, keeping the Queen's Peace by your wits as well as your weapons. But the wind of change was blowing hard, and 'colonial' was already a dirty word. It was clear that when independence came, those of us wanting to stay on would have to negotiate different terms.

Aid is the diplomatic pronunciation of 'dash', and there seemed an endless supply on offer. An acquaintance at the UK High Commission invited me to apply for the post of advisor in the agricultural division of something called the Bureau of Economic Co-operation. It was government-funded, he told me, delicately situated somewhere between the Home Civil Service and the Overseas Diplomatic Service so that its officials could operate with minimum red tape. I scented a rat immediately, and after ten minutes of my interview the smell was so pungent that I said to the interviewer, 'OK, expert you might be, but agricultural you're not. I doubt if you could tell beans

16

from broccoli if they weren't on your plate. So what's this really about?'

His name was Joe Lightoller, and to his credit he didn't mess about, but quickly confirmed what I'd already guessed. As our old colonies became 'foreign powers' it was imperative to set up a system to replace the instant access to influence and information we had hitherto enjoyed as a right. The Bureau had been set up at the end of the war to help cope with our security needs in the wreckage of Europe. Now, its influence was extending to the wreckage of Empire. My long connection with East Africa, my excellent contacts, linguistic expertise, plus (for I will not pretend this was altogether the seduction of an innocent) a certain aptitude for military intelligence work displayed during my stint with the KAR, had attracted their attention. The job was mine for the taking.

I didn't take long to make up my mind. I honestly thought I could do some good, and at the same time I rather fancied the excitement. Frankly, a career spent giving real agricultural advice, which I had to do as my cover, would have come, on the excitement scale, somewhere alongside a curacy in the Home Counties!

Another factor was that I liked, and was impressed by, Joe Lightoller. He'd been on the Bureau's African operation from the start in the West, when first Ghana, then Nigeria and Sierra Leone got independence, and was now following the hauling down of the flag in the East. His designation was Controller, Africa, a large-sounding title. Controller, I learned, was the highest rank of a field-man in the Bureau. I also learned that the term 'Bureau' was only used for official aid and advisory services. In its more obscure form, it was always called 'the Co-op' and its committees and working units, too, were called 'co-ops'.

Back in London, there was a Head of Africa section

17

who had responsibility for the overview of the whole continent, Commonwealth and not. Within a couple of years, Joe Lightoller was recalled to take over this job, and he got his knighthood with it, as a reward for the excellent work he'd done. This was a rare distinction, as honours usually only come with retirement. Even the lowliest and least regarded Co-op executive usually manages an OBE. To get a simple MBE you must really get up someone's nose!

When Joe, now Sir Joe, went, he was replaced in Nairobi by Archie Archbell, a character I shall have more to say about later. I missed Joe's light touch and easy manner. Archbell was harder to work under and eventually it was to gain a bit of at least temporary relief from him that made me accept the offer of a London attachment in 1968. Also, it had been more than five years since I last got back and I was keen to spend some time with my sister and my father, who was in failing health. I'd heard about 'swinging London' but this was the first time I'd experienced it. I was bowled over! After the initial shock, I found that, on the whole, I loved it. All the mean-spirited, joyless, repressive elements of British society seemed to have been swept aside in a great explosion of life and colour.

I was helped by being invited not long after my return to a party given by Joe Lightoller. It was a mixed do, with the oldies (every one of whom seemed to have made some concession, whether of hairstyle or shirt colour, to the spirit of the age!) being well diluted by a bunch of energetic youth. One of these was the loveliest girl I had ever seen, wearing a skirt which many tribes of Central Africa would have found too revealing. I was converted to minis and the permissive society instantly. I asked her to dance, then had to ask her to show me how. I was sure she would turn out to be a precocious sixteen-year-old, her head full of flower power and Sergeant Pepper.

Instead, she turned out to be twenty-three, a Cambridge graduate currently writing a doctoral thesis on D. H. Lawrence, and, best of all, she was Joe Lightoller's only daughter, Sarah. I asked her for a date. When I woke up the next day, I thought I must have been drunk to do it and delirious to imagine she'd agreed.

But there was nothing to lose by turning up at the place my delirium suggested for the assignation.

She was there, lovely and lively as I recalled. Madness turned to miracle, and six months later we were married.

I've brought you thus far in my life because the main part of what I want to write about begins thereafter. There'll be plenty of people who say I am bound by honour and by law to keep my mouth shut. But I have long debated whether a signature scribbled on a piece of paper a quarter of a century ago should bind a man to silence for ever about crimes committed in his country's name.

Crimes may seem a strong word. But wouldn't you say that assisting a man many think of as the black Hitler to gain and to remain in power was a crime? Or giving a helping hand to those breaking sanctions imposed against a country in revolt against the Crown? Or, to give a more recent example, when an undercover meeting is arranged with two ANC spokesmen and, on their way to the secret rendezvous in Botswana, their car is forced off the road and both are killed, wouldn't you then get a strong whiff of criminality?

But as I said earlier, I am no holier-than-thou saint. The public weal is certainly part of my motivation, but I won't hide the fact that private woe is there, too. Loyalty is two-way traffic. I have been treated shabbily, even dishonestly, by men who were my superiors. And if their honesty is in question in personal dealings, how can I accept their reassurances that whatever I found dubious in their policies and practices over the years was perfectly justifiable in some broader picture?

You must judge for yourselves. Me, I'm just an old Africa hand who got involved in what he thought was a game preservation safari, and can't understand why he saw so many leopard skins and elephant tusks being hauled back to the coast.

2

'Your father would like a word, I think,' said Fanny at breakfast one morning, about ten days after their return from Spain.

Sairey had little doubt what the word was about. She had tried with some success to conceal the worst effects of her lack of sleep, and her father's preoccupation with his memoirs might have enabled her to get away with it a good deal longer. But Fanny's keen eye missed little.

She went into her father's study and found it empty, but a still-smouldering cigarette promised he'd be back soon.

The study was very much a 'man's room', in the old-fashioned sense. A few tusked or toothy heads protruding from the panelled walls would not have looked out of place, but Ellis, fortunately, had never been that kind of white African. What did cover the walls were photographs. All his life, or at least its surface, was here. Like a visitor to an art gallery, Sairey wandered round the room.

Here he was, aged about five, with his father and sister, outside their farmhouse near Nyeri. Half a dozen Kikuyu farmhands grinned at the group from a respectful distance, their broad smiles contrasting with the Whites' solemnity. Sairey looked at the nineteen-year-old Celia and could already see in that slim, upright figure and thoughtful gaze the much-loved, middle-aged aunt who had once more taken over a mother's role, forty years on. A photo of her in her thirties on Camber Sands with her invalid father showed little change, but the crouched and wizened figure in the wheelchair was unconnectable with the broad-shouldered, vital man outside his Kenyan farmhouse.

Sairey let her gaze slip to the young Kikuyu. Had any of them been involved in the raid which destroyed his life, she wondered? But there was no way of looking beneath those smiling faces. She passed on.

Group photographs, formal and informal, dominated; her father tassel-capped at school, bare-headed at university, peak-capped in the KAR, bare-headed again at the hauling down of the Union Jack in Nairobi in '62, grey-toppered at his wedding . . . she moved her gaze rapidly on.

Here he was being married again, casually dressed this time in a light linen suit, with Fanny, cool in a flowered summer dress, by his side. There were no black faces in this group, except in contrast with Fanny's pale, flawless skin which was, apparently, impervious to the African sun. Nigel Ellis looked uncharacteristically nervous. Most of the surrounding guests looked suitably cheerful except for one, a bulky, snarling man whose head was thrust forward in the questing pose of a hungry bear.

She remembered noticing him particularly when she first saw the photo. He must have made a deep impression for, though it was years since she could recall looking at this group, she was suddenly convinced that this was the man she'd seen driving slowly round the Square that night the Dream returned.

She shuddered, and moved on in search of her father.

The very last of the pictures showed him alone for once, grey-toppered again, standing outside Buckingham Palace examining his retirement MBE. Sairey had taken a whole roll of snaps, but Ellis had shown little interest till Fanny said, 'In this one, you look as if she'd just given you a corgi dropping.'

'How apt,' he'd said, and chosen that photo as his record of the award.

The door opened and he swept in. Tall and rangy, with the deep tan of Africa hardly touched by seven years in England, he looked more like a bushranger than a civil servant, which is what appeared on his passport.

'Hello, sweetie,' he said, kissing her cheek. 'Not sleeping so well, I hear.'

'I'm all right,' she said. 'Just a bit of insomnia, that's all.'

'You reckon? Look, I'd like John Varley to take a look at you, OK? Now I know you're eighteen and, by one of those laws which they passed behind my back, that makes you adult and able to say yea or nay to being examined, but for my sake, just so that I can cross one worry off my list of a thousand, see John, will you?'

'All right,' she said. There was no way of arguing with him, or, at least, no way which would not leave her feeling more like eight than eighteen.

'Daddy,' she said, 'I was just looking at these old photos before you came in. This man at your wedding, who's he?' She pointed at the ursine man.

Nigel Ellis said, 'Why do you ask?'

'No reason. He just looks very . . . striking. In a rather nasty way.'

It was the right thing to say, it seemed.

'That's not so far from the truth. His name's Archbell. Archie to his friends, such as they are.'

'What was he doing at your wedding?'

'He was by way of being my boss in Africa. Also, Fanny was his secretary. So it would have been difficult not to invite him. If ever you meet him, run a mile, even if he does seem to be on a chain! Now I must dash. Got to see a publisher. Don't I sound high-powered!'

He swept up some papers from his desk and was gone.

This had been the pattern of their relationship for as long as she could recall – brief intense encounters, sudden departures. She wanted to explain to him that she needed long sessions of examination and reflection to get to know people. She'd made few close friends at school because the sheer pace of life and the multiplicity of personnel had made it difficult to work things through. His judgements were swift, piercing, accurate, but rather limited in their understanding of an opposite nature. She could have told him, of course, only there never seemed time. And also, perhaps because there never seemed time, she never felt close enough for the kind of openness such a telling would require.

Two days later, John Varley came. He was grey-haired, studiously tweedy, and smelt of <u>black twist</u>. He had been her mother's doctor and attended at her birth, so his face, his tweed, his tobacco, were among her very first sensations. His bedside manner was matter-of-fact and avuncular. Most people found it very reassuring. So, for colds and colics, did Sairey, but it was the magical end of medicine she felt in need of now.

He gave her a thorough check, prodding her with fingers and questions. She saw no reason not to answer honestly, except that she generalized the Dream into its vague swirl of supporting nightmares. Somehow, to be specific smacked, she didn't know why, of betrayal. Otherwise, she was quite open and John Varley listened very well. He knew a good listener was worth his weight in attendance fees.

The examination finished, he said, 'All right. Get dressed. Lovely tan, by the way. Bet you turned a lot of heads in Spain.'

He grinned and winked as he said it. Is he going to start asking about boyfriends, she wondered? Put it all down to Freud and hormones?

Instead, he said casually, 'Saw your grandfather the other day.'

'He's not ill, is he?'

'Sir Joe? Good Lord, no,' he laughed. 'We were playing golf. But he'd be pleased to know you'd be concerned.'

'Of course I'd be concerned. Just because he and Daddy . . . well, I make my own decisions now.'

She didn't believe it, and suspected Varley didn't either. Sir Joseph Lightoller, her maternal grandfather, hadn't figured large in her upbringing. He had attempted a takeover after his daughter died and Aunt Celia brought the young Sairey back to Britain. Celia had resisted politely, he had been foolish enough to persist, upon which she had let him see what a formidable woman she was.

There'd been two further causes of distancing. The first was Ellis's remarriage, and the second had something to do with work. Sairey took very little interest in her father's job, accepting at face value his offhand assurance that it was boringly centred on ploughs and oxen and crop rotation. But boring though it might have been, he'd certainly been furious when he was made to give it up and settle down to working in London, some years earlier. Nor did the pleasures of early retirement seem to have cooled that rage.

'Sir Joe was saying it's a long time since he saw you,' pursued Varley. 'Look, I don't want to interfere, and if there's an absolute injunction against you seeing him or me mentioning him, just say so. I always play house-rules.'

'I told you, I make my own decisions,' she said, pulling her tee shirt over her head, then reconstructing her olive-tipped spikes of hair in the mirror.

'You certainly do about your hair,' he laughed. 'He

feels concerned about you too, you know.' He glanced at his watch. 'Time flies. I may just have time to squeeze a gin and tonic out of that mean old parent of yours.'

'But what about . . .?'

'Nothing to worry yourself with,' he said cheerfully. 'I'll drop some gunge in. One of your spikes is wilting, I think! Bye.'

She heard his light tread run nimbly down the stairs. She counted to ten, then went out of the room.

Downstairs, John Varley was helping himself to his drink.

'What's the verdict?' said Ellis. 'Same as before?'

'Nothing's ever the same as before,' said Varley. 'But a not dissimilar syndrome, certainly, though rather more acute.'

'You said she'd grow out of it, then,' said Ellis accusingly.

'Did I? In some ways, of course, she's still growing. This started after your return from Spain, I gather, Fanny?'

'That's right.'

'So, tell me again exactly what's happened, what you've observed. It's no use asking that husband of yours. He wouldn't observe Christmas if he didn't get cards.'

Fanny talked, Varley listened. Finally, Ellis broke in irritably, 'Come on. What do you suggest by way of treatment?'

'It's not a dose of flu, Nigel,' said the doctor. 'I'd guess that her last year at school, full of "A" levels and entrance exams, took more out of her than you realized. She relaxed in Spain, but now she's back, she knows the work is all going to start up again. This is a very sketchy amateur analysis, you understand.'

'So what do you suggest?'

'Specialist help,' said Varley, very positively.

'A shrink, you mean?' said Fanny, raising her exquisitely groomed eyebrows. 'Wouldn't a couple of weeks in Kent with Celia do the trick?'

'A couple of weeks in Spain with you didn't,' said her husband sharply.

'Yes, but she's always got on so much better with Celia,' said Fanny, unaffected by the gibe. 'And honestly, Nigel, can you see the poor child talking to a stranger? It would be a waste of time and money.'

Nigel Ellis had no immediate counter to this objection, but Varley said, 'I wasn't thinking of a stranger, necessarily. I was wondering about Vita Gray.'

There was a pause. Fanny smiled expectantly at her husband, who said, finally, 'Would that be wise?'

'Because Vita Gray's a family friend, you mean? If you're going to object to both strangers and friends, that, of course, limits the field considerably.'

'No need for sarcasm,' growled Ellis. 'All right. Vita it shall be.'

Sairey went quietly back upstairs. On this occasion she felt no guilt at all about eavesdropping. At one point she'd felt like bursting in and demanding to know what the hell they thought they were doing making decisions about her health behind her back. She was an adult and entitled to make her own decisions. Except (and this was what kept her fury in check) that she didn't feel very adult, not unless depression and insecurity were adult conditions too, and she didn't want to believe that.

Back in her room, she sat on her bed. After a while, her father tapped at her door, but she called out that she was resting. She heard Varley leave. A little later her father, too, went out. She knew she was safe now for Fanny would not trouble her. But still she sat on the bed and thought of nothing. This was the nearest she dared come to sleep. How long it was before she lay down, she did not know. Suddenly she realized that instead of the wall, she was looking up at the ceiling, focusing on a patch of rough plaster, relict of some old repair, familiar to her as long as she could remember, and which had probably been there in those early, unrecapturable years before they'd gone to join her father in Africa. It was shaped like a star. She lay and looked at the star and concentrated on not falling asleep. But she was too exhausted to resist for long.

At first it was a new dream that came, strange but not frightening, its central image a face that came swimming out of darkness, the face of the boy in the park, but with eye and nose undamaged and only a smile on his lips, no blood. The contusion on his cheek had hardened into a star-shaped scar. She smiled back in pleasure and felt the warm stirrings of sexual arousal. But then he was gone and instead, she was in her father's arms and the face she was looking at was her mother's, deathly pale in her coffin. *Mummy! Mummy! Mummy!*

She awoke.

A heavy-featured woman with intense blue eyes was sitting by the bed, regarding her gravely.

'Hello, Sairey,' the woman said.

'Hello, Vita,' whispered Sairey Ellis.

3

'You must learn to love your dreams,' said Vita Gray, with no trace of irony. She was the most serious person Sairey knew. Her rare smiles were sunlight in a rainy country.

For the first time in her life, Sairey had described the Dream in detail to another person. Vita Gray's reaction had been disappointing, merely nodding as she made a brief note, then going on to ask about other dreams.

'I think you're missing the point, Vita,' Sairey had protested. 'I'm absolutely terrified!'

And this is when Vita had started her little lecture.

'Dreams *can* be terrifying, but they are not sent to terrorize,' she went on. 'Their function is to remind, or to warn, or to reaffirm. A child's mind is like an inexperienced voyager preparing for a long journey. Choice has to be made. Much that will turn out to be useless is lugged into the cabin and unpacked in full view, while much that will later prove essential to the traveller's well-being, or even survival, is stored far out of reach in the depths of the hold and marked "Not Wanted On Voyage".'

The phrase stuck in Sairey's mind, though it didn't seem to her, ten days later, that Vita was having much luck sifting through the luggage.

Phsyically, she was in better shape. Vita permitted the sparing use of some tablets which, for a couple of hours at least, could put her deep beyond the reach of the Dream. And she got plenty of fresh air and exercise, as many of her sessions with Vita took place outside and on the move.

Sometimes they strolled round and round the Masham Square park. Whenever they passed the flaking summerhouse, Sairey thought of the wounded boy. She had never dreamed of him again, but when she told Vita about him, the psychiatrist seemed far more interested than she had been in the Dream of Sairey's mother.

Occasionally, for a change, they headed further afield. Once they went to Kensington Gardens and watched the children sailing boats on the Round Pond.

'Do you remember, you and I once came here together before you went to Africa?' said Vita.

Sairey shook her head very vigorously, as if denying the truth of this assertion rather than just her own memory of it.

'Oh yes, we did,' said Vita firmly. 'We sat on that bench there, and waited for Sarah.'

Sarah was Sairey's mother. The pet form had differentiated the two, and there had been no attempt at upgrading since the need for differentiation vanished.

They sat on the bench indicated. Sairey waited a moment, as if seeking a message through the contact, then said, 'I really can't remember anything of those days. How should I? I was a baby! What should a baby remember?'

'Much,' insisted Vita. 'Babyhood isn't about blankness, it's about total sensitivity, about reception with, as yet, no built-in jamming.'

'I can't remember anything,' insisted Sairey.

'What about the voyage out? Did all those days at sea make no impression?'

'None, because we went by air,' said Sairey triumphantly.

Vita Gray smiled briefly, a glimmer in the rain-forest,

and Sairey said, 'Was that a trick question?' rather angrily.

'No trick,' said the older woman. 'Except insofar as all questions are tricks.'

She met Sairey's puzzled gaze with her customary alert passivity. Was she beautiful, wondered the girl? Her rather square face was framed in a coal-scuttle helmet of vigorous brown hair which, if not quite unkempt, was a long way from being kempt. There was no attempt to disguise the rather coarse texture of her skin with make-up. Heavy breasts and a thickening waist were neither concealed nor accentuated by a belted leather jacket over a heather-pattern wool skirt. She looked neither younger nor older than her forty-two years. Sairey knew the age because Vita and her mother had been born within a few weeks of each other, though how she knew *this* was not so certain. They had met at Cambridge, Sarah Lightoller and Vita Gray, became firm friends in their first year, shared a house in their second and third. Sairey had seen photographs. She was able to look at them with equanimity because her mind could form no link with the laughing girl with long, bouncy blonde hair, who always struck an outrageous pose as soon as she sensed the camera upon her. All memory of her mother was now compressed into that single, terrible dream image.

'I've remembered something,' she said suddenly.

'Yes?'

'In the Dream, her hair, it's smoothed down. Not like in the photos. It's flat. Like it was wet or something.'

'That's interesting,' said Vita.

'It's not interesting, it's awful!' shouted Sairey. 'When are you going to do something about it?'

'We've started. You're up and about and able to face the world.'

'Yes, but inside I still feel . . . oh, I don't know. And I

still have dreams. *The* Dream. When am I going to get better?'

'Perhaps when you decide what better really means.'

'Oh shit. You enjoy playing the sphinx, don't you?' exclaimed Sairey angrily. She intended insult, but as she spoke she realized how apt it was. The massive calm, the impenetrable mind – even the helmet of hair was not unlike the fabled beast's head-dress. There was no problem in recognizing Vita from those old photographs. Even at nineteen she had stared out seriously from the side of her posturing friend. Yes, she *was* beautiful. Sairey answered her own question, and, with the answer, wondered why there'd been any need to ask in the first place.

'We sat on this very bench,' said Vita, with a typical, dislocating leap to an earlier track of conversation, 'and saw your mother coming along that path.'

Sairey glanced round. There was a woman some distance away approaching them. She said, 'I can't remember anything,' and turned away to look across the pond. It was an overcast, blustery day with the water shivering to shrug off the wind. A few children played by the water. There weren't many adults, but there was someone standing on the far side of the pond with an absolute stillness that, at first, made him difficult to see but, once spotted, impossible to miss.

In this light, at this distance, it was hard to be forensically sure, but Sairey was certain it was the golden boy she'd left wounded in the park.

'It *is* you! I thought I recognized you. Hello!'

Sairey must have cried out in alarm, for the woman who had stopped to address Vita looked at her with open curiosity. She was middle-aged, perhaps older, slightly built, with a narrow, anxious face and wispy hair.

Vita said, 'Mary, how are you?'

32

'I'm pretty well, I suppose, as long as I keep moving.' But she showed no eagerness to keep on moving, rather regarded Sairey with interested, questioning eyes.

Perhaps she's some old flame of Vita's who reckons I've supplanted her, thought Sairey. It was an idea only slightly more charitable than her immediate suspicion that Vita had tried to contrive a bit of shock therapy by talking of meeting her mother, then having this woman approach along the same path and address them. But size, age, and colouring were all so wrong that she couldn't believe such a stickler for detail would have picked such a poor decoy.

'Sairey, this is Mary Marsden, an old friend. Mary, Sairey Ellis.'

'Ellis. Sairey Ellis . . . not . . .?'

Vita nodded.

'Good Lord,' said Mary Marsden, sitting down beside Sairey. 'My dear, I knew your mother.'

Immediately, Sairey's suspicions flooded back.

'How?' she asked with aggressive abruptness.

'I supervised her thesis. Did she never mention me? Of course not. Stupid of me. A doctoral thesis would hardly be the kind of thing you'd talk about with someone as young as you must have been when . . . oh, I'm sorry . . . it really was a first class piece of work, first class. She could have done so much.'

She looked rather wildly at Vita, who showed no sign of helping her out of her self-created predicament.

Sairey said, 'It's all right. But I think we ought to be going, Vita. Fanny said Daddy would like a word when we got back.'

'Perhaps another time,' said Mrs Marsden. 'Vita, we must keep in touch.'

She fluttered away. Sairey and Vita looked at each other in silence, then they, too, set off.

As they walked away, Sairey glanced across the pond. There was no sign now of the golden boy.

Back at Number 28, they found Nigel and Fanny having tea.

'Vita, come in, sit down, have a muffin.'

It was plain to Sairey that her father's hearty friendliness concealed certainly dislike and possibly fear. Fanny's welcoming smile wasn't so readable. She examined her stepdaughter, then said to Vita, 'She's looking awfully well. What do you think, Vita? A few days in Kent with Celia to blow off the last cobwebs before she gets down to her swotting again?'

She made it sound like a game, but it was hard to take offence as she made most activities, including her husband's memoirs, sound the same.

To Sairey's surprise and slight consternation, Vita did not disagree.

'Soon, perhaps. There's a conference I have to attend, so I would need to suspend treatment in any case. But as for swotting, as you put it . . .'

'I've been thinking about that,' said Ellis. 'How would it be if we put off Cambridge? It would have to be for a year, of course. You can't just miss a term, especially your first one.'

'Could she do that? Would the college agree?' wondered Fanny.

'Oh yes. Nowadays, they seem to prefer undergrads to have had some experience beyond school. You know, travel, a job, VSO, that sort of thing.'

He's checked it out, thought Sairey. He's got it all fixed, if that's what I want. What do I want?

She glanced at Vita as if in search of an answer, just as her father said, 'What do you think, Vita?'

Why the hell doesn't he ask me? But before she could voice her indignation, Vita said, 'What do you think,

Sairey?' and she found herself thinking with equal anger, that's typical! She always puts it down to me!

The incongruity struck her immediately, without lessening her annoyance, though she was no longer sure of its target.

She said, 'Yes, I think that would be fine. Also, I think it would be nice to go to Aunt Celia's. Vita mustn't let me get in the way of her real work. Now if you'll excuse me, I think I'll go and have a lie down.'

It was childish, she knew, but she felt as if she'd been treated as a child and she was not sure yet what the adult response ought to be.

Fanny spoke as she reached the door.

'By the way, dear, the oddest thing. That raincoat you lost in the park that night. It's turned up in a plastic bag on the doorstep. It looks as if it's been dry cleaned. The oddest thing.'

'Isn't it?' said Sairey, not catching Vita's uncurious blue eyes.

The coat was lying on her bed. She examined it closely, went through the pockets. There was nothing. She stretched out on the bed and pulled the coat over her like a blanket.

After a while she fell asleep.

When she woke up she felt refreshed, and it wasn't till she was standing under the shower that it occurred to her that, for the first time since her return from Spain, her drugless sleep had been completely dreamless.

At seven o'clock prompt, the door opened and two army captains came in, wearing full dress uniform. They were Nubis, with thin Nilotic faces and watchful eyes. One of them motioned Shem and me to stand close together. The other went quickly through the suite to check that we were alone. No attempt was made to check for listening devices, and I could only hope that this had been done earlier.

Satisfied, one of the Nubis went out into the corridor. There was a short pause, then Major General Idi Amin came in.

The first time I'd met him, I'd been a lieutenant in the KAR and he'd been a corporal. There'd been a lot of him then. As he soared up the promotion ladder after Independence, he seemed to put on weight with rank, and I reckon his general's uniform contained enough cloth to fit out a small platoon.

'Major Ellis,' he said, using my terminal rank. 'Nice to see you, Major.'

'Plain Mr Ellis now, sir,' I said, snapping him a salute. 'Nice to see you too.'

This struck the right tone and he shook my hand, grinning. His palm, however, was damp and I knew there was still work to do. Everything was perfect for a coup except Amin's nerve. Obote was in Singapore at the Commonwealth Conference, demanding that Britain should be chucked out because, within a month of Heath becoming Prime Minister, it had been disclosed that the UK was contemplating renewing arms sales to South Africa. This provided both the final provocation and the perfect opportunity to get rid of him.

'I'm glad to hear that your overtime dispute has finally been settled,' I said heartily.

Amin regarded me with that look of utter blankness with which NCOs the world over try to conceal utter incomprehension, then understanding dawned and he laughed loudly and said, 'Oh yes, Uncle Felix got that fixed OK.'

Felix Onoma, Amin's uncle, Minister of Defence, and Secretary General of the UPC, had just issued a directive saying that unless officers took leave in lieu of overtime payments immediately, they would lose it. By this device he had got most of those potentially loyal to Obote (mainly those from the northern tribes of the Acholi and Langi) separated from their troops. The Nubis (that is, Nubians, the army's non-generic name for the West Nilers who comprised most of the rank and file, and from whom Amin had caused officers loyal to himself to be promoted) naturally had not taken up the offer.

Now Shem Seligmann spoke.

'It would be surprising if the Minister of Defence's success did not inspire the Minister of Justice to greater efforts. I believe the investigations into Brigadier Okoya's murder and the army fund embezzlement case are both nearing conclusions.'

For a second I thought he'd gone too far, but I should have known my man. Shem was a soft-spoken Israeli who never started anything he was not confident of finishing. Just what evidence Mossad had implicating Amin in these crimes I don't know, but clearly the General acknowledged its strength. He took half a step towards Seligmann, with a look on his face which seemed to promise that in the next couple of minutes Shem was likely to become, in Amin's own favourite phrase, 'a gone case'. Then he relaxed.

'Major Ellis,' he said. 'This fella Heath going to give guns to B. J. Vorster, what's he going to give to me?'

We'd been through it all before. I rapidly reiterated that, in my strictly unofficial opinion, it seemed likely that HM Government would rapidly recognize, and thus help legitimize, any new Ugandan government which commanded popular support, and that future levels of aid would certainly not sink below past levels. The details had, of course, been hammered out with the politicians like Onoma. But Amin wasn't interested in those details even if I had the time, and he the brains, to understand them. What he wanted were promises that at the first sign of any threat to him personally, Britain and Israel would send in planes and tanks to put down the opposition.

My heart sank. A coup needed a figurehead but this could be a real mistake. I'm not saying I had any premonition of what was to come, but in my experience, a man who is brutal in authority and terrified in adversity is not good ruler material. As I looked at him, his great melon face oozing nervous sweat, I recalled the night of the 1968 attempt on Obote's life. A colonel went to Amin's house to tell him what had happened. Seeing soldiers pulling up outside his door, Amin panicked and made off out of the back, gashing himself badly as he clambered over his own security fence. It was after that, that his family name of Dada, which is Swahili for 'sister', came to have a mocking significance, though not many people mocked him to his face. Brigadier Okoya had tried that and he and his wife had ended up murdered.

Fortunately, or unfortunately, Shem Seligmann didn't share my scruples about giving reassurance. To his threats about incriminating Amin, he now added promises to protect him with whatever he needed, from ju-jus to jets.

Ten minutes later, we all shook hands, and Idi and his entourage resumed their interrupted journey to the night-club on the sixteenth floor. We were in Kampala's top hotel, the Apolo, changed after the coup to the Kampala International because Apolo was Milton Obote's middle name. It had been Shem's idea to meet here. As he said, when you're built like Amin, it's no use having secret meetings on a park bench. Shem, under his cover as an American businessman, had booked the suite on the tenth floor and Idi had simply stepped out of the lift and into the room.

'What do you think?' I said.

'A schlemiel. Let's hope you can control him.'

'You mean, *we* can control him, don't you?'

'Come on,' he grinned. 'You Brits still think of this as part of the family estate. You know why Obote finally got up your long thin noses? It wasn't because his Common Man's Charter was too Marxist, it wasn't because neither you nor the Kenyans want another socialist state tacked on to Tanzania.'

'All right,' I said, 'why was it?'

'Because the bastard ploughed up the Kampala Sports Club's cricket pitch to build his OAU Conference Centre!'

'Very funny,' I said. 'You staying?'

'Why not?'

'There's going to be a revolution, remember?'

'Bloodless,' he said. 'We were promised bloodless.'

'That just means the winners don't intend to get hurt,' I said. 'Shalom.'

'Toodle-oo,' he said.

I went down to the lobby. It was full of tourists. At the desk, a couple of Americans were debating whether to take the earliest flight to Cairo, which meant leaving that night. Hang around, I thought, and you may have a story to bore your friends with for years. They must have been telepathic for they decided to stay. I asked the clerk to get me a call through to Nairobi. I planned to be back there myself before the fun started, but I knew Archie Archbell would be sitting at the end of the line.

As I waited for my connection, which might take two minutes or an hour depending on vagaries beyond the grasp of British Telecom, a hand grasped my shoulder and a voice whispered in my ear, 'You're under arrest'.

I span round so violently I almost fell off my stool and the man who'd come up behind me had to steady me.

'Dear, dear,' he said. 'Who's got a bad conscience, then?'

'Bill,' I said. 'You bastard!'

Bill Bright was, for me, the perfect type of colonial Englishman, hard-working, fearless, fair minded; a little naïve at times, at others a compelling visionary, he loved Africa and its people with a real fervour. We'd first met as subalterns in the KAR mess, and kept in touch ever since. He farmed up in the northern region of Uganda now, and normally there was no more welcome sight than those broad shoulders and that mahogany tanned face with its thatch of sun-bleached hair. Tonight I felt like keeping as low a profile as possible, so my welcoming smile may have been a bit forced.

'Surprise, surprise,' I said. 'Bit early in the year for you to be visiting the fleshpots, isn't it?'

'Ocen got some unexpected leave. He loves to play farmer, so I thought I'd pop down to K and sort my bank manager out.'

This hit me like an accusation. Ocen Okoya was Bright's brother-in-law, and a captain in the Ugandan army. As an Acholi, and distantly related to the brigadier of that name whose death Amin had probably arranged, he was just the kind of officer the conspirators would want out of the way before the coup. And after? We'd been promised bloodless. I could only hope there were enough political restraints on Idi to force some kind of attempt to keep that promise.

'Is Apiyo with you?' I asked.

It had come as a considerable shock to the old white establishment when, shortly after Independence, Bill Bright had married Ocen's twin sister, Apiyo. She'd trained at Makerere as a teacher and was twice as clever as most of the white die-hards, but the best they could find to say was that maybe, with the uncertainties of post-Independence life ahead, wily old Bill was taking out a bit of extra insurance.

The only truth in this was that Bright, fearing a crack down on black-white relationships, had insisted on marriage, which was always what he'd wanted anyway. Apiyo had been the one to resist. I think it was possibly Bill's insistence that he wanted a family, but only in wedlock, that carried her. Bright was not the kind of settler who scattered little brown bastards all over Africa. Now they had a son, Allan, who was five or six.

'No. She's not crazy about Kampala and she doesn't get much chance to see Ocen these days. You must come and visit soon. And better still, when are you going to stop hiding this lovely wife and kiddie of yours at home and bring them out for a bit of sunshine?'

My marriage had surprised Bill almost as much as his had surprised the ex-pat set. Nor had he understood when I explained about Sarah having to stay in London to finish her doctorate. Then she became pregnant, and John Varley had been firm in his diagnosis that it would be most unwise for her to travel to a new life in East Africa till the child was born. With the Head of Africa as my father-in-law, there was no problem about a temporary home-posting, which I knew Joe would have liked to make permanent to keep his daughter and grandchild close to him. I liked neither the climate nor the routine work I was doing, but in the end I might have given way if the Tories hadn't got back in and started off that chain of events which was to throw the Commonwealth into such a turmoil. Archie Archbell had been adamant that he needed me. The situation was critical. This was no time for new boys. My experience and expertise would be invaluable. I suspect, also, that at a very early stage he'd got Idi Amin lined up as his boy and thought that my old acquaintance with the man would be helpful.

Reluctantly, my father-in-law had given way, bolstered by the fact that Sarah was remaining behind for a while to complete the PhD thesis postponed by the birth of our daughter. But now it was complete, and my doctor wife and baby daughter were flying out to join me.

Bill Bright was delighted when I told him, but disappointed when I added that, to start with at least, we would be setting up home in Kenya.

'But you've spent most of your time working in 'ganda since you came back,' he protested. 'Seems daft to be commuting over the border!'

'We'll see how things go,' I said. I couldn't tell him tonight that no sane man was going to bring his wife and kid into a country that had just suffered a military coup, not till the dust settled, anyway.

'Your call to Nairobi, sir.'

I excused myself and went to one of the phones on the wall beyond the desk. They were screened off from each other, but I was aware of Bill, standing within earshot, behind me.

'Archie,' I said. 'Just to say I'll be on my way back

42

tonight. I presented the figures on that new fertilizer spray and I think there's a real interest.'

'You reckon they'll want to go ahead?' growled Archbell.

'You always get some nervousness when something new comes along, but yes, I'm pretty confident.'

'So I should go ahead with re-routing the consignment, you think?'

'It would be silly not to make arrangements.'

We were talking about what would happen when Obote came hot-footing it back from Singapore, once news of the coup reached him. He wouldn't fly to Entebbe, that was sure. Most probably he'd end up at Nairobi, and while the Kenyans could not afford to be seen openly aiding the overthrow of a friendly neighbouring country's legitimate government, there were plenty of political and business interests there who'd be delighted to see Obote toppled. The longer the resistance to the coup was deprived of its main focus, the easier things would be, and, as any traveller knows, there are a thousand ways you can bugger a man around at an airport.

'Excellent,' said Archbell gloatingly. 'Good work. See you soon.'

I put the phone down. Bill Bright was looking at me speculatively. He never pried openly, but I sometimes got the feeling he felt I was a pretty odd kind of agricultural advisor. Perhaps the fact that he never talked farming with me was the biggest giveaway of his suspicions.

'Fancy a beer?' he said.

'Quick one,' I said. 'Down here. No time to go up to the night-club, if it was feathered fanny and fancy prices you had in mind.'

'No. I'll leave that to Idi and his mates.'

He would have noticed my shock if he'd been looking

at me, but when I followed his gaze, I realized there was nothing provocative in his remark. He was looking across the lobby to where Amin and his friends had just emerged from the lift. The waiting tourists parted before him like water before an oil tanker.

'Big bugger, isn't he?' said Bill. 'I don't know what he's like as a general, but he was a lousy cook.'

Bright, like me, had encountered Amin in the KAR.

I said, 'It's not like you, Bill, to carp at people getting on in their own country.'

He said, 'I'm no dewy-eyed liberal, Nigel. There's black shits as well as white, and some of the tales I've heard about our fat friend . . . What the hell! I'm not going to have to serve under him, am I? Let's go and get that drink!'

4

It was a world of infinite greens. They exploded against
her eyes, sparkling, bubbling, streaming, coiling; they
caressed her body, green fingers stroking, green lips
kissing, green tendrils grasping; they even sounded in her
ears, with a reef-like roar and a merman's whisper; and
she knew that all she had to do was open her mouth and
the green taste would, in a second, fill her belly and her
lungs and make her part of that greenness for ever.

She kicked hard, rose swift, and burst into the air.
Above her the blue sky, before her the yellow sands, and
all around the green Channel, rising and falling with lazy
strength, indifferent, alike, to the keels which laboured
through and the hulks which rotted beneath her restless
waters. Sairey threw back her head and sent a cry of pure
delight to join the scream of the gulls overhead.

'Good?' said Celia Ellis in her ear.

'Great!' exclaimed Sairey.

She hadn't felt like that an hour earlier when the alarm
had gone off. One of the penalties of staying with Aunt
Celia was that you were invited, in terms which brooked
no refusal, to join in her pre-breakfast dip. Considera-
tions of season or weather were rarely allowed to interfere, and Sairey could recall, as a child, running back to
Dunelands with goosepimples that felt like cobbles, while
Celia strolled behind in her ancient tartan beach robe,
oblivious to the cold.

'Don't overdo it,' said Celia. 'Floating in a Spanish
swimming pool's all right, but it's no preparation for real
water.'

Piqued, Sairey said, 'Race you to the shore!' and plunged forward in a furious crawl, which she kept up till she grounded in the shallows.

Shaking the water from her eyes, she stood up and saw her seventy-year-old aunt vigorously towelling herself down while her two dogs, Mop, a Sealyham, and Polly, a Red Setter, gambolled madly around her.

'You're better than you used to be,' said Celia. 'But more rhythm, less effort, would double your speed. Go on, you two. Get yourselves wet!' She hurled a stick into the water and the dogs rushed past Sairey in excited pursuit.

'Aren't they marvellous?' said Sairey, laughing. 'They never get any older, do they?'

'No?' Celia looked at her speculatively. 'It was Twig and Dancer when you lived here with me. They died within a month of each other, not long after you went back to Masham Square. You must remember that?'

'Of course I remember,' said Sairey indignantly. 'I didn't mean I thought Polly and Mop were the same dogs.'

This was true. She hadn't meant that, but she realized she had meant something even odder; that, just as this narrow English Channel stretching out before her was part of the one great sea, so the two dogs were part of that energy which involved all dogs, and from it they derived an immortality far more important than their limited lifespan. And herself? Such a context for herself solved all those problems of loss and gain, of past and future, which smudged the bluest of her horizons with threatening cloud.

At least for the moment, she was well. The Dream had not returned since the day her coat had reappeared, and the improvement in her health and spirits had been so marked that even Vita had seemed pleased. Typically, as

46

Sairey had come to view her departure to America with less and less concern, so Vita seemed to grow more unhappy about it.

'It's only for a short while,' she said. 'If there's any trouble, leave a message on my answering machine and it will get to me.'

'And what will you do? Drop everything and fly home?' asked Sairey gaily. 'Vita, I'll be all right. I can't tell you how much I'm looking forward to going down to *Dunelands*.'

It was true. In many ways it was like going home, for this, more than anywhere else, had been her home. Here her remembered life began when, after her mother's death, Celia had taken responsibility for her upbringing until her father had come back to Masham Square six years later with a new wife. London had been marvellous for an adolescent girl, but she had never lost her taste for the peace of *Dunelands*, the undemanding affection of the dogs and the uncomplicated directness of Aunt Celia's care.

It was only gradually that she came to realize what Celia must have given up to care for first her brother, then her father, and now her niece. Marriage, children of her own, possibly a career, perhaps (for she seemed to have few) even friends. It was easy to take such devotion for granted in the same way as she took Polly and Mop's. Perhaps her first mature thought had been her awareness of this danger.

She towelled herself vigorously, staring out to sea.

'I sometimes think it would be nice to stay in the water for ever,' she said.

'I thought that's what they called drowning,' said Celia. 'Let's get back and see what we can find for breakfast.'

As they walked up the beach towards the villa, Sairey

47

said, 'When you brought me back here from Africa, what was I like?'

'Good Lord, child, what kind of question's that? You were yourself, what you are now, in the making.'

'Was I very unhappy?'

'Of course you were unhappy,' snapped Celia. 'Your mother was dead, your father was still in Africa, you'd been uprooted and brought back to this cold climate by a tedious old aunt who didn't let you have all your own way. Hardly a recipe for unconfined joy, was it?'

'But I always remember being happy here.'

They had paused while Celia unlocked the gate in the fence which ran round *Dunelands'* large garden. The fence was tall and made of tungsten steel, with a double row of barbed wire at the top. The gate had a magnetic lock, and prospective callers at the house had to make contact through an intercom to be vetted before Celia activated the unlocking switch inside. The building itself had the same high standard of security doors and windows. When Celia had first required these, they had been regarded as evidence of mental eccentricity brought on by memories of the Mau Mau attack, but the intervening years had rendered them far less eccentric in rural England.

'I'm glad you were happy,' said Celia, urging the dogs through the gate. 'Children should be happy. It colours the whole of life. I tried to make your father's childhood happy after our mother died, but it wasn't always easy.'

'Well, you succeeded with me,' said Sairey. 'Aunt Celia, do you remember before we left Africa, Daddy showing me Mummy in her coffin and you having to take me out of the room?'

This was the first time she had ever hinted details of the Dream to anyone except Vita, and her aunt's reaction made her feel she'd been wise to keep quiet. Her face contorted with shock and pain, as though she'd been physically assaulted. For a moment she seemed unable to speak, and when she did, the words came out with a harsh force that made her customary brusqueness seem mild.

'No, I don't remember that. How could I, when it never happened? When they found her she'd been lying in the African sun with African wildlife . . . for heaven's sake, child, you don't think they were going to pretty her up for a lying-out, do you? There, don't upset yourself. I don't mean to be rough, but I know what strange things can get into a young woman's mind. I hope Vita Gray remembers, too. These psychiatrists love to make normal things seem odd. So wipe your eyes, or I'll make you go back and wash your face in the sea!'

Sairey had not been aware that she was crying, till Celia's comic threat made her laugh.

'There, that's real April weather for you,' said Celia. 'How like your mother you look sometimes.'

'I don't think so,' denied Sairey strongly. 'She had lovely long blonde hair and was so tall and willowy.'

'She was five feet seven and wore a thirty-six "B" cup,' said Celia dismissively. 'I helped her choose her wedding dress. About your size, I should say. As for the hair, if you didn't wear yours shorn like a convict, it would grow just like hers. Tall and willowy indeed. You'd think you were talking about Fanny.'

'Would you? Well, I'm certainly not!'

'You don't get on?'

'What is there to get on with?' demanded Sairey.

'Privacy is no crime,' reproached Celia. 'I treasure mine. But your father ought to . . . never mind. Listen, Sairey, don't rush to meet unhappiness. Fanny is Fanny. You are you. There's room for both of you in the world, isn't there, even under one roof? And never forget, this is your home too. And it'll belong to you one day, after I'm gone, as long as you take on these monsters with it!'

The dogs jostled to nuzzle at her hand as if aware they were being spoken of. Sairey reached forward, hugged the old woman and kissed her on the cheek. Celia, who never encouraged such open displays of affection, looked a touch disconcerted.

'What was that for?' she asked.

'For telling me this is my home. It's always felt like it. And for caring so much about me.'

'Lots of people care about you!' Celia said, almost angrily.

'Yes, I know,' said Sairey placatingly.

But she didn't.

5

On the second Sunday of her stay, Sairey might have been spared the morning bathe. Celia was going to early Communion – another form of ritual cleansing, she offhandedly described it – and felt that this was sufficient substitute for braving a drizzling dawn on the beach.

She left Sairey in bed, but shortly after the front door had clicked shut behind her, the sky brightened and the sun broke through and it suddenly seemed to Sairey that she could enjoy both moral credit and physical pleasure by taking her pre-breakfast swim anyway. Flinging off the sheet before she could change her mind, she pulled on her costume, grabbed a towel and headed out of the house.

Polly and Mop were there to greet her, barking impatiently at the security gate, as if they personally had never had any doubt about her intentions. The sun gave off a great deal more light than heat, and the proportions of moral credit and physical pleasure changed as she ran down the beach, determined to get it over with. But as always, once in the water, she found herself converted to a denizen of this three-dimensional world and most reluctant to leave it.

When finally she could no longer pretend that the water wasn't chilly and her skin wasn't starting to crinkle at the edges, she headed for the shore. And saw she wasn't alone.

A man was squatting on the sand next to her towel.

She halted, waist-deep in water.

The man rose, picked up her towel and came to the water's edge.

He was tall, broad-shouldered, narrow-waisted and very black. He was middle-aged with greying hair and a thin, almost ascetically serious face heavily scarred on the right cheek. He held out the towel towards her. A fine silver chain moved on his wrist. She heard its faint chime clearly and realized that the sea was at that brief still point which marks the turning of the tide.

'You'll get cold,' he said.

His voice was unaccented, unaccentuated, totally lacking in threat. But she remembered what the pangas had done to her mother, and the sea might as well have been concrete for all the power of movement her legs had.

'Come,' he said. 'You think because I'm black I must be lusting after your lily-white body? Be easy. From here, it looks more pink turning to grey. Also, I try to avoid ravishing before midday on the Sabbath. I only want to talk.'

'You can talk here,' she said, with only a slight tremor. The dogs had left the water and were gambolling happily round the legs of the man, in the hope of enticing him to play. It would be nice to think they were good judges of character, but she wouldn't bet her life on it.

'All right,' he said, shrugging. 'Though it's a little public.'

He stooped to pick up a piece of driftwood which he hurled into the water with Polly and Mop in close pursuit. Public? thought Sairey, looking up the empty beach. If this was public, what was his definition of private?

Then she glimpsed something in the dunes, a flash of light like sun glancing off a windscreen. At the same time, as though at a signal, water pulled at her legs. The tide had turned. Next moment, a vehicle came surging over the crest of a dune. It was some kind of jeep, with four-wheel drive, that ripped through the fine loose sand with hardly any problems of traction. For a second she thought that it had come in response to the black man's summons and she lay back in the water, preparatory to riding the tide out to sea if it came after her into the shallows.

But the man on the beach had turned in alarm as he heard the vehicle's approach and suddenly he was off, running parallel to the water's edge. He still carried Sairey's towel, streaming behind him like a banner, and Mop and Polly cavorted at his heels, delighted at this new game. He ran with a deceptively fast, high, loping stride, but the jeep was speeding after him on an interceptory diagonal, and collision seemed inevitable.

'Into the water!' screamed Sairey. 'Into the water!'

It was his only hope of escape, though why she should be concerned for a man whom a few seconds earlier she had found terrifying, she couldn't say.

He was splashing through the shallows now, but the jeep was almost upon him. It had two occupants, a big hard-faced man driving and, by his side, a slighter man holding what looked like a pistol. Not that he needed it. A few seconds more and they would run their quarry down. But just as impact seemed inevitable, the black man halted and leapt gracefully aside. Then, like a toreador making a pass with his cape, he laid Sairey's beach towel across the windscreen as the vehicle sped by within inches.

The driver's blindness was only momentary, but it was enough. The jeep ploughed into the water over the axles and came to a halt. The black man turned and loped up towards the dunes, with the excited dogs still in pursuit. In the water the engine roared, and the vehicle juddered, and for a while it looked as if it might have got firmly stuck in the soft sand. But slowly it came out backwards, then crashed into forward gear, and the chase was on again. By now, however, the black man was clambering up the dunes and as Sairey watched, he dropped out of sight. The jeep needed to take a more serpentine route but a few moments later it, too, vanished over the crest.

Now Sairey came out of the water and ran up the beach, desperate to catch the outcome of this drama. But when she had clambered up the highest dune and stood among the spikey sea grass, she found she was too late. There was the sound of a distant engine, or perhaps engines. A movement caught her eye, then the sound of excited barking, and Polly and Mop came back. It was easy to see they had a tale to tell, but whether of capture or evasion was impossible to make out.

She went back to the water's edge to collect her towel, which was floating in the shallows. This, and the jeep's tracks across the sand, were the only proof she had of what had taken place.

But what *had* taken place? A black man on a beach, some more men in a jeep, a chase, a disappearance, and nothing left to show but some tyre tracks in the sand.

She ran back to the house with the excited dogs at her heels. But as the gate came into view her pace slowed, and after a few steps she halted.

The gate was open. She was sure that she had at least pulled it to, and almost certain that she'd locked it. The dogs were looking up at her, hopefully scenting a new adventure. Then a figure stepped out from the shadow of the porch and the dogs bayed excitedly, sensing the tension of her muscles, the imminence of action.

'Sairey! There you are. I was beginning to think I'd dropped in on the *Marie Celeste*!'

She relaxed, walked forward. The dogs, disappointed, attacked each other in compensation.

'Hello, Grandad,' she said. 'What on earth are you doing here?'

Sir Joseph Lightoller was a small, slim man. As a child, Sairey had been fascinated by the lines of black hair which fanned out from his wrists and ran along the backs of his fingers. This, and the monocle he sometimes affected, had seemed the most distinctive things about him. But with age, she had observed the way he held himself very straight and erect, as if to make the most of his few inches, and also a slight staginess in the way he projected both himself and his voice socially.

She took him into the house and made coffee. He told her that he was motoring down to Brighton and had diverted on a whim, to look her up.

Some whim. Some diversion, she thought.

She said, 'You must have set off early.'

'Only way to avoid the coast traffic on a Sunday,' he said.

'But how did you know I was here?'

'The small estrangement between your father and myself does not mean that I cannot ask, nor he reply, to civil questions. Are you not glad to see me?'

'Of course I am,' she replied, but when she consulted her inner litmus she found its colour ambiguous.

Perhaps she had never seen enough of him to get very close to him. And she could still recall Aunt Celia's reaction to the days she spent with him. Gifts were dismissed with a cold, 'very nice,' and questions about her activities seemed less concerned with her enjoyment than with the things her grandfather had said.

On her move to London to join her father and his new wife, it had seemed likely she would see rather more of Sir Joe. Then something had happened at work which provoked her father to storm around the house promising

55

all kinds of unpleasant things to his father-in-law. And to someone called Archbell, she now recalled. The man in the wedding photo. The man in the car, that night in the Square.

She'd understood none of this; she was a child then, knew herself to be very much still a child even now, and was concerned only with effects, not causes. But a time was fast approaching when she would have to face up to the cause of things.

'Aren't you going to change? You'll catch your death,' he said.

She was still wearing her bathing suit. The run up the beach and the warmth of the house had dried her off to some extent, but she was beginning to feel a little chilly.

She hesitated and said, 'How long can you stay?'

Sir Joe laughed and said, 'You're more of a diplomat than your father. What you mean is, do I want Celia to find me here when she returns from her devotions, which is what I presume she is at? No, I suppose I don't. I have once before been accused by Celia of trying to win you away by stealth to a better life, and I don't care to repeat the experience.'

'You mean, you no longer want a better life for me?' joked Sairey.

'No. I mean that your choices are now your own. Or ought to be. Are you looking forward to Cambridge?'

'I suppose so. I mean, I am, but we've put it off for a year.'

He frowned and said, 'You've not been well, I gather.'

'How do you know?'

'I had to be away on business for a while, and the first thing I always do on my return from a trip is check up on those nearest and dearest, which, in my case, is you.'

'Oh. Well, yes, I wasn't too good. I couldn't sleep. But

I'm fine now. Truly. Grandad, why have you and Daddy fallen out?'

She only asked the question to change the subject, but then she realized she wanted to know.

'We haven't really. Your father has fallen out with his old employer, that's all, and I'm the nearest thing to a senior executive for him to vent his wrath on. It will pass. Listen, Sairey, I must go soon. It's always been a matter of regret that I've never been able to do as much for you as I wished. Now you're eighteen, I can at least make my offers direct. Except, I find myself uncertain what to offer! You're all that remains to me of your mother, just as she was all that remained to me of my wife. I should like you to be able to love me, but we can't dictate these things. Nor, I am very much aware, can we buy them. So there is no motive other than my love and care for you when I say that, if you would like to spend a bit of time travelling before you settle to the books, even unto a trip around the world, then regard me as your Cook, Thomas or Captain, whichever you prefer. Open offer. No time limit. No hooks. Only, I should prefer your acceptance outside the hours of one to five A.M. I need less and less sleep as I get older, but what I do need, I need badly.'

The joke was meant to dilute the emotional intensity of his words, but it was too late. Sairey's eyes had already filled with tears. She came and knelt beside him and pressed her face into his tweed jacket.

She said, 'I do love you, Grandad, only . . .'

'Yes?' he prompted.

'I don't really know you,' she said hesitantly.

'You mean, not like you know your father, say?'

She raised her head to look into his face, and surprised a savage smile. It faded as she watched, and he said, 'Loyalties, loves, we have so little to say in choosing them that it seems most unfair when circumstances force us to

57

rank them. Now, I must go before your guardian dragon returns.'

'She's nothing like a dragon,' protested Sairey. 'You're not afraid of her?'

'Afraid of having a sweet interlude soured, that's all,' he said, shifting her gently and rising. 'Will you tell her I've been?'

'Do you not want me to?' asked Sairey.

'I don't mind. I was just interested. Everything you do, Sairey, must be of interest to me. No, don't come out. The sooner you get under a hot shower, the better.'

At the door he paused, looking out across the dunes.

'I thought I saw a jeep or a sand buggy roaring around here when I arrived. Do you have much bother from that sort of thing?'

She said, 'Hardly at all, really.'

'Good. I should hate to think that Celia's little plot was finally being invaded, though it would need an armoured division to take the house! Bye now, darling.'

He kissed her quickly on the cheek and walked away, his back straight as a soldier's. Sairey watched him out of sight then went in and showered. She was quite unconscious of any debate in her mind, but when Celia returned from church and said, 'Just got up, have we?' all she replied was, 'Not really. Me and the beasts have been for a swim, but apart from that I must admit we've been pretty lazy!'

That night, the Dream returned, with all its associated, less coherent nightmares. She concealed it from her aunt for three days, but then her tired appearance and her mental withdrawal made concealment impossible. But at least the delay had won her goal.

'Please,' she said, 'don't ring Daddy. Vita will be back now. She was due home this week. Ring Vita, please.'

'Vita may be tired after her flight and busy after her absence,' said Celia dismissively. 'She'll probably have neither the time nor the energy to cope with you.'

But she rang, all the same.

The phone was answered on the second ring. Vita Gray listened to Celia's explanation without speaking, but when the older woman started to list the many reasons why it was unlikely Vita would be able to help, she interrupted brusquely.

'I'll come down this evening. I'll stay overnight, then take Sairey back to town with me tomorrow. Don't make a meal for me.'

'I'm quite capable of dropping a handful of nuts into a bowlful of lettuce,' said Celia, with heavy irony. But the phone had gone dead.

'Hello, hello,' said Celia, jiggling the receiver. Suddenly the line came back to life and she heard a voice that wasn't Vita's, but was, nevertheless, very familiar.

'. . . handful of nuts into a bowlful of lettuce.'

And then the line went dead again.

6

'Hitherto, the occasion of these attacks has been clear . . .'

'Attacks?' interrupted Celia. 'Isn't that putting it a bit strong?'

'Dreams are the attacks the subconscious makes on the psyche,' said Vita Gray. 'Believe me, it's a perfectly apt metaphor.'

'But it's not an illness in the strict sense, is it? Can't she be treated, then, by, I don't know, by . . .'

'By love and fresh air?' said Vita. 'You've offered her plenty of those, yet still the attacks recur.'

'That word again. It makes it all sound so dangerous!'

'Believe me,' said Vita fiercely, 'it *is* dangerous. These attacks are like someone beating at your door with growing ferocity. Either you open that door or it will eventually be smashed down.'

The two women were sitting on either side of a glowing fire, made necessary by a stiff easterly blowing along the Channel. Sairey had reluctantly gone to bed half an hour earlier, and Celia would have swiftly followed if Vita hadn't indicated an untypical readiness to talk.

'You say the course of these . . . attacks . . . has been clear, hitherto. How?' asked Celia.

Vita never wasted words on things like, 'Isn't it obvious?' but she let her eyes say it for her, even as her voice patiently rehearsed the past.

'Sairey was three when she and Sarah went to join Nigel in Kenya. Her world was her mother. A child's world usually is, at that age, but even more so in Sairey's case as she had seen very little of her father in those first three years.'

'He was a busy man. His work took him abroad. Important government work. He couldn't refuse to go,' said Celia defensively.

'I'm explaining Sairey, not accusing Nigel,' said Vita. 'Her physical environment changed dramatically, from that gloomy house in Masham Square to East African heat and brightness. But her mother was there, so the change was readily accepted. More difficult to assimilate, perhaps, were the new relationships . . .'

'Her relationships? Nigel, you mean? He's her father!'

'She'd seen little of him in her short life. And, from what I gather, she continued to see little. All right, I know, he was a busy man. Would you call him an open, outgoing man?'

'Of course. He has always been incredibly popular, at school, in the army, in his job. What are you trying to say?'

'Not say, discover,' said Vita, frowning in concentration. 'I know how much you love him. You practically brought him up, didn't you? All I'm saying is that Nigel was possibly still a rather ambiguous figure in Sairey's mind when . . . it happened.'

Such a turning away from plain statement was so untypical as to catch Celia's attention.

'She was very dear to you, wasn't she, Vita?' she said gently.

'To us all, I hope,' said Vita curtly. 'Nigel must have been distraught when Sarah vanished. It was fortunate you happened to turn up at that time.'

'I didn't happen to turn up. It was planned. I was invited,' said Celia. 'I had to go to Nairobi to settle some legal business which had come up in regard to my father's estate, a matter of some property which he'd let on a lease which was now up.'

'Couldn't Nigel have dealt with it?'

'I was my father's executor,' said Celia. 'Nigel was still a minor when the will was made. Our father saw no reason to change things later.'

'No. So you had arranged to fly on to Kampala after your business in Nairobi was done?'

'You sound more like a detective than a psychiatrist, Vita,' said Celia tartly. 'Or are the two things the same? The answer is no. First, I'd planned to go up to Nyeri for a couple of days to take a look at the old farm, see Mother's grave, that sort of thing. But at the last moment I changed my mind.'

'Can I ask why?'

'With or without permission, you seem to be asking,' retorted Celia. 'The simple truth is, I lost my nerve. This was my first time back in Kenya since we'd got out in the fifties. Some memories are best left unstirred, that's what I felt.'

'And still feel?'

'Perhaps. So instead of heading north to Nyeri, I got a seat on the next flight for Entebbe. I sent Nigel a cable, of course, but I'd gathered that Uganda wasn't at its most efficient just then, so I wasn't much surprised when there was no one to meet me at the airport. I made my way into town and to the house. There I found Sairey in the care of some ancient servant, Nigel was out on business and Sarah, well, Sarah had, in fact, set out to pick me up. I thought she'd probably had a puncture or something. It wasn't till much later that I began to get worried . . .'

The two women sat in silence for a while after that, each face composed to conceal whatever thoughts and emotions surged within.

'Did you see Sarah after she was killed?' asked Vita suddenly.

'No!'

'Did Nigel tell you about her injuries?'

'Yes. No. I don't know. He might have done. What . . .'

'Was she raped?'

'For God's sake, woman!' exclaimed Celia, in horror. 'What are you getting at?'

'Nothing. I simply wondered whether the autopsy report said she'd been sexually molested by her attackers,' said Vita equably.

'If any such vileness was discovered, no one mentioned it to me,' said Celia, her voice trembling with barely restrained emotion. 'Now, I think this has gone far enough. I can see no reason for stirring up these painful memories and I can't begin to understand your motives in wanting to do so. I invited you here because I thought it might help my niece, but . . .'

'That's what I'm trying to do,' said Vita. 'All I want to know is the kind of thing Sairey may have picked up about her mother's death.'

'Picked up? You don't imagine we ever talked about such things in front of the child . . .'

'Adults talk in front of children far more often than they suppose,' said Vita. 'Children have the gift of invisibility when they want it. Friends, relatives, priests, the press, they all required information, both in Uganda and when you got home. It's incredible what babies can pick up and retain. And Sairey was no baby. Also, like many children she was, and probably still is, an instinctive eavesdropper.'

Celia glanced in alarm at the door. Vita said, 'It's all right. I gave her a pill. So you brought her back to

England and set up as a surrogate mother for the second time.'

'Second?'

'You brought up Nigel, didn't you?'

'What are you saying? That I did things wrong?' demanded Celia.

'Far from it. It's quite clear that living with you at *Dunelands* was probably the best thing that could have happened to Sairey. Your love, the steady pattern of your life, the dogs, the sea, these were, and still are, of the greatest importance to her. If she could have stayed on here . . .'

'Nigel came back from Africa. He had remarried, could offer a proper home. He was her father, he loved her, of course she had to go to him,' cried Celia.

'Of course she did,' said Vita. 'But look at it from Sairey's viewpoint. Age nine, and her world is turned upside down again. She has to return to Masham Square which she'd only ever known when her mother was alive. But now, instead of her mother there was her father, whom she most closely associated with her mother's death, and this new woman, who was usurping her mother's place and function. That's when these mental and emotional disturbances started, wasn't it?'

'Yes, but they were just nightmares. Children do have them, you know. John Varley didn't think there was anything to worry about. He prescribed a tonic, said she'd grow out of them. And she did,' said Celia accusingly.

'It was John Varley who prescribed *me* this time,' Vita reminded her. 'Did she ever talk to you about her dreams, in detail I mean?'

'No, never.'

'In the principal one, Nigel is holding her over her

mother's coffin to see Sarah's face. Then he hands her to you. Celia, are you all right?'

The older woman had gone quite grey, and rocked forward in her chair as though she might slide off.

'I'm fine,' she said, recovering a little. 'It's just that earlier, a few days ago, she asked me whether she ever saw her mother in her coffin and I was quite sharp with her. Poor child. Is this what she's been dreaming? But why?'

'The simple answer is fear,' said Vita Gray.

'Fear?' exclaimed Celia. 'What of, for heaven's sake?'

'Of ending up like her mother, perhaps. No, hear me out. Remember what happened last time she changed her environment. She met her father, and her mother died. Now, after several stable years, she returns to the house where she was born and has to start life again with her father and a mother substitute. Her head is stuffed with nightmarish fragments of knowledge of how Sarah died. She has probably been told a thousand times how like her mother she looks – she wore her hair very long, very blonde, as a child, didn't she? In her mind, she begins to confuse herself with her mother, so the dreams start. That's what I mean by fear.'

Celia reached forward to poke the fire.

'How you psychiatrists love to complicate things,' she said. 'I'm almost afraid to speak to you for fear of what you'll read into it. But I daresay you'd make even more of my silence. You're wrong about one thing. Sairey didn't think of herself as resembling her mother in any way. Just recently she talked of Sarah as being tall and willowy!'

'And you corrected her?'

'Of course. Shouldn't I have?'

'I really can't say,' said Vita. 'But it was as Sairey got older and started her physical development that the dreams began to fade, wasn't it? A good bust, wide hips, these set her so far from her mental picture of Sarah that she began to feel safe. And how old was she when she chopped her hair off? Twelve? Thirteen? The last physical link. She was herself, and safe at last.'

'So what started it all again, in that case?' said Celia, with undisguised scepticism.

'Cambridge was part of it,' said Vita. 'The same university, the same college, the same subject, perhaps even the same room, as Sarah. How often do you imagine this was pointed out to her? But perhaps it didn't become a reality till she came back from Spain. And there was Nigel, too, talking about his memoirs. She felt huge pressures in both directions – back towards that traumatic loss, and forward in her mother's footsteps towards a nightmare end she could only dream of.'

'How absurdly you perceive life, Vita. But if there is any truth in what you say, the solution is simple. Cancel Cambridge and cancel Nigel's memoirs!'

Vita said, 'I must leave you to deal with your brother, but Cambridge, by being postponed, has already receded as a threat. This latest attack has clearly been stimulated by something new. This is the trouble. It is no use simply trying to isolate Sairey from danger like isolating a haemophiliac from cutting edges. What is troubling Sairey's unconscious is more like the first stirrings of a cancer cell. Leave it untreated now, and in a few years it could destroy her.'

She spoke with a quiet vehemence that was more persuasive than rational argument. Celia sighed deeply and shook her head, not in denial but at some inner tribulation.

'What will you do?' she asked quietly.

'I'll take her with me. To Britt House, my place in Essex. No, before you say it, it wouldn't do for her to stay on here. I need to be able to be in charge of her environment. Don't worry. She'll still be getting plenty of good fresh air. We'll make an early start, so I think I'll say goodnight.'

Vita rose as she spoke, and headed for the door.

'And love?' said Celia.

'Love?'

'You said she'd still get plenty of good fresh air. I wondered if she'd get plenty of love, too.'

Vita considered this, then nodded.

'Oh yes,' she said. 'I love her for her mother's sake. Just as you love her for her father's.'

'I love her for her own sake,' said Celia angrily.

'That, too,' said Vita Gray.

After the younger woman had left, Celia sat still for several minutes staring into space. Then she rose, went to the old oak bureau which was the one piece of furniture to survive the burning of her father's farm, took out a pad of paper and began to write.

Dear Vita,

So what do I think of life out here, now that I'm an old Africa hand of more than six months' standing? It took three of those for me to leave the bungalow by myself, and not just from fear of wild animals or cannibal natives. No, it was mainly simple dread of driving! As you know, I've never been a keen driver, but out here the combination of terrible roads in the sticks and even terribler drivers in the town looked set to keep me stuck on my verandah looking across the Great Rift Valley (which is just that, by the way, a bloody great rift), until Nigel came home to rescue me. And as he has to spend so much time away just now, that meant a hell of a lot of rift! So, finally, I took my life, and the wheel of the Land Rover, in both hands, and now the twenty miles to Nairobi is as nothing and even matatu drivers keep out of my way (matatus are communal taxis which use the pavement as an extra highway). Thank God, I can now subject Sairey to a bit of urban antidote to all those ghastly rural impulses which drove poor Wordsworth dotty!

Not that Nairobi is entirely on the side of sanity, though, in fact, it would be quite pleasant if it weren't for the tourists, the beggars and the old ex-pats, not necessarily in that order. It's incredible how quickly you become possessive enough about a place to object to tourists, isn't it? But the very sight of a new safari outfit or a tee shirt with an elephant on it or a fleet of those awful striped buses they chase the poor animals in, sets my teeth on edge. The beggars, I suppose, are worse, because you feel guilty about being revolted by them. From time to time they are cleared away, but they always come back. Where else have they got to go? As well as the usual disabilities and deformities, there are some which are uniquely African, like a living government health warning to keep taking the tablets and never drink the water. I saw a man the other day with his head twisted round by what looked like a monstrous carbuncle on his neck, so that he was permanently regarding his left shoulder. Easily put right at the hospital, I was assured, but why give up your meal ticket? I said I just couldn't believe this, and I got the usual pitying laugh and assurance that once I'd been here long enough to really understand the African mentality, I'd believe anything! I thought of you, Vita, and wondered what you'd make – will make – of all this when you come.

My 'expert' was of course an ex-pat, perhaps the worst group of the lot because at least you can recognize tourists and beggars by their cameras or their sores. Colonial nostalgia and racist paternalism don't manifest themselves till you've been lured into a drink or a meal. The few diplomatic types I've met seem almost as bad. I'd imagined our social life out here would be one long round of garden parties and receptions, but happily, Nigel doesn't seem to get involved very much in that kind of thing. The only Establishment figure we've seen much of is his immediate boss, and that was a pleasure I could have done without. There was a singer once, Rudi Vallee, I think, they used to call the man with a cock in his voice. Well, Archie Archbell has got his in his eyes. It's like a couple of cannon running at you out of the ports of a warship! To give the man his due, he can be very entertaining in a brutal kind of way, but the constant threat of ocular orgasm is very disconcerting!

Now to my big news. I've got another child. No, not a miracle, and certainly nothing to do with optical interference! It came to pass like this. You remember I mentioned the Brights in my last letter (months ago: sorry!). He's an old chum of Nigel's, and they sent Sairey a really lovely present on her birthday, with apologies for not being able to come to the party, which, as they live God knows how far away in Uganda, was hardly surprising. Well, they did turn up for a visit rather unexpectedly as it happened, but they're as nice as Nigel promised, fortunately. *He* looks type-cast for the role of Old Africa Hand, but beneath the bush-hat he's sensitive and civilized. *She's* black and bonny, a touch serious perhaps, but then she trained as a teacher. They have a boy, Allan, five or six, gorgeous looking, but a handful. Introducing him to Sairey, Apiyo, his mum, said, 'Here's a little sister for you to be lapidi to.' (In her tribe, a lapidi is a kind of juvenile nurse, a child who carries a baby around so that Mum can get on with her work.) Young Allan was greatly offended and ran off yelling, 'I don't want to be lapidi. Lapidi's for girls. I want to be a soldier like Uncle Ocen.' I could see this upset Api but thought it was just good manners, or perhaps gender stereotyping, that was bothering her.

A couple of days later, however, it all came out and I realized that, to some extent, they'd been summing me up before speaking. Also, they were probably waiting to catch Nigel who, as usual, was running around like a scalded cat, never sitting in one place for half an hour at once.

It was at dinner. Bill said abruptly, 'We wondered, would you two mind looking after Allan for a while?'

I was taken aback. I liked them well enough, but after a couple of days hardly felt I was on child-minding terms.

Nigel said, 'What's up?' He's like you, V, when he wants to be, straight to the point.

'They've arrested Ocen,' said Apiyo.

Ocen, her twin, is a captain in the Ugandan army.

'Good Lord,' said Nigel. 'Why?'

'Because he is Acholi. Because Amin and his Nubis are persecuting anyone they think may be loyal to Obote.'

Nubis or Nubians is the general name given to southern Sudanese settlers in Uganda, who traditionally provided the army's other rank cannon fodder. The upper reaches were predominantly Acholi and Langi (Obote's tribe), both from the East Nile. Amin is a Kakwa from the West Nile, a backward superstitious people rated not much higher than Nubis when they join the army. I got this historical background by dint of frequent interruption, which irritated the others, but I wasn't going to sit quiet and uncomprehending like some of those old Cambridge farts wanted us to in their so-called classes!

'Amin has always made allies with the Nubis,' said Api. 'Now he is putting them in all the top jobs.'

'But what else do you expect?' said Nigel. 'If Ocen, say, had led a coup, wouldn't you have expected to see his fellow Acholi shooting up the ladder with him?'

'Please do not try to be reasonable with me, Nigel,' said Apiyo. 'This has already gone far beyond reason. In barracks, many Acholi and Langi soldiers have been beaten, even killed. And now there are Nubi regiments in our tribal areas massacring our menfolk indiscriminately.'

Very reasonably, I thought, Nigel asked if there was any proof of this.

'There are strong rumours,' said Bill Bright unhappily.

'Rumours?' exploded Api. 'You can see the crocodiles in the Nile gorging on those rumours. And it's no rumour about officers being arrested. Ask Ocen. If he is still alive to ask.'

'What do you mean?' I said. I think I was still hoping this was some kind of colonial, post-prandial game.

'We heard that some senior officers were executed at Makindye,' said Bill quietly. 'And at Malire prison there was a large explosion. The authorities said it was just some faulty explosive being disposed of. My info is that several Acholi and Langi officers were put in a room and simply blown up.'

As you can imagine, by now I'd quite forgotten my hostessy duties and the food was congealing on our plates.

'Surely you're not suggesting that any of this, if true, is anything more than the excesses of a few wild men, temporarily let off the leash by the coup?' said Nigel.

'The coup's been over for months,' said Bill. 'The UK has officially recognized the new regime, for God's sake!'

'This all starts from the top. Amin is a monster!' cried Api.

'Look, aren't you looking at this a bit too, forgive me, tribally?' said Nigel.

Before Apiyo could reply, her husband said, 'If it's tribal, it's because the old colonial admin boys liked to keep things tribal. Divide and rule, soldiers from the north, civil service from the south, ne'er the twain shall meet. But forget tribes, Nigel. This Amin's always been a mad bastard, you know that as well as anybody.'

'Why should Nigel know so much about Amin?' I interrupted.

'Hasn't he told you about his guilty past?' said Bill. 'We were both in the KAR at the time that Idi was making his way up through the ranks. There were plenty of active operations, Mau Mau here in Kenya, and later there was a lot of cattle-rustling going on up in Karamoja. Idi made quite a name for himself in the regiment. His favourite method of interrogation was to make suspects lay their dongs on a table while he stood by with a machete. If they didn't answer . . .'

He brought the side of his hand down sharply on the table, making the plates jump.

'Then in '62, there was that Turkana massacre . . .'

'Massacre?' said Nigel. 'Hardly. A dozen suspects died, resisting arrest.'

'There was a court of enquiry,' said Bill.

'Which exonerated Amin.'

'You do recall quite a lot about him, then?' said Bill, with an edge to his voice.

'Enough not to accept without query your allegations that he's some kind of mass murderer,' retorted Nigel.

I suddenly realized that instead of doing my duty and rechannelling the conversation to how warm it was for the time of year, I was sitting there like a spectator at a prize fight. I exchanged glances with Apiyo, but it wasn't a meeting of minds. She was eager to get in there alongside her husband.

Bill took a deep breath and said, 'Look, Nigel, we didn't come here to ask you to send a gun boat or even a diplomatic note. We came to ask you a simple favour as a friend.'

Nigel was instantly, almost dramatically, stricken.

'Oh, Christ. And here am I acting like a petty official. Forgive me, Bill. Api, too. Forgive me. What can we do for you? You've only got to ask.'

'They've asked, dear,' I pointed out. 'They want us to look after Allan.'

'It would mean so much to know he was safe,' said Api, addressing me.

'Safe from what?' I said. I really didn't know what to make of all this. 'They surely wouldn't harm children?'

'Believe me, no Acholi male is safe, especially not if his uncle is an army officer.'

'You, then, what about your own safety?'

'I have to go back to see if I can help my brother,' she said.

'And it's our home,' said Bill. 'But it would be a great comfort to know the boy was safe, in good hands.'

'Then of course he shall stay. And I guarantee I'll turn him into Sairey's lapidi before you see him next,' I said.

That was a good hostessy thing to say. The atmosphere lightened several watts, and we were able to proceed to our pudding in some kind of order.

There, don't I lead the exciting life, then? Nigel assured me in bed that it was all much exaggerated and things would settle down in Uganda as soon as the teething troubles were past. In fact, he's so certain of it that he's talking about transferring us all to Kampala at some point. That's where he was based for a time, and he talks almost nostalgically of the place.

We shall see. And if you're going to see this in the near future, I must finish, or else I'll miss the boy with the cleft stick.

Vita, I refuse to congratulate you on this new job you've got, (a) because you're so vague about it. I'm sure it must have something to do with watching rats running around mazes which you know I hate, and (b) because it's taking you off to America and preventing you from visiting us here. I know you're not crazy about Nigel and it must nark you that I am, but I promise not to show it if you tell your bosses that you can't fly with your back to the sun and have to travel to the States via Africa. Do try, darling.

My love to all who deserve it. If you see Mary Marsden tell her I've hardly opened a book since I've been here, but I'm continually thinking unutterably deep Laurentian thoughts!'

And, of course, my fondest love to you, dear Vita,
Sarah.

7

Essex had a different sky, a different air, and, though the Blackwater at Maldon was already tidal, it promised a very different sea from the one that Celia had urged her into every morning.

Vita Gray imposed no such strict physical regimen.

'Do what you will,' she said. 'Only, let me know if you're going off by yourself. And try to keep a record of what you see, what you think; not everything, just anything that strikes you as worth noting.'

'Why?' asked Sairey.

'To help me understand the cast of your mind, that's all,' said Vita. But Sairey did not altogether believe her. She'd told Vita about the incident on Camber Sands which had preceded the return of the Dream, and she guessed that the older woman wanted to keep a check on her activities, without seeming to do so.

Already the shift of location had resulted in a slackening-off of the nightmares. Vita corrected her when she said this.

'Not "resulted in" but 'been coincident with",' she said.

'Oh, Vita, sometimes you sound a real old pedant!' laughed Sairey.

'Do I? Pedantry is often the name the slipshod give to the words of the precise,' said Vita. 'Your mother used to call me pedantic, too.'

'Did she?' Sairey felt her usual impulse to slide away from talk of her mother but this time she forced herself to say, 'And did you think she was slipshod, too?'

'*Too?*' said Vita. 'I try always to say what I mean, Sairey, but there's no legislating for sloppy listening. But yes, to be honest, I did think Sarah was slipshod in certain ways, though I only ever said that to her once.'

'When she told you she was going to be married,' Sairey guessed.

'You're right,' said Vita, after a tiny pause. 'You see how very sharp your mind can be. Again, just like your mother's.'

'But not when it came to marriage?'

'I didn't think so.'

'Why? Because of Daddy? Or were you jealous?' blurted out Sairey.

'I think that last question could be more precise,' said Vita.

'All right,' snapped Sairey, furious at not being able to match Vita's control. 'Were you in love with Mummy? Is that precise enough for you?'

'It's certainly vehement enough. No, I was not. Though, of course, I did love her. I think that leaves just one question unanswered. "Because of Daddy?" you asked. Yes, partly. There now, I think that does it. Anything more?'

'Not for the moment,' said Sairey. 'Vita, why do you do it? Why do you treat me like a little child asking foolish questions?'

'I'm sorry that's how you feel,' said Vita Gray. 'But you're wrong. You feel like that because I am treating you as an equal. I could make you feel as if you were being treated as an equal, but only by approaching you as a child. It's easy for me not to make you angry. What's hard is for you not to get angry. Sairey, I think it's time we got down to some serious work. Would you like to come to the consulting room?'

She led the way upstairs, to a room at the back of the

old clapboard house. It was a long rectangular room, low-ceilinged, like the rest of the building. A wide, shallow window was heavily curtained so that Vita had to switch on the lights as they entered. The lighting was concealed, casting a dim, suffused glow not much this side of crepuscular. The carpet and curtains were dull beige, and the walls were painted mushroom and hung with a couple of fuzzy abstracts which looked as if they'd been painted with a sponge. At one end was an office desk with a swivel chair behind it. At the other end were three armchairs upholstered in dark tan leather. They were oddly arranged, two quite close and facing each other, the third a little apart and facing the end wall, on which hung a school-room clock.

'Sit down,' said Vita.

Was it a test?

'It's not a test,' said Vita. 'Sit there.'

As Sairey sat in one of the two chairs facing each other, Vita went to the desk and pulled open a drawer. A moment later she came and sat opposite Sairey. In her hand was a portable cassette recorder.

'What do you think of my consulting room?' she asked, checking the sound level.

'It's very . . . neutral.'

'Good, we don't want a room taking sides, do we?'

'I didn't realize you worked here, Vita. I mean on a regular basis.'

'You thought you were uniquely privileged, did you? Don't be piqued. Sometimes my work requires a degree of confidentiality that can't be guaranteed in London. Here, I'm not a well-known consultant psychiatrist, I'm merely that slightly dotty old Mrs Gray's slightly dottier daughter.'

'This is your family house, you mean?'

'Yes. I was brought up here.'

'I didn't know. Did Mummy ever come here?'

'Yes. She used to come and stay in the vacation sometimes. My own mother was alive then, of course. Oddly, I lost her at the same time as you lost yours.'

'I didn't know.'

'Why should you? She was very fit for her age, loved to walk around the estuary. It's strangely beautiful down there. You must go. But take care. Those long levels of wet mud can be almost hypnotic with the sun glancing off them. It's easy to forget the tide. Mother did. Then she panicked. Got stuck in the mud. The tide came up, and she drowned.'

'Vita, how dreadful!' exclaimed Sairey. 'No one ever said.'

'What was there to say? Sarah, your mother, was killed at almost exactly the same time. I would have flown straight out in normal circumstances, but it wasn't possible. There was too much to do here.'

It sounded almost like an apology, but the topic was clearly exhausted for the moment as Vita proceeded to say briskly, 'Let me give you a full picture of what will go on here. Normally, we shall sit as we're sitting now, facing each other. Sometimes I'll ask you to sit in that chair where you won't be able to see me as we talk. And sometimes if the situation seems to require a touch of official distancing, I will sit behind the desk. I'm telling you all this so that your active little mind won't be burrowing away after my motives all the time. We have to have an equal trust. The recorder will provide us with a record, so there can never be any doubt as to what precisely was said, though of course there may be debate about meaning. All right?'

'Vita,' said Sairey uneasily, 'where is all this leading?'

The older woman held up the recorder and switched it

on. She spoke the date and the time then set the machine on the table between them.

'Where do you think it's leading, Sairey?' she asked.

'I don't know. It's like trying to find a way through a labyrinth,' said Sairey, self-consciously dramatic, still aware of the recorder.

'A way? Which way?'

'Is there more than one way?'

'There's a way out. And there's a way to the centre.'

'You mean to the monster? Is that how you see yourself, Vita? As a dragon-killer?' said Sairey, trying for mockery.

'Not necessarily,' said Vita. 'It's too easy to forget, in all branches of medicine, that there's nothing can be killed inside you that isn't part of you. Let's talk about your dream, Sairey.'

They talked on, and off, for the next few days. Sairey could discern little pattern in their talks, but she found that she looked forward to them. She admitted to this rather shamefacedly and was rewarded by one of Vita's rare smiles.

'You have a curiously puritanical notion of medicine,' she said. 'If it's not nasty, it can't be doing you any good! Your mother was the same. Whatever you did for pleasure should be explored to the full, but whatever you did for your health had got to be painful.'

'Am I really like her?' asked Sairey.

'Do you feel as if you are?'

'How on earth should I know that? All I know about her is what people have said, and that hasn't been much!'

'I expect people were worried about hurting you,' said Vita. 'But don't underestimate how much you know about Sarah. You came out of her. You spent more time with her in those first five years of your life than with any other person then or since, and she with you.'

'I was a baby, an infant. That's not knowing, that's just dependency!'

'That's a motive for learning, isn't it? The need to know.'

'I thought that was a security term for limiting knowledge, not extending it.'

Vita said, 'Knowledge is like water. You can map out boundaries, but lines on paper don't hinder currents and tides. People must start understanding this.'

'In security?'

'In psychology. Sairey, would you like to hear yesterday's tape?'

Sairey hesitated in her reply. Vita's normal technique was to wait for desires to emerge, wishes to be stated. She must have strong motives for making the suggestion herself, and Sairey relished this brief moment of control. But she lacked the will to say no, which in any case would only mean postponement. Better to accede with dignity now than feel herself nudged into it later.

'All right,' she said.

They listened for half an hour. Sairey was aghast. At first, she sounded more or less like she expected to sound, a young woman talking to an elder about her life, her hopes, her fears, her likes and dislikes, then gradually she became less coherent, more emotional, and towards the end there was a long silence of perhaps a minute where it seemed she had lost the power of speech altogether. Then Vita's voice said, 'All right, Sairey. That will do for today,' and her own voice, sounding quite normal again, replied, 'Oh, good. It looked as if the sun was going to come out earlier. I thought I'd take the rowing boat out and see how that family of coots is getting on.' Then Vita pronounced the date and time and the tape went dead.

'Well?' said Vita.

81

'I was awful!' exclaimed Sairey.

'It wasn't an audition,' said Vita.

'That makes it worse. I mean, that was really me, wasn't it? How can you bear to spend so much time listening to such drivel?'

'I wouldn't call it drivel,' said Vita.

'No? The best thing in it was when I finally gave up and shut up at the end. Vita, I don't remember that at all, that's what makes it even worse. Was I just sitting there with my mouth open, drooling? That's what it sounded like.'

'No,' said Vita. 'The truth is, you were hypnotized.'

'I was what?' Sairey looked at the other woman in amazement.

Vita said, 'Hypnotism is a technique I sometimes find useful. But, of course, I would never use it without the patient's permission.'

'You didn't have my permission!' said Sairey indignantly.

'No. But I wasn't using the technique as part of your treatment. Yet. I said that it wasn't an audition, but in a way that's precisely what it was. Not everyone is susceptible to hypnosis, so, where possible, I like to be sure in advance that it is feasible before worrying people by suggesting it. You would, I believe, make an excellent subject. But rest assured, if you refuse, I won't try to put you under again. Not that it would be very easy, now you've been alerted.'

'You mean if you'd wanted you could have had me quacking like a duck or singing "Rule Britannia", like they do in the theatre?'

'That's almost as offensive as pointing out to an anaesthetist that he could slip between the sheets with you once you'd gone under,' said Vita caustically.

'You know what an anaesthetist is doing when he starts

doping you,' retorted Sairey. 'Look, Vita, this is a bit of a shock. What exactly is it you want to do with me?'

'I want to take you further into the labyrinth,' said Vita Gray. 'We're already in there, beyond the reach of simple memory. And I'm beginning to feel that I'm getting beyond the point where dreams cast sufficient light.'

'You mean you want to take me back to childhood? Like in the movies?'

'I'm not sure which movie you're referring to,' said Vita. 'I know of none which doesn't sensationalize, or worse, trivialize the technique.'

'Is it dangerous?'

'Not in the sense I think you mean,' said Vita hesitantly. 'I certainly don't anticipate unearthing a previous incarnation or putting you in touch with the Devil. But there's a danger in expecting too much. Often the technique merely seems to reinforce the mind's subconscious defences. And sometimes the realization that the past isn't dead, but still lives within us, can be devastating.'

Sairey rose and went to the window and drew back the curtain to let in a haze of lemony sunlight. From here she could see the Blackwater winding towards the estuary, where the mudbanks basked like sleeping whales. Somewhere along its course, one summer day a thousand years ago, the English had defended a ford against marauding Vikings. There'd been no difficulty in holding them at bay till the English leader, over-confident of his strength, had permitted the enemy to cross and fight on equal terms. A short time later, his force was routed and he himself was dead.

Why should she feel this old story as some kind of parable?

'The past still exists, you say?' she delayed.

'Somewhere, though it's not always possible to find it.'

'But if it exists, then it doesn't. I mean you can't have a past that isn't past.'

'I'm not a semiologist,' said Vita. 'Just a simple psychiatrist.'

'When would we start?' asked Sairey.

'I think we've started already.'

Sairey didn't argue, but slowly drew the curtains across the uneasy sunlight.

'*Where* shall we start?' she asked.

'East Africa, 1971, the year you and your mother arrived in Nairobi. Do you remember much about Nairobi?'

'Nothing.'

'No? You were just a baby, of course, but a little older when you moved to Kampala. Do you recall anything about Kampala?'

'Just that it's where Mummy died.' The effort of keeping her voice controlled produced a slight tremor, but Vita didn't seem to notice.

'But you'll have read something about Uganda, I'm sure. About Obote and Amin and the coup and the reign of terror and the hostages at Entebbe . . .'

'No! Nothing!'

'Nothing? You surprise me. I thought that school history courses had shaken off their old prejudices.'

'Not the kind of school Daddy sent me to,' said Sairey aggressively. 'Vita, can we get on? I mean, don't you want soft music, flashing lights . . .'

'A jewel on a pendulum, swinging before your eyes? That *can* help, a focus, a point of concentration. Perhaps we shall need it, perhaps we shall not. I didn't need it last time but then you didn't know I was trying to hypnotize you. Now you're on your guard, even though your conscious mind has agreed to co-operate. The voice alone may not be relaxing enough, the voice and this warm

84

room and this comfortable chair and the river outside winding slowly to the sea . . . are you sure you've read nothing about Uganda, about Obote and Amin and the coup and the reign of terror and the hostages at Entebbe . . .'

'Yes, of course I've read about them,' admitted Sairey wearily.

'But you can't remember anything about your own time in Africa?'

'No. I can't remember.'

'Of course you can't. Not at your age. You were only a baby then. Let's go back through those years. Nice and slowly, no need to rush, you're seventeen . . . sixteen . . . fifteen . . . say the figures with me . . . fourteen . . . thirteen . . . twelve . . . ten . . .'

'Ten,' said Sairey, 'nine . . . eight . . . seven . . . six . . . five . . . four . . .'

'. . . three . . . two . . . one . . .' said Vita softly. 'And now the year is nineteen seventy-one . . .'

'. . . nineteen seventy-one . . .'

8

Sairey stood by the window and looked out towards the river, from which the morning mist had given up the struggle to arise. Behind her, for the third time, the tape of last night's hypnosis session played.

'*There's a light in the air, moving. I want to catch it.*'

'*Just one light? A flame, maybe?*'

'*Yes. A flame. It's quite close. I'm in Daddy's arms. And then he blows. I feel his breath. And the light goes out. People laugh. But I want the light back. I struggle and he gives me to Mummy and she takes me away from the noise to a place where there's nothing but me and Mummy and a great darkness full of air and strange faraway sounds . . .*'

Sairey switched off the machine. She and Vita had agreed that it would be best for Sairey not to hear these tapes immediately, but to listen to them the following day when she would be fresh and Vita would have had time to analyse and interpret.

There was a tap at the door, but Vita did not come in till Sairey called out, 'OK.'

The older woman had two cups of coffee in her hands. Sairey drank greedily, then burst out, 'Was that really me remembering my birthday?'

'Remembering?' said Vita doubtfully. 'Yes, but just because this is recorded under hypnosis, don't think that your memory's precise as a tape. The technique can bring back forgotten tunes, but it can't remaster them to get rid of all the hiss and crackle and distortion.'

'That's your job, then?'

'Our job,' said Vita.

Sairey turned to face her.

'Vita, this is taking up a lot of your time. I mean, is it worth it? People go around with lumps of shrapnel in them all their lives. Why can't I manage with one bad memory?'

'I could explain that, but are you sure that's really what you mean?'

'Christ, Vita, it does get irritating you telling me what I really mean all the time,' exclaimed Sairey angrily.

'I'm sorry,' said Vita. 'You're right. My task is to make you understand what you mean, not simply to tell you.'

Sairey mastered her extra irritation at this Vita-ish apology, and said with a wry smile, 'There you go. It's not the telling which is irritating. It's the being right. So, what I really mean is, why all this bother? You don't like Daddy much, so it's hardly a favour to an old friend. On the other hand, because you dislike him, you're probably too proud to charge him, so you end up doing it for free anyway.'

'It's not Nigel I'm treating,' said Vita.

'Yes, but I wonder how much you really like me,' said Sairey. 'I know you've always been a kind of aunt, but . . .'

'A bit weird?' said Vita. 'Not a big-cheque-at-Christmas and cream-tea-at-Fortnum's kind of aunt? You mustn't be worried about people liking you, Sairey.'

'Am I worried?'

'Tell me one person you're absolutely sure loves you, warts and all, for your own sake.'

Sairey thought about this for a long time, realized it was too long, and said quickly, 'Celia, I think.'

There was no triumph in Vita's face but Sairey felt triumphed over.

'What about you, then?' she demanded. 'Can you do it?'

'Probably not,' said Vita Gray with one of her smiles. 'But the difference is, I'm not worried about it. Now, you won't forget that Fanny and Nigel are coming for tea?'

'For a progress report, you mean?'

'This is not a school and they're not coming on a half-term visit,' said Vita. 'If asked, I shall say you seem in good health and reasonable spirits. For detail, I shall refer them to you.'

'Thanks,' said Sairey. 'Vita, you managed to avoid saying how much you liked me.'

'Think of me as a mirror, Sairey,' said the older woman. 'I like you as much as you like me. Now, let's talk about the tape.'

Sairey went out for a walk in the afternoon. It was a murky day, with sight and sound muffled in a clamminess that was not quite rain and not quite mist. She walked by the brown swirling river, lulled by its gurglings into a melancholy near-trance which she couldn't break free from, though she was much more aware of it than she ever was of Vita's hypnosis. In its grip, she walked further than she intended and realized she was going to be late back for her father's visit. Or perhaps it wasn't unintentional. That was one thing a deal of Vita's company did for you. It made you mistrust the apparent causes of things.

She set off back at a brisk pace. In a rutted and muddy lane about a furlong from the house, she thought she heard a sound ahead of her. She paused. She could hear nothing, but her straining eyes caught a movement in the gloom. Someone was approaching, so far nothing more than an eddying of the vapour which seemed to fill the hedge-lined track like a horse's trough. A foot splashed in a puddle. To her left was a gate into a field, horrent with young wheat. Crossing it diagonally would bring her straight to Britt House. Normally such a damaging trespass would have been unthinkable, but now she was over the gate and into the field before she'd even begun to wonder what she was running from.

Not that she was making much of a show of running, with every step on the sodden furrows skidding and sliding back almost as far as it took her forward. She'd forgotten what a huge field it was. The air was clearer here but she could hardly make out the boundary hedge ahead. She glanced behind her to take encouragement from the distance she had covered. Instead, she found terror. The figure in the lane had entered the field too. Now it had shape and bulk, possibly exaggerated by the distorting glass of the air, but she wasn't going to wait in the hope that closeness might cut it down to size. She threw back her head and tried to sprint for the security of the house, which she could now see, apparently floating on the vaporous air. It was like running through the shallows at *Dunelands*, except that there it was joy that exploded in that huge waste of energy, and it was Polly and Mop who loped along behind her, barking their delight at the game.

She looked back no more, and the pounding of blood in her ears shut out whatever noise of pursuit there might have been.

Finally it was there, the boundary hedge. She burst through it, heedless of damage to herself or the hedgerow, ran up the tussocky lawn and came to a halt against the french window. There was no time to compose herself. Inside, with the light unseasonally on against the dusky day, she saw her father with Fanny and Vita. Vita was pouring a cup of tea, her father was nibbling gingerly at a slice of the coarse seed cake which was Vita's sole concession to the demands of hospitality. Fanny was doing nothing except look beautiful and composed.

It was, of course, Fanny who saw her first. Her eyes registered her stepdaughter's strange apparition but her expression of gentle amusement did not change. Sairey wanted to slip away out of sight but she was certain there were sounds of pursuit close behind her. She seized the handle of the window and pushed it open. Only her father showed any surprise.

'There you are,' he said. 'No one can say you're a fair-weather walker.'

She stepped into the room and at last felt brave enough to turn round, fully expecting that her pursuer would have evaporated into one of her wispy fantasies.

But there he was, standing in the open doorway, bold as brass. The next shock was that she recognized him. That young dark face with its star-shaped scar. It was the wounded boy from the Masham Square gardens. And the third shock came from her father.

'So you found her, Allan. Well done. Did you recognize him, Sairey? Probably not. He looked a bit different last time you saw him! But don't stand around, you two. You're dripping all over Vita's carpet. Get those wet things off and have some tea!'

9

By sitting quiet and listening carefully, Sairey learned a lot.

'Did you meet Bill Bright, Allan's father, when you came out to Kampala?' Nigel Ellis asked Vita.

'I never came out,' said Vita. 'I was planning to, but Sarah died.'

She had no use for euphemism.

'Yes, of course . . . well, you'd have loved old Bill. Real Empire-building stuff, all the virtues, none of the flaws. The salt of the earth.'

Against Vita's directness, Sairey weighed her father's ability to produce clichés with all the vibrant sincerity of new coinage, and declared a draw. Her father reminisced on, giving Sairey the facts to work out that her 'wounded boy' was six years older than she was. But with those fine features, that golden skin, he really didn't look any more than sixteen or seventeen. He must have got the best of both parents, whereas she . . .

'I seem to recall Sarah mentioning Mr and Mrs Bright somewhere in her letters,' said Vita.

'Yes, she would,' said Ellis. 'Allan lived with us for a while. He and Sairey were great friends.'

'She doesn't remember,' said Allan, smiling at Sairey, who shook her head.

'Perhaps Vita will help bring it all back,' said Fanny, speaking for the first time since the young people had arrived.

'Perhaps,' said Vita. 'Your parents are dead, Mr Bright?'

'Yes . . .'

'It was tragic,' intervened Ellis sharply. 'I'm sure Allan doesn't want to be reminded of it.'

'It's a painful memory,' said the young man. 'Mr Ellis was tremendously helpful afterwards. I'll never forget what his friendship meant to my family.'

Looking rather embarrassed, Nigel Ellis went on, 'You can imagine how delighted I was, Vita, to hear from young Allan a few weeks ago. And when I realized he was between jobs, I snapped him up to give me a hand with my memoirs.'

'As a secretary?' said Vita.

'Secretary, researcher, editor – remember, though young, he was actually around during that last, most frightening period of my time in Africa.'

'Yes, he would be,' said Vita. 'Tell me, Mr Bright . . .'

'Allan.'

Vita considered this, as she considered all things before making a decision.

'Allan,' she said experimentally. 'Tell me, Allan, what jobs are you between?'

'Before, rather than between,' he said. 'I did a degree at Makerere, then came to London to do postgraduate work, which I've just finished. I hadn't really made up my mind what to do next. I suppose what I mean is, I haven't really made up my mind whether I'm European or African. Running into Mr Ellis was a lucky break. It gives me a breathing space as well as some really interesting work to do.'

'What is your subject?' asked Vita.

'Literature,' said Allan. 'In particular, the African novel.'

'Then you'll have a lot in common with Sairey. She's going to read Eng. Lit. at Cambridge. Like her mother.

There were many who felt she had the finest critical mind of her year.'

Sairey bowed her head so that her hair, had it been long, would have screened her face. The movement drew Fanny's attention and she said, 'At least you seem to be having a good influence on Sairey's hair, Vita. A few weeks ago it was just a fluorescent stubble!'

'Yes,' said Sairey, 'I thought I'd try it long. If I don't run out of patience.'

She caught Vita's eye and forced herself not to look away.

After tea, a wind blew up from the south and transformed the murky afternoon into a comparatively pleasant evening. Underfoot, it was still soggy and the hedgerows left damp fingermarks along any sleeve that brushed against them. But the palling mist was gone, and the big East Anglian sky slipped away on all sides to horizons so distant as to be foreign.

Sairey and Allan walked together beside the river. Vita had proposed it. Sairey had looked at her father, thinking that perhaps he was hoping to get her on her own for a while, but he had smiled and said, 'More fresh air? Best tonic there is – when you're young. When you're my age the only good tonic comes with a lot of gin in it. I'm sure Vita's about to satisfy my needs. Off you young things go, and satisfy yours.'

Now as they paused to watch a pair of tufted ducks diving for their supper, Allan Bright said, 'Which of your needs shall I satisfy first?'

'Is that meant to be a pass?'

'I'm merely obeying your father's instructions.'

He smiled as he spoke, but Sairey was looking beyond the joke already. Could it be that her father thought that she might be more forthcoming with someone of her own age group, and would debrief Allan later?

She said, 'Curiosity, then. What were you doing in the Square that night?'

He said, 'You didn't mention seeing me?'

'No. You were a needless complication. And I didn't know who you were, of course.'

'Will you mention it now?'

'Not without cause.'

He didn't ask what the cause might be, but said, 'It was an amazing coincidence, that was all. I'd been at a party and I was on my way home. I've got a flat in Victoria. I was walking, because I thought the air would do me good as I'd got a bit tiddly at the thrash. Then I ran into this bunch of yobbos. There was the usual provocation, *where you been, nig-nog?* that sort of thing. Sober, I'd have put my head down and kept going. But I let them get to me. There was trouble. They soon sorted me out and about ten minutes too late I decided to run. They came after me. I turned into Masham Square, went over the rails into the gardens, and lay still as a mouse under a bush till I was sure they weren't still looking for me. Then I got up and started cleaning myself under that tap when suddenly I heard you. I nearly dropped dead from fright. I was sure those bastards had come back.'

It rang true, but not wholly.

'And you didn't know who I was?' said Sairey.

'No. How should I? But when your father called to you, that voice rang a bell. I had the coat cleaned and left it on the step. And I found out from the postman that the family who lived there was called Ellis. It seemed so unlikely a coincidence that I hung around the house from time to time till I got a glimpse of your father. He's changed a little, of course, but I still recognized him.'

'I can see why you should want to have a look at Daddy, but why did you spy on me?'

'You saw me, then?' He smiled. 'Curiosity. To get another look at this strange creature who runs around parks in her night-clothes and doesn't scream rape when she bumps into a bleeding black man!'

'So. All coincidence. But bumping into Daddy, I take it that the coincidence had stopped by then?'

'I'm afraid so. Though if I'd known he was living in London, I'm sure I would have looked him up a great deal earlier. After all, he and my father were very good friends. Look, I'm not trying to worm my way into his affections and get you disinherited. Anything he gives me, I'll have worked for!'

The vehemence with which he spoke took her by surprise.

'What on earth are you talking about?' she asked, annoyed. 'Do you really think I see life like a Victorian novel?'

'No. But you may see it like a medieval mystery.'

'What's the difference? They're both rigid with moral lessons, aren't they?'

'In one, coincidence is a writer's trick, in the other it's an act of God.'

'I don't believe in God.'

'If I walked across this river on top of the water, would you believe in him then?'

'Perhaps.'

'Then I shan't do it.'

'Why not?'

'Because I don't believe in God either and it would be immoral to persuade you of a lie.'

'Even by a miracle?'

'Especially by a miracle.'

* * *

The visitors stayed to an hour which would have forced an invitation to dinner from most hostesses. But meals at Britt House were as irregular in timing as they were eccentric in menu, and Vita didn't even feel called upon to reissue the seed cake.

As they left, Nigel Ellis embraced his daughter warmly and said, 'It's good to see you looking so well. We must see what we can do about sending you on a long holiday soon. No, don't say anything now. Think about it. How about the States? You'd love it over there.'

Fanny offered a non-contact kiss, then produced a book from the car and presented it to her.

'I thought you might like to have this. I enjoyed it when I was a couple of years younger than you.'

It was a leather-bound copy of Karen Blixen's *Out of Africa*. It was inscribed, *To Fanny, Happy Birthday, with much love, Uncle Arch.*

'But I can't take this,' protested Sairey conventionally. 'It was a birthday present.'

'You grow out of things,' said Fanny. 'That's what birthdays are all about. If it bores you, dump it.'

Allan shook her hand.

'This is a strange place,' he said. 'In Africa it would be a magic place. Don't get on the wrong side of the natives.'

That night, after a late supper of carrot soup and blackberry pie, Sairey and Vita sat together in companionable silence before the embers of an unseasonable fire and drank the herbal tea which was Vita's inevitable nightcap.

'What do you make of coincidence, Vita?' asked Sairey.

One of Vita's merits as a companion was that she never expressed surprise at a turn of conversation, so you didn't have to waste time on pointless prolegomena.

'In my line, it's accepted wisdom that all accidents are

significant. Perhaps this should be applied in general as well as in particular.'

'God's purpose at work, you mean?'

'Do I? You're thinking of Allan Bright, I suppose. For a young intelligent man to end up studying in London, where he looks up an old friend of his father's, seems too forecastable a sequence to partake of the coincidental. Unless there is an element I don't know about.'

Sairey sighed, and lied.

'No. It's just that I'm here because of my dreams, and Daddy brings Allan, who is part of the past you're trying to get me to relive.'

'Recall. If we could relive we could change. Change is an illusion sometimes known as hope.'

'What's the point of chasing the past then, Vita?' cried Sairey.

'So that the present can live in the truth.'

'But that must affect the future. Surely that gives us hope?'

'Why should truth bring hope?' said Vita sombrely.

'If it doesn't, if truth has no spin-off in the future, what *is* the point of seeking it?'

'I didn't say it had no spin-off.'

'What, then?'

'Justice,' said Vita Gray.

Sairey digested this. Then she said, 'By the way, you mentioned some letters of Mummy's. You said you recalled something about the Brights . . .'

'Yes. Your mother was not a very regular correspondent, nor have I been very meticulous in preserving private correspondence, but I daresay I could lay my hands on the letter in question. Would you like to see it?'

'Yes,' said Sairey. 'Yes, I would.'

'All right. But not tonight, I think. Drink up and let's get to bed. I'd like to start early tomorrow, while young

Mr Bright is still in your head. Coincidence or not, he may prove a very useful trigger.'

Triggers fire guns. Sairey didn't speak the thought out loud, but she saw Vita regarding her thoughtfully, as if she had.

no Panel Beaters today ... lost track time ... only
regulator ... moved ... where? ... window ... too high
... clothes ... no shoes watch wallet but biro in lining

sun through window in morning ... cried ... breakfast
mangoes ... ate ... was sick ... ate again ... guard
took bucket ... brought back more bog paper ... I
laughed ... first in how long ... was sick ... but no
beatings ...

stronger today ... may try clothes on later ... something
meaty in mealies ... tried clothes ... trousers beyond
me ... guard helped ... Gregory ... always smiling ...
why not? ... asked where? ... shook head ...

this cell better than last ... dried blood not mine ... and
window ... could reach window standing on bed ...
tried ... fell off ... Gregory came very concerned and
scolding ... said no release if not look well ... release?
... daren't hope ... asked Gregory about Apiyo ...
shook head ... safe? ... pray God ...

Gregory knows I'm writing. Caught me today. Looked
other way, very obviously. Brought more bog paper.
Thanked him. He shrugged, said plenty paper this month,
no coffee. In Uganda! Outside noises, shouting, laughing.
Shrieking.

This morning, Gregory muttered, 'visitor today, look good, hold tongue.' Ready to explode in rage and indignation. But when door opened and slim moustachioed man with Arabic features said, 'Good morning, Mr Bright, how are you?' I stuttered, 'Quite well. Improving.' Like to think I was clever, best way to get out. Truth is, terrified going back to Makindye and Panel Beaters. He said, 'Good. Your case is under review' and left. Gregory more smiles than ever. I'd been good boy, done well. Shame gave me strength. Later, I climbed on bed, pulled myself up to window. Compound of one-storey buildings overlooking courtyard. Main road visible to right. The Jinja road! I'm at Naguru in HQ of Public Safety Unit. Has anyone been told I've been shifted from military custody at Makindye?

Noises in compound again. Climbed up, looked out. Lots of guards standing around, smoking, laughing. Two men brought from building, hands tied behind backs, clothes in tatters. One made to sit in middle of compound. Guards took other aside, talked to him. After a while he nodded. Cuffs removed. Guard gave him sledgehammer. Stealthily he approached other prisoner. They'd promised freedom if he killed other man! Seated man attracted by guards' laughs and cries of encouragement. Tried to struggle to feet, shrieking, but man with sledgehammer rushed on him. Not strong enough to do it with one blow. Raised hammer again and again and again. I was shouting, but drowned by dying man shrieking and cheering from the guards. Along the road from Kampala to Jinja went a bus. I could see passengers' heads turn. Now I was crying. Body dragged away. Killer congratulated, led to shady corner near compound gate. Invited to sit. Needed to. Poor wretch was exhausted. I wondered what he would feel later when price of his freedom struck him. Then I noticed another prisoner being brought out. Guards pointing to man in

100

corner, offering sledgehammer . . . I threw back my head and shrieked, 'No!' Then I was pulled off bed by Gregory no longer smiling, very angry. He said, 'You see that, you stay here always,' and chopped his hand at his throat like a panga. 'People on the bus saw it,' I argued. He smacked his lips derisively to show what was thought of the obser-vations of people who travelled on buses. Then he made me lie on the bed making soothing noises as if I were a child. 'Rest man. Get some sleep. You OK. You got friends.' I felt exhausted but I couldn't sleep. I put my hands over my ears, but all through the long afternoon I heard the shrieks and the laughter and the cheers from the compound beneath my window.

I asked Gregory who my friends were. 'Important person,' he said. 'Else you dead.' He's guessing, I think. But it makes sense. Someone must be pulling very hard on a string to drag me back from where I was not long ago. Ellis is the only one I can think of. God knows what he really does, but if anyone has the pull, it's him.

Today I tried bribery on Gregory. All he's done so far has been from natural kindness, but kindness stops way short of taking risks for a stranger. Thought of promising money but that rang false. Finally I decided. 'Gregory,' I said, 'There are many bad things happening here.' He looked at me uneasily and shook his head and said, 'You do not see. Big trouble for you if you see.' I said, 'Big trouble for you, Gregory, whether you see or not. When Obote returns, big trouble for all PSU men.' 'Obote finished for good,' he said without conviction. 'If not Obote, someone,' I said. 'Idi Dada cannot last for ever. Then he will go somewhere far and safe with all his wives. But where will you go, Gregory?' He looked so unhappy that I knew that this wasn't the first time such a thought had occurred. I said, 'These papers you see me write, in them I say that my guard, Gregory, is a good man, a kind man, who deserves reward, not punishment. When I leave here and return to my own country and talk to the enemies of Idi Dada, that is what I will tell them also. So when the change comes, whoever else is punished, my friend Gregory will be rewarded.' His eyes lit up. I don't honestly think he'd had any ulterior motive for his kindness, so the idea that it might actually benefit him, filled him with a novel delight. Now was the moment to strike, though I felt quite ashamed. But I had to know. 'Gregory,' I said, 'I need your help. I must know about my wife. She may be in danger. She is Acholi woman.' I could see from his face that he knew this already and knew also how very great the danger must be for an Acholi married to a suspect white man. If he'd known about Ocen, I doubt if even natural kindness plus, now, self-interest would have made him co-operate. But I told him where I wanted him to go and what I wanted him to do and after a while he nodded and left me. I was eager to learn when he could go, when I could hope to hear something, but I know that here in Africa such European needs for reassurance would only cause a re-appraisal of the danger involved. I had to stay still and look confident. I had to wait.

Gregory came back after several days off. When I tried to ask him about message he turned evasive. In the end he said yes, he'd delivered it and all was well, but I can see he's lying. Something's happened. He must tell.

Gregory ran into the cell and said the Panel Beaters were here. But the Panel Beaters are SRC. Besides nothing has

bastards bastards basta

10

Reading her mother's letter was an experience almost as devastating to Sairey as the Dream. She had to put it down halfway through and walk around her room till its furnishings became familiar once more. Picking it up again was like touching a live wire. She felt the tingle of pain course up her arteries towards her heart, but this time she got to the end. Instantly she re-read it, concentrating now on the meaning of the words instead of drowning in her awareness that these attenuated curves of fading blue had been inscribed by her mother, that here she had paused, here refilled her pen, here spilt a small drop of liquid. Tea, more likely than tear, she told herself angrily, and just as probably from Vita's cup, reading, as her mother's, writing.

Vita had waited forty-eight hours before giving her the letter. Far from being a trigger, Allan's image seemed to have been a block, and the next two sessions had been fruitless.

'You're sure you want to read this?' said Vita.

'Does that mean you don't think I should?'

Vita gave her that puzzled look she reserved for any suggestion that she had not made herself crystal clear.

'No,' she said. 'You say you've never read anything your mother wrote?'

'Never. I've never even seen her handwriting, to the best of my recollection.'

Vita had placed the letter delicately on the table-top as if she wanted to make it absolutely Sairey's choice to read or not to read.

'You must have seen it in Africa,' she said from the doorway.

'I said, to the best of my recollection, which, as you know, doesn't include much of Africa.'

But as soon as Sairey looked down at the letter, she recognized the writing. And now, as she read through it for the third time, she began to hear the voice. It was quick, expressive, ranging from a surprising depth at moments of serious reflection, to a skylark trill at points of high frivolity.

It reminded her of her own voice on Vita's tapes, except that there wasn't much at the upper end of the register there.

As she finished her third reading, there was a knock at the door.

'May I come in?' called Vita.

If she said no, Vita would go away. Questions were never simple social formulae with Vita.

'Yes.'

She didn't, in fact, come in, but stood in the open doorway.

'You've read it.'

'Yes.'

'And what is it that makes you angry?'

Until this moment, Sairey hadn't identified anger as a component of her emotions. Now she acknowledged that it was certainly there, though not predominant.

'Because she doesn't say much about me, I suppose,' she replied thoughtfully.

'She knew I wasn't baby-centred,' said Vita.

'Was that why you didn't go to visit her in those early years? Because I was still a baby?'

It was a ludicrously egocentric question, but Vita gave it her usual close attention.

'No,' she said. 'I didn't go because I was busy with my new job.'

'You were busy for three years?'

'Longer,' said Vita. 'But I was planning to go late in '75.'

'You must regret not going sooner,' said Sairey, trying to make it sound non-accusatory but not certain how much she succeeded.

'Yes, I must,' said Vita. 'By the way, Celia's here.'

'Aunt Celia?' exclaimed Sairey in surprise.

'Yes, Aunt Celia. She's in the garden.'

Celia was sitting on a copy of the *Daily Telegraph* spread over a rustic bench under a magnolia weary with half a century's struggle against an unsympathetic east wind. Celia looked to be in much the same state, though today neither had much cause for complaint, as the wind was still and the morning had been pleasant enough for Sairey to breakfast in the garden, albeit in a thick sweater.

She'd been reading Fanny's present of *Out of Africa* and Celia had the leather-bound volume in her hand. She laid it on the garden table as Sairey approached, and leaned forward to be kissed.

'Careful,' she said, as her niece made to sit down. 'You don't want to risk rheumatics. Here, you can sit on the parliamentary news, that should be dense enough to keep the damp out.'

Sairey laughed and said, 'Honestly, Auntie, it's perfectly dry. But if you're so worried, why not come inside?'

Celia shook her head and said, 'Unhealthy place, Essex. They used to get malaria here, did you know? And I don't like being inside these clapboard houses. They must soak up the wet. You can almost see them contracting.'

'It's lovely to see you, Aunt Celia,' said Sairey, sitting. 'Really great.'

'But why have I come? Can't an aunt come to visit her favourite niece?'

'Her only niece,' said Sairey.

'Same thing, then. Vita said she'd bring me a coffee. It'll be the real thing, I hope. None of your decaffeinated herbal muck.'

'I expect she's being diplomatic. Letting us have a few minutes alone. So you can tell me why you've come.'

'You're like your father sometimes. Worrying away at things, like Mop with a bone.'

Sairey ignored her cue to ask how the dogs were. Exposure to Vita had certainly made her much more aware of conversational directive.

'More like Daddy than Mummy, you'd say?'

She had countered with a negative cue, knowing that Celia was far from keen about discussing her dead sister-in-law.

'Nigel came to see me,' said Celia.

'After he'd been here?'

'Yes. He was worried about you, Sairey.'

'But why? He seemed happy enough when he left. What is there to worry about?'

'I don't know. I think he's like me. He finds this part of the world depressing; flat, damp, dripping. I think he feels a change might do you good. New contacts, new impressions, less isolation.'

'But I'm not isolated,' protested Sairey indignantly. 'Vita's here nearly all the time.'

'Even so. Just look at that house. No security. Anyone could get in.'

Vita's arrival with two mugs of coffee and a plateful of her seed cake interrupted expansion of this curious observation.

'You'd be more comfortable inside,' she said.

'You think so?' said Celia, sniffing at the steam suspiciously.

'You'll stay for lunch?'

'I thought I might take Sairey out somewhere. For a treat,' said Celia. 'I hope you haven't prepared something.'

'For lunch?' Vita looked amused at the idea. 'No. I believe the Old Viking does a nice meal. Shall I ring and book you a table?'

'That would be kind. It is brick-built, I take it?'

'It appears so.'

'In that case, thank you.'

'Don't I get consulted?' Sairey burst out.

'I assumed you had been,' said Vita. 'Will you go?'

'Yes,' said Sairey, not knowing how to push the issue without seeming petty. But she didn't feel petty.

Vita returned to the house. Celia tasted the coffee, nodded approvingly, frowned at the mug and said, 'Good enough to serve in a decent cup. But what do you imagine *this* is? Does Vita perhaps wish us to feed the birds?'

'It's quite nice, actually,' said Sairey, surprising a feeling of defensiveness about Vita's seed cake.

'You say so? I read in a magazine that people make cakes out of marijuana. I have never seen such a cake, of course, but I would not be surprised to find it resembled this.'

'No such luck,' said Sairey provocatively, if dishonestly. She had tried it at school a couple of times and been obliged to fake the spaced-out condition achieved by most of her friends.

It occurred to her that she was being diverted again and she said, 'To get back to Daddy . . .'

Celia drained the hot coffee at a draught and said briskly, 'We'll talk at lunch. We're really being very rude

107

sitting out here like this and ignoring poor Vita. Let's go inside.'

The Old Viking was neither very old nor, save for the motif of a horned helmet on the crockery, particularly Nordic, but the dining room was airily anonymous enough for Celia to feel safe from Essex, and the food was all right.

'Your father and I were wondering if perhaps you'd like a trip to America. I think he probably mentioned the idea to you. There are some friends of his from San Francisco, the Dooleys. I believe they once came to Masham Square on a trip to London. I gather they would be delighted to entertain you.'

Sairey remembered the Dooleys, or at least recalled a pair of terrifying children a couple of years younger than herself who, far from showing the respect eight-year-olds ought to have for ten-year-olds, had treated her like a mental defective.

'Why should they want to have me?' she asked. 'Daddy hasn't been in touch with them already, has he? How could he, without asking me first?'

Her indignation at this second instance of non-consultation was not to be held in like the first, but before she could give it full vent, Celia said, 'Don't be silly. What would be the point of suggesting something to you that we didn't know was possible? Now, listen. I understand perfectly well that you are not a piece of baggage to be shifted round at the whim of your elderly relations, and so does Nigel. So come down off your high horse. Mop's like that. Let the lead go taut and he'll dig his heels in, even if you're leading him to his favourite meal!'

Suddenly Celia broke off, staring over Sairey's shoulder. Then she rose and, without a word, strode rapidly towards the door leading to the bar. Sairey turned to watch her with an anxious surprise, clearly shared by their waiter.

A few seconds later she returned and sat down, shaking her head.

'Aunt Celia, is something wrong?'

'I don't know. I think perhaps I'm beginning to hallucinate. A couple of times recently I imagined I saw this black man hanging around the beach at Camber, watching me.'

'A black? What did he look like?'

'Tall, skinny, hair turning grey. In his forties, I'd say. Then I thought I noticed him at Liverpool Street station today. And now, to cap it all, I was sure I spotted him peering through the door of the bar!'

'And was there anyone there?'

'Not a soul. Not a soul,' said Celia. 'Now where were we . . .?'

'You were trying to persuade me to drop everything and head for America. And I was telling you I wasn't going. No, please listen, Aunt Celia – I love you dearly, and I'm very grateful to you and to Daddy for all your concern. But there's something very odd been going on in my brain for a long time. And I feel that here with Vita is where I'm going to get it right, not swanning around some beach in California.'

'You feel Vita's helping you?' said Celia doubtfully.

'Well, she's got my hair straightened out, at least,' laughed Sairey, running her palm across her fast-growing hair.

She felt Celia's opposition start to slip away like morning mist.

'Getting you better's the only thing. The only thing,' said Celia. 'Nigel must see that. I'm sure he will see that. But you'll take care, dear? Don't exchange one disease for another that may be worse.'

'No, of course not,' said Sairey, touched by the deep concern on her aunt's face.

She reached across the table and clasped both the elder woman's hands in her own. Thus they sat for a little while, till Celia withdrew a hand to wave at their waiter who came to the table instantly.

'Bill, please,' said the old lady.

The waiter said, 'Is everything all right?' anxiously.

Sairey said, 'Auntie, aren't we having anything else?'

And Celia's hand flew to her mouth as she looked down at the remnants of the avocados with which they'd started their meal, and she said, 'How very silly of me. Forgive me, dear. I must be getting old.'

And for the first time ever, with a pang of affectionate pain, Sairey saw that it was true.

11

After lunch, Celia paid the bill and asked the waiter to ring for a taxi.

'I shan't come back to the house, dear,' she said. 'Give my apologies to Vita. If I'm lucky with connections, I can get back to *Dunelands* before Mop and Polly start tearing the place to pieces. Come and see us soon.'

'I will,' promised Sairey.

She stood outside the restaurant and waved till the taxi was out of sight. Behind her there was a discreet cough, and a voice said, 'Miss Ellis.'

She turned and found herself looking at the thin, greying black man she had last seen running along the sands at Camber.

'As I was saying before we were so rudely interrupted,' he said gravely. Then he allowed a brilliant smile to split his face.

Sairey did not respond.

'What are you doing here?' she demanded fiercely. 'What do you mean by frightening my aunt?'

'Yes, she was frightened, wasn't she?' he said reflectively. 'I could see that, even at a distance. I'm sorry she feels like that about black men.'

'It's nothing to do with colour,' retorted Sairey. 'No one likes being watched, that's all. And followed. You did follow her, didn't you?'

'Yes, I did,' admitted the man. 'I went back to the beach a couple of times in the hope of resuming my talk with you, then started hanging around the house. It took me a little while to work out you'd actually gone. Slow learner, that's what they said about me, right from the mission school down to Balliol.'

If this was meant as a credential, it wasn't going to work, but simple curiosity was more than enough to make Sairey's reluctance merely token when he went on, 'Let me buy you a drink. That pub across the road serves nice beer.'

'Now ain't dis de life,' he said, as he placed her glass inside the brass guard-rail that ran round the top of the wrought-iron table. 'The black boy's dream, sitting in an English pub drinking English beer with a beautiful blonde English girl.'

Sairey, finding it difficult to feel insecure in such surroundings, said with a crispness Aunt Celia might have envied, 'Look, can we drop this inverted racism and get down to business? Who are you? What do you want with me?'

He sipped his beer and said, 'Well, well, you're your father's daughter, surely.'

'You know my father?'

'We've met. A man of fierce passions. But even fiercer loyalties. I wonder if his ex-employers understand that? And what of you, Miss Ellis? What do you understand?'

'Less, every time you open your mouth. Who are you, anyway?'

'I'm sorry. Peter Kanyagga. Peter to my friends.'

It sounded vaguely familiar but she couldn't work out why.

'And your business, Mr Kanyagga?' Again, pure Aunt Celia.

'Information officer with the Kenyan High Commission,' he said. 'Basically, I'm a journalist. I cut my teeth on student papers at Oxford twenty years ago. Happy days. Swinging sixties, flower power, love, love, love. A time of hope. Where has it all gone?'

He looked at her appealingly, and she said in irritation, 'That's for your generation to answer. You're the ones who lost it. Anyway, you seem to have done all right for yourself.'

'Because I'm here enjoying European comforts instead of squatting in a mud hut back home? Perhaps you're right, but it sometimes seems a paradox to me that education should qualify a man not to live in his own country. Perhaps not to die there, either. Do I sound maudlin? It's your strong beer. Also, I'm a long way from home.'

'What do you want with me, Mr Kanyagga?' demanded Sairey.

He played with his glass and said, 'I'm a man beset by uncertainties, Miss Ellis. Perhaps you can help resolve them. Your father is writing his memoirs, I believe. What do you know of them?'

'Nothing,' she said forcefully. 'And certainly nothing I'm going to tell you.'

'If that's all you know, then I cannot feel deprived,' he said. 'Let me tell you something, then. My country has been in a delicate position since the Big Man died. You know, Jomo Kenyatta, our great leader whom you British locked up for so many years. Since his death, things have been . . . uneasy. Ordinary men will stumble in a big man's shoes, eh? But things usually work themselves out. Unfortunately these years have seen the emergence of an anti-government group, Mwakenya. Constructive criticism is always welcome, of course, but this organization is basically a bunch of left-wing terrorists funded by the communist regime which now governs our neighbour, Uganda . . .'

'Yes, I do read the papers,' interrupted Sairey. 'And I've got a slightly less biased view of the situation. But what has it got to do with me or my father?'

'I'll tell you. It's rumoured that in his memoirs, your father makes allegations about eminent Kenyans – politicians, public figures, businessmen – which could seriously damage their reputations, and possibly destabilize the country.'

'False allegations, I presume?' said Sairey. 'And where is all this leading?'

But Kanyagga had suddenly lost interest in her. He was looking over her shoulder and not liking what he saw. Then his face split into a welcoming smile, like a politician's who sees the TV camera swing towards him, and he stood up and said, 'Well, hello. Nice surprise. What are you doing in this neck of the woods?'

Sairey turned, to see a man bearing down on them. He was burly, with a thatch of thick, silvering hair on his bear-like head. She recognized him at once, though it took a second longer to find his name.

Archbell. Archie Archbell, who'd been her father's, and her stepmother's, boss in Africa. He was shaking Kanyagga's hand and saying, 'I've got a little boat moored down here. Try to get down whenever I can for a spot of sailing. What about you?'

As he spoke, Archbell's eyes were greedily quartering her. He quite literally looked hungry. Then his gaze met hers, locked, and in a blink became avuncularly jovial.

'Bless me, isn't it Nigel's girl, little Sairey? I'm sorry, not so little now, but when I first knew you, well, good days, good days, long gone, alas. You probably don't recall me, my dear?'

'You're Mr Archbell,' she said.

'You do remember,' he said delightedly. 'Once seen never forgotten. But you two . . .?'

'I also knew Mr Ellis, back in the old days,' said Kanyagga. 'I saw him recently and he said Sairey was staying down here, suggested I should look her up.'

It occurred to Sairey that this pair were lying like mad and, stranger still, that each knew the other knew he was lying, but didn't care.

She stood up. Whatever Kanyagga had been going to say, he clearly wasn't going to say now, and she felt a strong desire to be out of Archbell's company.

To her surprise, the Kenyan seized her arm and said, 'No. You stay and finish your drink. I really should have been on my way five minutes ago, but my sexist upbringing made me unwilling to leave a lady unescorted in a drinking house. Now, however, if Mr Archbell doesn't object . . .'

'Object? A pleasure, dear boy.' But Archbell's eyes as he watched Kanyagga leave were hard as a hunter's watching his prey escape. He now bought himself a drink and sat down next to Sairey.

'Strange coincidence,' he said. 'Meeting like this, out here in the sticks.'

'Very strange,' agreed Sairey. 'Are you still in the Diplomatic Service, Mr Archbell?'

'What? Oh yes.' He seemed amused. 'Not all of us can afford to take early retirement like Nigel.'

'Afford? But Daddy's always complaining what a miserable pension he gets.'

'We only get what we pay for, Sairey,' said Archbell. 'But if he sold that mausoleum in Masham Square and set up house somewhere like this, he could live comfortably on the change.'

'I doubt if Fanny would like that.'

'Fanny? Oh yes. I was forgetting he'd married again. How is she, dear little Fanny?'

There was an undercurrent of malicious laughter beneath almost everything he said, and his eyes were roaming once more, like hands in an Italian disco.

'She's OK,' said Sairey, rising abruptly. 'I've got to go now. Goodbye.'

'No, wait,' said Archbell. 'Let me give you a lift. My car's outside.'

'It's no distance. I'll walk.'

'I insist. There's something I want to say to you. About your father.'

It was the only formula which could have made her get into his car, which turned out to be not the lecher's limousine she expected, but a muddy Land Rover, smelling of fish. She sat as far from Archbell as she could manage, but in any case he turned out to be a careful driver, keeping both hands on the wheel and his eyes on the road.

'Your father and I used to be good friends,' he said. 'But we've drifted apart. No one's fault. When you leave an organization, you often feel excluded by the mere fact that life goes on within it as if you'd never existed. Biggest sacrifice a man makes is to give up the key to the executive washroom.'

'Look, I'm sorry you and Daddy should have fallen out,' said Sairey, 'but what's it got to do with me?'

'Nothing, of course. But running into you like this made me wonder if perhaps you might not be ideally placed to act as a sort of go-between.'

'For a reconciliation, you mean?' said Sairey, surprised into amusement.

Archbell chuckled and said, 'Hardly. For a warning, really.'

'A warning? About what?'

'He's rather irritating some of his old colleagues. You probably know how abrasive he can be. They are men of influence. They can choke a man socially with very great ease. Shut off contacts, depress perks, make life less comfortable. I speak from sincere friendship.'

It didn't sound convincing.

Sairey said, 'Is this about the memoirs?'

'Memoirs? Good Lord, is he writing some memoirs? I expect I'll figure somewhere in them.'

Again the mocking undertone, the deliberate lack of effort to sound convincing.

'What precisely do you want me to say to him, Mr Archbell?' she asked.

'Nothing. No need to make a production number out of it. Just tell him we had a drink, I ran you home. Oh, and don't forget to tell him you bumped into Mr Kanyagga too. But he'll probably know that already, as it was his suggestion that Kanyagga should look you up, isn't that what he said? Well, here we are!'

He pulled into the narrow driveway alongside Vita's house, jumped nimbly from his seat and was round at Sairey's door before she'd unfastened her belt.

As he handed her down, Vita appeared from the rear garden. She stood in front of the Land Rover with that utter tranquillity which was equally far from vulgar curiosity and rude indifference.

Sairey said, 'This is Mr Archbell. He used to work with Daddy. This is Vita Gray.'

'Delighted,' said Archbell.

'Come into the garden and have some tea.'

She led the way into the back garden. The *Telegraph* had been removed from the bench, but *Out of Africa* remained on the table.

Vita said, 'Sit down. I'll fetch another cup.'

She went in to the house. After a moment, Sairey said, 'Excuse me,' and followed her.

'I'm sorry,' she said.

'What for?'

'Bringing him back.'

'He brought you, I thought.'

'Yes, but . . . look, do you mind if I duck out? I wouldn't mind having a bit of time to myself. I've got things to think out.'

'Of course,' said Vita, putting a slab of the infamous seed cake on a plate. 'I'll take care of Mr Archbell.'

'Thanks,' said Sairey. 'Oh, and Aunt Celia's gone straight home. She sends her apologies.'

'For going home?' Vita allowed herself a smile. 'Someone should write a paper on English occasions of apology.'

Up in her room, Sairey busied herself tidying her tangled bed clothes. Mrs Teal, Vita's local cleaning lady, had enquired if she should put the newcomer's room on her list, but Sairey, whose experience of cleaners was that they always wanted to 'do' you at the most inconvenient moment, had said no. The result was that she lived in some chaos.

As she worked, she let her mind drift round and round Kanyagga and Archbell. Both were trying to use her in some way, but she could not see how. Was there some link between their appearance and her father's wish to pack her off to America? Selfishly, she felt that these were complications she could do without. Getting herself right was the important, the *necessary* thing. Right, she could face up to anything life might throw at her. Till then, she didn't want to risk any encounter which might bring back nights of terror and days of weariness.

She stayed upstairs for twenty minutes, till she heard Archbell's Land Rover grind away. As she went downstairs, she felt such a tremendous sense of relief at being alone with Vita once more that when she met her in the kitchen, she impulsively hugged her and kissed her cheek.

She felt Vita go tense for a moment, then relax, but it was controlled relaxation and Sairey stepped back saying, 'Oops. Sorry. Patients must not hug their therapist, right?

118

But I just felt so safe with you, Vita, and wanted to say thanks. Is that OK?'

Vita said, 'What therapists want is to hear patients saying goodbye, because they feel so safe with themselves.'

It was a typical rejoinder but not delivered with her usual, calm detachment. She replaced the untouched seed cake in its tin and went through to the living room. Sairey followed.

Vita said, 'It's been a broken kind of day. We'll try a session tonight, if that's all right with you.'

'Whatever you . . . Yes, that's fine with me,' said Sairey. 'That's fine.'

The session went well. Sairey had come to be able to interpret Vita's reaction as she came out of her trance, even though it was a matter of a millimetre's difference in the compression of her lips and a few degrees of difference in the angle at which she held the cassette as she said, 'Now?'

Though it was their usual practice that Sairey didn't listen to the tapes till the following morning, Vita always made this offer, insisting that the tapes were Sairey's property.

'No, thanks,' she said. 'I think I'll get an early night. It was all right, was it?'

'I don't understand the question,' said Vita. 'By the way, you've left a book on the garden table and the dew won't do it any good.'

Feeling reproved, Sairey went to collect *Out of Africa*. The night was warm for the time of year. There was a full moon, but some trick of the atmosphere seemed to distort it so that it looked rhomboid rather than round, and its light was draped like a gauze curtain over the countryside, concealing as much as it revealed. There were sounds, rustlings and scutterings in the grass, and Sairey thought of the night she had run across the road into the park and met Allan Bright. Perhaps if she walked across the garden now, beyond the old magnolia tree towards the smudgily silhouetted hedgerow, she would find him again . . .

It seemed to her as she looked that part of the hedge detached itself, rose, sank, and became part of the hedge again.

She went back into the house and locked the door behind her.

When she got into bed, she felt too tired to read, and had switched off the light, when it drifted into her quiescent brain where her familiarity with Kanyagga's name came from.

In *Out of Africa* there was an old man called Kanyagga whose adopted son was tragically killed in a shooting accident.

She sat up, put the light on and picked up the leather-bound volume to check her memory.

It fell open at a thin airmail envelope which she had no recollection of using as a bookmark. She took it out and noted with the lack of surprise that comes with a sense of nightmare logic that it marked the passage in which Kanyagga dictated an account of the expenses incurred in bringing up the dead boy. And on the thin blue paper was printed FOR YOUR FATHER TO COUNT THE COST.

She tore the envelope open. It contained several sheets of almost transparently thin paper. She unfolded them and sifted quickly through them. They all bore a stamped heading – COMMISSION OF HUMAN RIGHTS – KAMPALA – 1987. The first was a photocopy of several passages of minuscule handwriting of various lengths. The others, using a typeface almost as small, were transcripts of the handwritten passages, or so she worked out from an eye-straining comparison of first lines. She got out of bed and held the sheets under the bedside lamp to aid her reading.

It started . . . *no Panel Beaters today* . . .

When she had finished she sat perfectly still and tried to concentrate on comprehending what she had read. But all the time, a strong sense of resentment came welling up inside her. It wasn't fair that this day, which had started off with her mother's letter, should end with this. All she wanted was to be left alone to heal. All these interruptions, mental and physical, were too much to bear. She tried to channel her resentment towards reason. Who was responsible for putting this load on her? Who had been here today. Celia? No, she couldn't believe it. Archbell? Of him, she could believe anything. And Kanyagga? There was nothing to stop Kanyagga from slipping into the garden, dropping his message and slipping out again.

In fact, there was nothing to stop anyone. But she was certain it was one of the two men. Kanyagga had been interrupted in his talk with her. Perhaps he had intended to hand the envelope over in the pub. Its position in the book pointed to him. But Archbell was the one who'd definitely been in the garden. She tried to recall anything significant in their conversation as they drove to the house, but all she could remember was her distaste for his company.

Vita would help her sort all this out, she decided, heading for the door. Vita understood everything.

Then she paused, and at last remembered something significant about her drive with Archbell. He hadn't once had to ask for directions.

That meant, at the very least, he had been watching the house.

At the very least.

She went to the window and looked out into the night. The cloud was low and there was no starlight or moonlight to reflect off the river.

It was alien and sinister and dark as Africa.

Chapter 10

In 1975 my wife died in tragic circumstances. She was found dead, by her burnt-out car, in a deep gully off the Jinja road. Suggestions that this might have been one of the arranged 'accidents' by which Amin's hatchet men tried to cover up some of their more notorious murders seem to me to have no foundation. There was no reason for my wife to be a target; the timing, with the OAU conference in progress in the city, would have been stupid; and in any case there was no attempt to disguise this as an accident. The police put it down to the activities of a notorious band of kondis to whom, paradoxically, the increased security demands of the conference had given greater freedom of movement. Ali Towelli, Head of the PSU, admitted to me himself that the protection of delegates was making such demands on his manpower that other spheres of work had to be neglected. This semi-apology rang ironically in my ears in the light of subsequent events. But I have to say that the PSU, licensed killers though they certainly were, seemed to pursue this enquiry with real diligence, indeed with greater diligence than I cared to know about. No one was brought to trial but Towelli assured me that the perpetrator had almost certainly been punished, by which I assume he meant that there had been a general slaughter of kondi suspects.

After the funeral, my sister, who was paying us a visit

at the time, took my daughter back to England. I, myself, was naturally devastated by what had happened and would have flown back with them, except that my masters had other ideas. One thing was clear, whether I went or stayed – it was far too dangerous for Ocen to remain in the house. Paula, our houseservant, was an old Bagandan woman, fat and lazy, but with the precious virtue of keeping her mouth shut. There was no way, however, that she could be involved in looking after a fugitive Acholi. This task had been Sarah's. With Sarah gone, and the PSU's attention focused closely on my household, it was imperative to get Ocen out.

Apiyo was contacted and she made arrangements immediately for Ocen to join her. She was hiding out in a friend's house, so overcrowded that one more or less would hardly be noticed. It wasn't the place for a man needing nursing, but Ocen was nearly recovered now and in another couple of weeks the plan to smuggle him back to Zambia would be complete.

I also contacted Archie Archbell in Nairobi to let him know what had happened to Sarah. And I told him I wanted out. I needed time to reassemble my life. I needed time to see that my little girl was adjusting to the loss of her mother. I needed time away from this madhouse called Uganda, a madhouse I had been crazy to bring my family into.

Archbell flew to Entebbe within hours of hearing from me.

'So you need time,' he said. 'How much? A week? You can have a week.'

'A week? I need a year at least,' I protested. 'I want a temporary UK assignment.'

'Impossible. We need you here too badly.'

'What the hell for? Isn't it time we were thinking about breaking all connection with Idi, official and covert? He's close to running amuck. This OAU conference has been like a three-ring circus. You must have seen the pictures of those half-witted whites carrying him around on a litter? And did you hear about the bombing display he laid on over the lake? There was an island, supposed to be Cape Town. Every single bomb missed! I gather they had a hard time hitting the lake. Guweddeko's been sacked as airforce chief. I reckon he'll be dropped in the lake himself, before long.'

'All right,' interrupted Archbell. 'But we can't break before the black states do, otherwise they'll all cry imperialism and form a common front.'

'Then we'll wait for ever,' I protested. 'Christ, they even put up with being made to sit and watch Idi get married to his go-go dancer! Unity, economy, sheer bloody terror, I don't know what it is, but Zambia and Tanzania apart, there's no sign of opposition. And all the time he's getting more and more tied up with the Libyans. No, it's not just me that should be wanting out. HM Government en masse ought to be setting an example to the world and packing their diplomatic bags. Once the public realize what's been going on here, they'll be sick to their stomachs we stayed so long, appeasing a lunatic.'

Archbell replied (I made careful notes immediately after the meeting, as I always did when something seemed particularly important): 'All right, so he's a fuck-ing lunatic, but he's still *our* lunatic. Back home, we've got all those bloody socialists thinking they're cracking the whip. Well, they won't last. Most of them are commies and we've got some of our best boys working night and day to get the proof. Meanwhile, we've got to keep our money on Amin. All right, he'll have to go eventually, but if he goes now, HM Commie Government will co-operate with their black Marxist friends, Kaunda and Nyerere, in sticking Obote, or even someone to the left of him, back in power. All I'm saying is, we need to buy time till we've got a nice pro-Western black boy ready to take over, and a good true blue majority to make sure he does.'

'You're very sure the Tories are going to get back in next time,' I said.

'That big wet nana, Heath, managed to make the unions popular last time, didn't he? But don't you worry. Things have been arranged so that nothing like that will ever happen again.'

'They can do that? With Labour holding the strings?'

I was genuinely amazed. Archbell laughed and winked.

'Depends what's at the end of those strings, doesn't it? They haven't managed to stop oil getting to Rhodesia or arms to SA, so why should they have any better luck with votes? The bastards aren't fit to govern!'

It wasn't till later that I was to discover the full extent of the covert aid to the Rhodesians and the South Africans and how far it went beyond oil and arms. All that concerned me now was that the bastard had cunningly got me sidetracked into a policy discussion.

I said bluntly, 'Archie, I'm not in a fit state to carry on here. And Sir Joe will want me home to talk about . . . what happened.'

He replied, 'I've been in touch with Sir Joe. He agrees with me. There's no one fitter. Idi still respects you, that's clear. Look at that message of condolence. Look at the way the PSU are investigating Sarah's death. You're our best hope of keeping some control of the man. If you go, there's no possible replacement, you must know that.'

I knew that outright refusal was tantamount to resignation in the Service. I continued arguing. I even told him that I'd been concealing a political fugitive in the house, hoping to persuade him that I might already be compromised in security terms.

He looked furious as I revealed this breach of regulations, but all he said was, 'Give me details. I'll check it out.'

'How, for God's sake?'

'You think you're the only one who can see Amin's on a downhill course? There are a few wise heads in the SRC who know the day will come when they'll be needing a few favours themselves.'

I gave him the details, but, to tell the truth, I was already resigned to staying. Something had finally given way inside of me. I was into the penumbra of despair, and in that strange light, all landscapes are the same. I might as well rot in Kampala as anywhere else. And despite what I said about Sir Joe, I had no real desire to face my father-in-law just now.

Two final blows completed my disintegration. First, as Ocen and Apiyo moved out on the first stage of their trek to Zambia, they were spotted by a PSU patrol, who opened fire. Ocen was killed and Apiyo seriously wounded. She was taken straight to PSU Headquarters for interrogation, where she died within an hour. When I heard the news, I was sufficiently roused to remember Bill Bright. I'd brought considerable pressure to bear on the authorities to have him released, and several weeks earlier I had been assured that his papers would be processed as soon as he recovered from a debilitating fever he'd contracted. I understood the shorthand by now and knew this meant they were just waiting till the more obvious marks of their brutality had faded. Now, I drove out to Nagaru to check on his progress and to bear him the tragic news.

The commandant told me gravely that Bill already knew. In fact, as Apiyo had died in the Headquarters, they had brought Bill from his cell to identify the body. I then asked if I could see him.

The commandant said, 'You must have seen him already! His release order came through today and we loaned him a car to drive back to Kampala. You must have passed him on the way.'

'I didn't notice him,' I said.

'It is a busy road,' said the man. He rose and shook my hand.

'I would like to commiserate with you on your own sad loss, Mr Ellis. And to thank you, for all the assistance you have given the PSU. This is the way a multi-racial society should work, isn't it?'

Then he lowered his voice and added, 'Incidentally, I hope your friend Mr Bright was in a fit state to drive. He was naturally very distressed. We offered him a chauffeur but he insisted on driving himself.'

Then he smiled slightly. I knew at once what he meant. And when I saw the ambulance and the police cars by the roadside as I returned to Kampala, I didn't even slow down.

The news of his death was in the paper the next day. The news of mine never made the headlines, as I was still walking around and functioning normally, but it wasn't till after Entebbe, a year later, that I started to come back to life.

12

The advance towards her mother's death was slow and
circuitous. Sairey preferred to accept Vita's line of
approach with blind faith. Too close a questioning would
be like glancing over your shoulder to make sure the
ghost you were raising from the underworld was actually
following. But at last they were into 1975 and the house
in Kampala.

The curtains were drawn, but it's light outside and the
bright sunshine sneaks in to edge the bed with light. There's
a figure in it, a man. He is asleep. He moves as I enter,
but doesn't wake up. I squat in a corner and watch.
Is he black or white?
Black. But his arms and chest are wrapped in white
bandages, very white against his black skin.
How long do you sit?
A long time. Then Mummy comes in. She has a basin with
steam rising from it. She doesn't see me, but sits on a chair
by the bed. After a short while, the man wakes up. He
says something and she says something back. I can't hear
what. Then she begins to unwrap his bandages. Next, she
starts to wash him from her basin. It hurts, for he cries
out, and she says, 'Sorry', and I see her gently rub his
shoulder like she rubs me if I've got a pain and she wants
to make it better. I must have moved then, for she turns
and looks at me. Then, smiling, she comes to pick me up
and takes me to the end of the bed. The man looks up at
me. There is a hole in the upper part of his arm and it
looks red and angry. Mummy says, 'This is your Uncle

Ocen come on a visit. He's Allan's uncle really, but I don't suppose he'll mind sharing him.' I say, 'Where's Allan?' And she laughs and says, 'You miss your lapidi, do you? Don't worry. You'll see him again soon, I promise.' And I feel perfectly happy because whatever Mummy promises always comes true.

When the tape finished, Sairey let the silence wash over her till the birds on the roof and the wind in the eaves and the internal creakings of the old house forced their way to the surface and her mind to the present.

Vita knocked. Somehow, she seemed to know the exact moment when Sairey was ready. As she came in, Sairey said, 'Can I really remember all that?'

'I've told you. Nothing is forgotten, just mislaid. Old people, as the short-term memory fades, often find the most distant past coming up sharp and vivid.'

'But the words . . . are they what Mummy actually said?'

'It's interesting,' said Vita, studying the file containing her close analysis of all Sairey's sessions. 'Whenever your mother is speaking, you seem to give the minutest detail. Often, I catch her turn of phrase, her actual intonation. All this points to accurate recall.'

She spoke in her usual calm, measured manner, but Sairey thought she detected an undercurrent of emotion. It occurred to her that in some ways, all this was perhaps just as painful for Vita as for herself. Once thought, this idea was so obvious that she instantly dropped the perhaps.

She said, 'You mention intonation. Why don't I sound like a four-year-old child, then?'

'You're thinking of those movies again,' said Vita. 'Yes, there have been cases where psychological regression has been induced so completely that infant speech patterns have appeared. In some cases, I don't say all, I suspect that these are not so much an echo of how the subject actually spoke at the regressive age as the way in which the conscious mind, now temporarily reduced to the status of the subconscious, imagines the subject *would* have spoken at that age. Even where childhood recordings exist for comparison, this proves little except that the subject has had something to mimic. For me, the stress is always on bringing to the surface what is hidden below, not sending the subject to walk on the bottom of the sea.'

This powerful image came out with a vehemence which made Sairey guess that Vita was rehearsing a case made out already, in the company of her peers.

She said, frowning, 'If the conscious is still playing a role, is that why you gave me Mummy's letter to read? I mean, would I have remembered about Ocen if I hadn't been reading about him just recently?'

Vita said, 'Who knows? The mind is not a fixed state. Everything new alters the whole of it. Everything you do, everything you read, can affect, not the truth, but the order and the intensity of your recollection.'

Sairey thought of Bill Bright's tortured scribblings, still hidden in her bedroom. Three days had passed and she still hadn't made her mind up what to do. Archbell, Kanyagga, even Aunt Celia, these were all little hooks drawing her back into a world which, from her present vantage point, looked even more confusing than it had in the past. Basically, she felt she would be foolish to attempt to deal with that world before she was 'better', whatever that meant. And getting better was in Vita's gift, no one else's, of that she was certain. Hence the need for blind faith. But even the faithful are not entirely free from the irritation of uncertainty.

'Vita, is this really getting us anywhere?' she asked

sharply. 'I mean, what's the use of memories when half the time I don't understand what it is I'm remembering. What was Ocen doing wrapped up in bandages in our house, for instance? What does it all mean? Why can't we just hop straight to the point where Mummy died and see what my memory makes of that?'

'Because after a landslide, you've got to clear away a whole scatter of rubble before you get near the point of maximum damage,' said Vita. 'Sairey, you've been looking a bit strained these past couple of days. Why don't you have a day in town, do some shopping, have lunch with your father? Too much rural tranquillity can be as nerve-jangling as too much traffic.'

The suggestion came like a thought-reading.

'Yes,' said Sairey briskly, like a young woman who could easily make up her mind. 'I'd like that. I'll ring Daddy straightaway.'

When the Masham Square phone was answered, Sairey didn't recognize the voice, and hesitantly repeated the number.

'Sairey, is that you? It's Allan Bright.'

'Of course, I'm sorry, I didn't recognize . . . how are you?'

'Working hard. Your father's out, I'm afraid, but Mrs Ellis . . .'

'No, I wanted Daddy. I'm coming up to town and hoping to bum a lunch from him.'

'You could always bum a sandwich off me in St James's Park. Cheese and pickle, very thick. Yes? No? Hang on. You're in, or out of, luck. That's your father now, so you're saved from making a decision. Here he is. Bye.'

A moment later Nigel Ellis came on the line. He sounded his usual breezy self, 'Lunch, darling? Why not, though it may be brief. I'm meeting someone for a drink in the Ritz at noon, so let's make it their restaurant at quarter to one, shall we?'

For once trains, taxis and traffic were all on her side and she was walking into the Ritz at half past twelve. It was not a place she was familiar with, and as she made her way hesitantly through the foyer it was with some relief that she glimpsed her father in a tall-backed chair leaning forward to talk to someone she couldn't see. He looked up, spotted her, glanced at his watch, then made a gesture which probably meant she should go and make herself comfortable elsewhere till the time of their appointment came. Pique and curiosity drove Sairey on, and when he saw she was not to be deterred, he spoke to his companion, then rose to his feet.

'Hello, darling. I never thought I'd see the day when any woman in my life was on time, let alone early. You know Mrs Marsden, I think.'

Sairey found herself looking down at the thin wispy woman she'd met in the park with Vita.

'Hello again. Your father tells me you're staying with Vita Gray down in that draughty hole of hers in Essex. How is she?'

'She's fine,' said Sairey.

'Good. She's an interesting woman. You should get her to talk to you about Lawrence's sub-text. Some marvellous insights among all the psychoanalytical claptrap. Now I must be on my way, Nigel. I've a paper to prepare.'

'Please, don't let me interrupt,' said Sairey belatedly.

'No such thing. I think we'd exhausted what there was to say. Goodbye, dear. Remember me to Vita.'

She gathered up a handbag, a scuffed briefcase and a Fortnum and Mason carrier bag and went out with a list to starboard, like an overladen dhow.

'What on earth were you talking to her about?' said Sairey.

'I hope this isn't what passes for good manners in Essex,' said Ellis dryly.

'Oops. Sorry. It was rather rude. But it's just that I didn't know you had any burning interest in academic Eng. Lit. That's what she is, isn't she? Some kind of professor.'

'She has held a chair. Now she freelances, if that term applies at that level.'

'So why were you seeing her?'

'She might, of course, be my mistress,' he said, leading her towards the restaurant, ordering her a glass of wine and himself a large gin as the waiter sat them down.

'Thank you for looking dubious,' he went on. 'In fact, one of the many strings to her bow is the post of editorial advisor to a big publishing house. Lit. crit. stuff mainly, but I thought as an aspirant author, I might as well use what contacts I've got.'

'And how did she react?'

'Rather like talking to a puffball. You feel if you exhale too hard there'll be nothing there. But enough of me. What brings you to town so unexpectedly?'

Briefly, she described her encounters with Archbell and Kanyagga, pausing only when the waiter brought their drinks. 'And again,' said Ellis, downing half of his at a swallow. 'And we'll have the cold beef salad.'

She didn't argue, but continued with her account.

When she finished, he said, 'Busy day.' She tried to examine him as Vita would have done and concluded that he was concerned but not surprised.

'Do you know this man Kanyagga?' she asked.

'I know someone who fits the description. Only he doesn't work for the High Commission. He's a supporter of Mwakenya. And an active member of the ANC.'

She said, 'Then you didn't suggest he should look me up? Nor, presumably, has Archbell got a boat down there.'

He replied with sudden savageness, 'That bastard's probably got boats everywhere. He'd have come dry-arse from the *Titanic*.'

'You don't like him?' said Sairey.

He smiled crookedly and said, 'Love him like a brother, as Cain said to the Lord.'

The new drinks arrived. Sairey hadn't touched her first, but Ellis was ready.

'Why do you want me out of the way, Daddy? Has it something to do with these two men? And why involve Aunt Celia? Did you think she'd have more chance of persuading me out of the country than you?'

He considered this, then, to her surprise, nodded and said, 'Perhaps I did, at that. You've never been what you'd call a doting daughter, have you?'

The unfairness of this hit her like a whiplash.

'Perhaps you need a doting father for that,' she retorted. 'Or even a present one.'

'Fine, fine, fine,' he said, with more irritation than remorse. 'You're right. Mea culpa. Look, Sairey, you must have gathered all this has got something to do with my memoirs. Various people, including my former employers, don't like the sound of them, but it's all under control, believe me. Only, I don't like you being harassed. So why *not* take a little holiday in the States? You'd love it.'

'I haven't finished my treatment yet with Vita.'

'The way you're squaring up to me, I'd say she'd got you back in full fighting trim,' he said dryly.

Their salads arrived. He pushed his plate aside impatiently and ordered another drink. Sairey said,

'Daddy, how could an agricultural advisor's memoirs upset so many people? What exactly was your job?'

He said, 'If I tell you, will you go to America?'

'No. Don't you think I've a right to know what it is you don't want me mixed up in?'

He smiled without much humour and said, 'Your mother used to say things like that.'

'Perhaps if you'd told her, she might still be alive.'

It was birdshot fired at random, but it hit some mark. His face went stiff and dark and suddenly she was afraid of discovering where the wound was.

She said, 'There's something else, too. Someone left this in a book of mine lying around the garden. It could have been anybody.'

She passed over the airmail envelope, with a feeling she identified as relief. When she'd spoken to Allan Bright on the phone and he'd invited her to share his sandwich in the park, she'd known she couldn't go, not even if her father had been unavailable all day. These were Bill Bright's last words on these thin sheets, she had no doubt of that. Allan was entitled to read them, yet they were addressed to her father, and that's where her first loyalty must lie. But she still felt ashamed.

She watched him read. His face gave nothing away. As soon as he had finished she said, 'This Commission? What is it?'

'It was set up by the NRM, that's the National Resistance Movement who're in charge in Uganda, to investigate what really went on during the Amin regime.'

'How did Bill Bright die? Was he executed?'

'Oh no. They rarely executed whites. That would cause too much fuss. He died in a road accident. There were many such accidents.'

'But they didn't bother to arrange one for Mummy?'

He raised his hand to massage his brow, covering his eyes.

'Her death wasn't an official killing, so there was no need to stage a cover-up,' he said.

She accepted this, glad of an excuse to move on from the topic.

'But what about the wholesale massacres of the Acholi and Langi? They couldn't pass all those deaths off as accidents, could they?'

His hand moved and his gaze met hers again.

'Madmen like Amin think that the deaths of unimportant people are themselves too unimportant for anyone to bother about,' he said. 'You seem pretty well informed on what went on, I must say.'

'Students of literature need "O" level History to get into Cambridge,' she said. 'Who were these Panel Beaters he talks about?'

His gaze fell away.

He said, 'At Makindye prison, where Bill was held when he was first arrested, there was a system whereby new inmates were beaten up three times a day, regular as mealtimes, by a special team of half a dozen men, hired solely for this purpose. Their nickname was the Panel Beaters. I thought I'd achieved something when they moved Bill out of Makindye, which was military, into PSU custody. I thought . . .'

He finished his drink.

Sairey said, 'Daddy, with things like this going on in Uganda, why the hell did you take me and Mummy back there with you?'

'Because that's where my job was,' he said flatly. 'I was going to be stuck there for the foreseeable future. Your mother didn't care to be left in Nairobi. If she was going to be a grass widow, she said, she preferred the green grass of St James's. I didn't want that kind of distance between us again. So I took you both to Kampala.'

'Despite the danger you must have known existed?' said Sairey accusingly.

He sighed and waved his glass at the waiter, who took it with a reproving glance at their untouched salads.

'Sairey, you see things differently when you're close up to them. Yes, things were bad, but we were looking at them still in political terms. They were bad because Uganda was slipping away from us. Amin was coming more and more under the influence of Libya who wanted him to establish a purely Muslim state. Even before the Tories got dumped in '74, they were beginning to wonder if there weren't perhaps some things worse than socialism. And with Labour back in power, the political point of view changed completely. But there was still work to do. Damage limitation. And there were still strong British interests in the country, British businessmen working there, British settlers . . .'

'Like Bill Bright.'

'Yes.' His drink came. He drained half of it. 'In 1975, the OAU conference was held in Kampala. Amin was the Organization's president then. He was photographed being carried on a litter by a bunch of grinning Brits. It got in all the papers. Public opinion at home saw him as a clown. Informed opinion saw him as a menace. Only a very few were prepared yet to see him as a monster. So Kampala seemed as safe to me then as many other capitals, certainly safer than Belfast. Also, I was an old army mate of Idi's, a man of influence and privilege. Invulnerable, they told me. That was why I had to be their man in Kampala. I reminded them later.'

He spoke bitterly.

Sairey said, 'They? Archbell, you mean? And . . .'

'Yes, your grandfather. Sir Joe.'

'He didn't want you to take us into Uganda?'

'Not a lot.'

'And you reminded him that he'd reassured you it was completely safe?'

'I didn't take you and your mother to join me to spite Sir Joe, if that's what you're sniffing around, Sairey.' He glanced at his watch and said, 'I've got to go.'

'But you haven't had your lunch.'

'No? Then you must regard this as a simple retreat, darling. There are things I'm not yet ready to talk to you about. You're quite right about America. It would please me to have you safely out of the way. And if you weren't, in the eyes of the law, an adult woman, I'd parcel you up and pack you off screaming and kicking and weeping. For your own sake. Because I love you.'

He folded Bright's notes and put them in his briefcase.

'Will you show that to Allan?' asked Sairey as if she hadn't heard his last words.

He looked at her in surprise and said, 'You're very cool, I must say.'

'Perhaps I've learned to look behind displays of emotion,' said Sairey.

Nigel Ellis considered.

'Vita, I suppose? Don't get too perceptive, darling. Remember, gold does glister, too. Will I show this to Allan? I don't know. I'll tell you when I've made up my mind. Meanwhile, think seriously about America. It would please me enormously if you went. Goodbye, Sairey.'

He rose, leaned over the table and kissed her.

'Sorry about the lunch. Have anything you like. It's taken care of.'

'It always was,' said Sairey, as she watched him stride through the door, still athletic and attractive, still distant and unreadable.

139

The waiter was at her shoulder, looking questioningly at the untouched plates.

'Can I get madam anything?' he asked.

Sairey began to shake her head, then stopped and smiled at him. It occurred to her that St James's Park was just around the corner.

'Yes,' she said. 'Some doggie bags to put this stuff in. And a bottle of house white – no, make that Chablis – with the cork loosened. Some rolls. And a couple of glasses, too.'

13

At first she thought Allan wasn't in the park, then she saw him on a bench, half hidden by a newspaper. He didn't seem to notice her approach but when she reached him he looked up without surprise and said, 'Hello.'

'Hello. Finished your lunch?' she answered.

'Wasn't very hungry. The ducks did well,' he said.

'Let's see if this can tempt your appetite.'

It did. She watched him eat and drink. Occasionally, their eyes met and he smiled. Finally he said, 'You're not eating much.'

'No. I'm enjoying watching you.'

'Is this the new voyeurism, then? All the kicks of eating with none of the cholesterol?'

'Is that what a university education does to you?'

'What?'

'Make you a smart-ass.'

He grinned and said, 'I'm ready for coffee now.'

'I'm sorry, I didn't bring any coffee.'

'No coffee. Pity. It's attention to details like that which turn a nice thought into a work of art. Fortunately . . .'

He reached into the briefcase which rested against the side of the bench and produced a flask. They had to share a cup. The coffee was strong, black and bitter.

'Ugandan?' she asked.

He gazed at her with an ironical twist of the mouth, and for the first time looked his age.

'Instant,' he said. Then he smiled properly and was a boy again, open, eager, exuberant – and very attractive. Sairey hadn't considered this before. At their previous encounters he had been a mystery, a menace, a surprise; now, though those elements had not been entirely dispersed, he was also an acquaintance who might possibly become a friend who might . . .

He reached across her and his sleeve brushed her breast. Instantly, their relationship retreated two stages, but he was only claiming the plastic cup from her.

'What happened to you when my father transferred to Kampala?' she asked.

'You remember I didn't go with you? Ah, what an impression I made on that funny little girl!' he laughed.

She smiled her agreement. It didn't seem the moment to point out that the only recollection she had of him, or those times, was under the prompting of Vita's hypnosis.

'You won't recall all the background, of course. Not even Nigel Ellis's daughter could be as precocious as that. What happened was, Uncle Ocen got released from his first arrest. He wasn't a big fish, you see. Even then, it must have cost my father a small fortune in bribes. Ocen headed south immediately, into Tanzania. Obote was there under Nyerere's protection, training his fellow refugees for a counter-coup.

'With Ocen out of the way, things settled down a bit for my parents. My father was a hard man to mess with. He'd been around a long time, was liked and respected by everyone. Also, he had been an officer in the KAR, which always impressed Amin. I think they even thought of bringing me home. But during '72, Amin was getting closer and closer to Libya and further away from his early allies, Britain and Israel. He broke completely with Israel first, denouncing it in a joint communiqué with Gaddafi, then chucking all Israeli personnel out of Uganda. Britain, he was more careful with. There was the question of aid, also of Commonwealth relations. But he chucked out all the Asians holding British passports that summer and carved up their property among his own men. Shops, businesses, hotels, transport firms, all in the hands of men who didn't have the first idea how to run them. The result was a rapid collapse of the economy. The black market became a way of life. The official supply of goods was just crazy.'

'No coffee, but a surplus of toilet paper,' mused Sairey.

'That's right,' he said, looking at her shrewdly, as if sensing a hidden significance. 'Then in the autumn, Obote's supporters launched an invasion from Tanzania. It was a miserable failure but it drove Idi wild. Various rebel leaders were identified, among them Ocen. Suddenly, instead of wondering if it was safe enough to have me home, it became imperative that my mother herself got out! Friends and relatives of known rebels were disappearing at a terrifying rate. So Apiyo came to live with your family outside Nairobi. Surely you must remember that?'

Sairey smiled ambiguously. Something was stirring in the depths, she felt, but what it was, she could not yet say.

'We were both with you for almost a year. Our mothers became close friends, I think. My father came as often as he could. All Uganda's supply lines run through Kenya, so it was politic to keep on good terms. I think your father used his influence to make mine appear more influential than he was, so that his trips to Nairobi had official blessing in Kampala.'

'It all sounds so . . . convoluted,' said Sairey. 'So devious.'

'So dirty?' suggested Allan. She didn't contradict him. 'Yes, it was. Kenya's whole attitude to Amin was devious and dirty. There was little love for Obote, you see. One socialist neighbour to the south was enough, without having another spring up in the west. They couldn't get rid of him quickly enough when he flew into Nairobi after the coup. As for Amin, the fact that he was a child as far as proper government went was, if anything, a plus factor. The worse state he got Uganda into, the fatter the pickings for the men who controlled his lifelines. As for the monster inside the child, as long as he restricted his nasty games to his own side of the border, what business was it of big business? The only positive action they took against him was in '78, when they switched off his oil supply till he changed his mind about a territorial dispute. Just think what they could have done from the start if they'd wanted!'

He spoke with a bitterness which took him far beyond his own age, into a timeless grief and rage.

Sairey took his hand.

'I'm sorry,' she said.

'For what? For having lost only one parent?' he snapped.

She tried to pull her hand away but he held on to it.

'Wait, wait, wait,' he urged. 'Don't pay any heed. I'm sorry, too. Sometimes it hurts so much thinking about it that I just lash out.'

She let her hand rest loose in his.

'Tell me the rest,' she ordered, suddenly feeling herself emotionally in charge. 'What happened to you and your mother after we went to Kampala?'

'We took a flat in Nairobi. My mother got a job there. She was trained as a teacher, you know. Again I think your father used his influence. He was a powerful man.'

'Powerful?' Sairey thought this was a strange word.

'Oh yes. He still is, I think. In office, the power comes from knowing how to keep secrets. Out, it comes from knowing how to tell.'

'You don't sound as if you like my father much,' said Sairey.

144

'Don't I? That would be strange, as I have so many reasons for being grateful to him. Perhaps today I've found one more.'

He squeezed her hand and she pulled it away sharply, realizing even as she did so that his suddenly unctuous tone had been a parody of Hollywood sentimentality and that he was laughing at getting a raise out of her. But she also realized that this was another successful diversion.

Allan was serious again.

'I went to school in Nairobi. I enjoyed myself as boys do. I missed my father, of course, though I did see him a couple of times when he managed to fly over from Entebbe. And I even missed you sometimes, though I was glad not to have that undignified *lapidi* label stuck to me any more! I daresay you missed me, too?'

She smiled enigmatically, but this time it wasn't enough. He examined her face till she felt herself flush, then he said, 'You don't remember me at all, do you?'

It seemed pointless pretending. She shook her head and said, 'I remember nothing of those times.'

'I thought not. Was it your mother's death . . .?'

'They think so.'

'You were very young. It was different with me. It's the times after my parents' death that I've forgotten. But earlier, that long stay at your parents' bungalow, that year with my mother in Nairobi . . . I can recall every moment.'

'Why did she go back to Uganda?' asked Sairey.

'They caught Uncle Ocen again. He'd infiltrated from Tanzania to make contact with Obote supporters still in Kampala. But four years of Idi had changed people. He was betrayed. They stuck him in Makindye military prison to start with. My mother returned as soon as she heard, unofficially you understand. My father was making the loud official protests about Ocen's imprisonment.

145

And then Ocen escaped, or was rescued, as the military were handing him over to the SRC, that's the State Research Centre, Amin's gestapo. He was badly injured and had to lie up somewhere till he recovered . . .'

'He was in our house,' said Sairey. 'I remember that. He was in bed, all bandaged . . .'

'Yes. Your parents took him in,' said Allan. 'And the authorities took my father in on suspicion of complicity in the escape. He was in Makindye, too, then they moved him . . . I don't know what happened after that, except that he died.'

'And your mother and uncle?'

'Caught as they tried to get out of Kampala.'

'And you heard nothing more?'

'Crocodiles don't send messages,' he said savagely.

Her shock must have shown.

He said, 'Look, I'm sorry, but you asked. There was a letter, actually. Just one. No date, nothing specific, in case it got intercepted, but it seems to have been written between the time Ocen was fit enough to leave your parents' house and the time they got caught. I'll show you it if you're going back to the Square. Your father borrowed it.'

'Why?'

'When people write their memoirs I suppose they get obsessive about documents. It's all evidence in case someone accuses them of lying. Are you coming back?'

'Yes,' said Sairey. 'There are a couple of things I'd like to pick up.'

They walked back to Masham Square in silence. Allan, she was interested to see, had his own key. The house was empty, at least, no one answered her call. He went into the study while she ran upstairs to her bedroom. Here she started digging round for heavy sweaters and thick trousers. This Indian summer couldn't last for ever.

'Here it is,' said Allan.

She hadn't heard him come into the room. He handed her a transparent plastic folder, inside which she could see a letter, written in lovely flowing copperplate.

'Your father is very protective about documents,' said Allan.

She sat on the bed and started to read. He stood at the window with his back to her, looking down into the little park where they'd first been reunited, the innocent child and her guide, her lapidi.

When she finished she didn't know what she ought to say, so she said what she felt.

'Allan, that's a lovely letter. I wish that I had something like that. I wish . . .'

She stopped. There was no wish that expression didn't make more painful. She sat perfectly still on the bed. She wasn't crying, because what she felt was beyond tears. He came and sat beside her, expressing neither bewilderment nor concern, but simply putting his arm around her shoulders and turning her face towards his.

They were almost too close for proper focus but, curiously, her mind seemed to be seeing things in perfect rational detail. Her sexual experience was limited to medium-heavy petting and she'd not felt a deal of impatience to push back those limits. But it had to happen some time. If so, what better place than here, in her own room? What better partner than this golden boy whom she had adored in her forgotten childhood?

What better time than now?

She moved her face an inch nearer his and it was hint enough. His lips were soft without being sloppy, his mouth tasted of the salad dressing they had shared for lunch, his hands moved from caressing cloth to caressing flesh with little or no fumbling, and hers slid down to his crotch with no fear. He rolled her on to her back and she

147

spread herself on the narrow bed where she had hugged her dolls and listened to the rain on the window-pane and known that it was the noise of scrabbling fingers . . .

There was a noise now. A door shutting. Her fingers dug into Allan's slim shoulders, but he had heard it too and lay quite still above her, their flesh touching but not yet joined. Suddenly, she knew she would have to wait for a better time, a better place. In unison, their heads turned towards the door.

Fanny was standing there, regarding them, as if she'd come upon a pair of children playing snakes and ladders. On her face was that faint smile which looked like the surface manifestation of a deep private amusement. Seeing their eyes focus on her, she nodded pleasantly and moved away.

Physically, it was still possible, but there were imperatives beyond the needs of the flesh.

By mutual accord, without a word spoken, they rolled off the bed and began pulling on their clothes.

My dearest boy,
I have only little time to write as I have just heard of a friend who will take this over the border with him, not straight to you, for there are many enemies there, though smiling as friends, but south, where all are friends. Soon we shall follow, if God permits. Your uncle is well again and is living with me till the time comes to go. Before that, he was at the house of your little 'sister' where he was nursed with great kindness. Never forget that kindness, my son, even though it should stop. Sometimes goodness leads to evil and friendship to enmity because we understand ourselves even less than we understand each other.

Your father is not with us now, but I know he will be thinking of you with love. Remember, we talked of the bad men who are running our country? Well, there is much talk against them and I do not doubt that in a very short time the good people will throw them out and we can live here happily again as before. Meanwhile, though, your father has been taken by the bad men, but your little 'sister's' father promises he will be all right and I believe him. I know you are all by yourself over there, but you must be brave. Remember that part of you is Acholi. If you had been brought up in my village, at the age of thirteen or fourteen you would have moved out of the family dwelling and your father would have helped you build your own hut to sleep in. This is how you must think of yourself now, as an Acholi boy, building for himself, a little younger than his cousins around Gulu, and without a father's help. During the day at school, you must be still your father's son, learning quickly all the modern knowledge which will help you in your future. But at night, remember your Acholi ancestors, practise the steps I taught you of the Larakaraka dance and imagine you can hear me singing you an Apiti song.

Now I must finish. My kind messenger is ready to go. He takes with him all the love of your mother and of your father, my little Acholi, my little European.

14

'Vita. Was my father a spy?'

It would be nice, one day, to amaze Vita Gray. Sairey had not asked her question with that intent, but if she had done, she would have failed.

'Was?' said Vita, not raising her head from the book she was reading. 'There are some professions, like medicine and priesthood, where the past tense is not strictly applicable.'

'*Is* then?'

Now she looked up.

'He *is* a man with a very high security clearance,' she said.

They were sitting after supper in front of a smokey, not very warm, greenwood fire. Sairey had told Vita nothing of her meeting with Allan. She had lain awake all that night thinking at first of the sex act which had come so close, but then, and more disturbingly, of Apiyo's letter to her son. It was the only letter he had received. There was no way of knowing if it was the only one she wrote. Her messenger may have been caught. Whatever happened to Ocen and Apiyo and Bill Bright, happened after this letter. To Allan, reading it now must be like looking over the edge of a black pit. What lay down there? Did he want to know what lay down there? She thought of the prison notes she had passed on to her father and was glad that she would not be the one to bring them to Allan's attention. They had talked very personally after Fanny's interruption, as if offering each to each a compensatory intimacy of mind. He had listened to her history of the Dream and said bitterly, 'It seems a small price for the privilege of not remembering.'

'What do you remember, then, that's so terrible?' she demanded, stung by this downgrading of her trauma.

'I remember saying goodbye to my parents and never seeing them again. I remember getting that letter from my mother and counting the days till she came back to me. I remember the day my mind ran out of numbers. I remember your father coming to see me and telling me they were dead, and I remember not believing him. I remember running away from the people I was staying with and trying to get back to Uganda. I remember how their patience ran out after my third or fourth attempt and they showed me a photograph your father had left. It was a photo of my father, dead in his coffin.'

Instantly, the Dream rose in Sairey's mind, sharp and clear though she was broad waking.

'Are you all right?' said Allan.

'Yes,' she lied. 'It's just so horrible. How could they do such a thing?'

'It worked,' he said in a matter-of-fact voice. 'He wasn't easily recognizable, but one look and I knew. After that, I settled down.'

It sounded very cold, but when Sairey looked into his face she saw that it wasn't coldness but control.

'You waited,' she said.

'That's right. Till it was over. Or at least, the part which involved Idi Dada was over. I went back, then. What was I looking for? Revenge? The consolation of shared grief? I found neither. Amin and his henchmen had fled. I went north, even though it was not yet safe. I went to my mother's village. She had reminded me I was an Acholi boy, that I must be true to both sides of my inheritance, so I went in search of the only people I knew as family. The village was a scatter of cold ashes. I found out then what I presume my mother had long known, that after the coup, soldiers had ranged through Acholi land, killing the young men. More recently, Amin's army in retreat had passed this way again, completing the job. So I went back to Nairobi, unavenged, unconsoled, and completed my education.

'That is what I remember.'

She had wept then, and taken him in her arms and pressed him close. There had been no further sign of Fanny after her ill-timed appearance, but neither of them felt inclined to let this new closeness rekindle desire.

He had said, 'Don't cry, little Sairey. I am still your lapidi. I'll keep harm from you if I can.'

'And if you can't?' she had answered, trying to struggle back to self-control.

'Then you, too, must be true to your inheritance. Be subtle as the snake, sharp-eyed as the hawk, patient as the crocodile which lies beneath the water waiting for the dik dik to stoop and drink.' His tone was both serious and joking, but she could not see the joke.

'That's no part of my inheritance,' she protested.

'You think not?' he said, all serious now. 'We are all half and half, Sairey, even if it doesn't stand out so clearly as with me. These are your father's gifts. Use them.'

So here she was, staring into a dull fire, half her mother and half her father, and in no position to understand either half.

'Why do you ask about your father?' said Vita.

Sairey realized that by drifting off into this maze of thought, she had unconsciously turned one of Vita's techniques against her, forcing a response by a long, absorbed silence.

'I don't know. I seem to spend all my time chasing after Mummy, trying to get a good look at her. Yet even

153

when I'm sitting opposite Daddy, I'm not sure I really know him any better.'

'So that makes you think he may be a spy?'

'No. That would be silly. It makes me feel he judges very carefully how much of himself to show. I think he'll always keep a piece in reserve, for a rainy day.'

Vita was amused by the expression and showed it in a gentle crinkling of the cheeks.

'That's still a long way from espionage,' she said.

'Is it?' said Sairey. 'I don't mean a spy like James Bond or Burgess and Maclean. But something on the shady side of diplomacy. No one's going to be much bothered by the memoirs of an agricultural advisor, are they?'

'It takes a dumb man not to give offence and a deaf one not to take it,' said Vita, as if she were quoting. 'Has your father said something particular which has roused this interest?'

'He would like me to go to America,' said Sairey.

'For a holiday?'

'For safety, I think.'

Vita nodded, as if this confirmed something.

'Did you find out whose?' she asked.

'What do you mean? What are you getting at?' Sairey felt a sudden surge of indignation and rushed on. 'Just because you don't like Daddy, that's no reason always to attribute the worst motives to him!'

'I don't,' said Vita. 'Nor, however, do I always attribute the best. Did you accept the offer?'

'No!'

'So the situation, whatever it is, remains unresolved. What will he do now?'

'What can he do?' demanded Sairey.

'He could give up his memoirs.'

'I don't think he'll do that.'

'Probably not,' agreed Vita. 'On the other hand, I

think he knows that a direct threat to you would be a last resort. You told him about meeting Kanyagga?'

'Yes, of course.'

'And that you'd met him before in Kent?'

'Yes. And about the men in the jeep chasing him off.'

'Did he seem surprised?'

'No. Hey, perhaps that was Daddy's doing – perhaps he's been protecting me all along.'

She looked triumphantly at Vita, who nodded and said, 'Perhaps. Certainly it was after that he agreed you should come here, which did require some explanation. But now he wants you further, safer, in America, which means . . .'

'What?'

'That he has decided to resist the other pressures that are being brought to bear.'

'What other pressures, Vita? You talk as if you know something.'

'Do I? I suppose the steps of reason have always smacked of secret knowledge to the unsophisticated mind. Which is why women, clever beyond their class, used to risk being burnt as witches.'

'All right. I'm back in my place,' cried Sairey. 'Reason or knowledge, what are these other pressures he's resisting?'

'Blackmail. The law. The threat of personal violence. Which leaves violence against those near and dear. To wit, you.'

'And Fanny. And Celia.'

'Of course. I'd almost forgotten Fanny and Celia.'

She sounded, not puzzled, but interested as to why she should almost have forgotten Fanny and Celia. The ailing fire wheezed out a dying breath of sweet-smelling smoke. As it wreathed around Vita's uncaring face, it struck Sairey that so she would probably have looked on a witch's pyre, observing and analysing the reactions of the spectating citizenry.

'Oh, this is all so silly,' she suddenly burst out. 'I'm sure there's some simple explanation. All this business about his memoirs will turn out to be a load of rubbish. Don't you think so, Vita? Isn't it possible?'

Vita regarded her rather crossly.

'There are two main stages of female maturation,' she said acidly. 'In the first, the child often plays at being adult. In the second, the adult finds it convenient to play at being a child.'

'Just women? Not men?' interrupted Sairey, anticipating and hoping to divert criticism.

'Men rarely pass the first stage. The best women reach a third, in which they are content to be themselves.'

'You're saying I'm playing at being ignorant? Why should I do that?'

'Because you've lost your mother and want to hang on to your father, even though you're not absolutely certain he's worth hanging on to. A child seeks reassurance, not knowledge.'

'And a woman?'

'Learns to live with truth.' Vita closed her book. 'I think I'll go to bed now. We'll make an early start tomorrow, if that's OK. I have to be in town in the afternoon.'

'We're still going on, then?'

'Of course. Unless you don't want to. That's the only reason I'll stop. Why do you ask?'

'I don't know, I just thought maybe you felt, I mean . . .'

'Sairey,' said Vita patiently. 'Why do you ask?'

'What? Oh. I see. Really *why*, you mean? I suppose . . . I suppose because I want reassurance.'

Vita stood up, stooped, kissed Sairey on the forehead.

'Goodnight, my dear,' she said.

After Vita had left the room, Sairey sat staring into the dead fire. Life seemed a long uphill struggle, particularly if all it promised was learning to live with the truth. What the hell was wrong with wanting reassurance? And what was so difficult about giving it?

She noticed that Vita had left her book on the arm of her chair. Usually, as in the case of Sairey's *Out of Africa* left on the garden table, she was fussy to the point of obsession about the need to return books to their proper places. Perhaps, like the goodnight kiss, this was a sign of human weakness. Whether such a sign would be welcome, Sairey wasn't sure.

She reached out and picked up the book. It was an edition of Dante's *Commedia*, nicely bound, with gilt lettering. She let it fall open. Hadn't this been one of those texts they used for the *sortes*, that random opening which hopefully revealed a passage of particular significance to the troubled opener? Not that *she* had much chance of finding guidance. *Her* Italian stopped at menus!

But the book fell open at a page of the English editor's commentary, and Sairey started reading. It was clear why it had opened here. Vita must have been looking at this section recently, for the pencil she always held as she read had underscored a passage.

'The Ninth Circle is reserved for traitors who are trapped in the frozen lake of Cocytus. Its outer region, called Caina, after Biblical Cain, is reserved for those who betray their own kin. The next region, Antenora, named after Antenor, in the *Iliad* a wise Trojan councillor, but by the Middle Ages pilloried as the man who conspired with the Greeks to bring about the downfall of Troy, holds traitors to their country. Dante, with his usual keen perception of human failings, shows us how eager this type is to divert attention from its own crimes by pointing to the treacheries of others.'

Carefully closing the book and leaving it on the chair as she had found it, Sairey went to bed.

15

The following day, they resumed the hypnosis sessions. If Vita had hoped that the brief break from routine would reinvigorate Sairey, she was disappointed. Her normal, post-trance reaction was a slight lethargy. Now she was hot and sweating and felt as if she'd just climbed a steep mountain. Worse, the tapes contained little of value. Her response to Vita's calm questioning was irrelevant and incoherent and Vita ended the trance very quickly.

'Why don't you try longer?' asked Sairey, on the morning after she'd listened to the third of these abortive sessions.

'You're fighting against regression,' said Vita. 'Hitherto, there's been full co-operation, so no trouble. Now . . .'

'But I *am* co-operating!' insisted Sairey.

'Your waking mind is, though even there . . . it's very complex, Sairey. That's why I don't keep pressing. Only a fool thinks the best way to cross a minefield is fast.'

Sairey digested this.

'Why am I not co-operating?' she asked finally.

'Because we're getting close. So far you've been travelling hopefully. Now you're not sure you want to arrive. If I seem to be expressing myself over-figuratively, it's because linguistic precision might give the impression that I know a great deal more than I do. This time there's no reassurance coming from anywhere, Sairey. This time I can only open the door. You have to go through by yourself.'

Another metaphor. Like the one she'd used right at

the start. Not wanted on voyage. Now here she was at the bottom of the hold, prising open all the crates, looking for . . . God alone knew what.

She went out for a walk. The river was brown and sullen and there was a faint smell of stagnation. Perhaps Celia was right and Essex was unhealthy. What was it she said? That Essex was the last place in England where malaria was endemic. Whereas Kent had always been famously bracing! Dear old Celia. Perhaps if her father had never come back from Africa, perhaps if she could just have gone on living with Celia at *Dunelands* all through her teens . . .

She passed some children playing on the river bank, two boys and a girl. She watched them for a while, but her presence inhibited them, or perhaps it was guilt at being where their mother had forbidden them to play, and finally they ran off. Sairey resumed her walk. Then up ahead she saw another figure, sitting on the bole of a tree which bank erosion had drawn down so that the lowest branches were trailing the water.

It was Peter Kanyagga.

He looked cold, despite the sheepskin jacket he was wearing, with the big furry collar up around his head.

'Good day to you, Miss Ellis,' he said. 'Quite nice for this time of year, wouldn't you say?'

'I'd be surprised to hear you say it,' she replied.

'Not very convincing, you mean?' He laughed. 'One thing I hope, Miss Ellis, is I get to die at home. It's not just nostalgia. Before the mission man got to them, my people believed a man's spirit needed time after the shock of death to prepare itself for leaving the body. No guaranteed paradise for the poor black man. You'd be amazed what dangers lurk to ambush the unready soul. Perhaps the Boers are right and there's apartheid even after death! The point of these ramblings is that the quicker a corpse stiffens, the less time the spirit has. Worst of all is to be trapped in the body before you can escape. And that, I feel sure, would be my fate if the Good Lord took me now.'

'I think you're mixing your mythologies, Mr Kanyagga,' said Sairey.

'Why not? From the behaviour of the whites on our continent, it seems possible to be a good Christian and a bad pagan at the same time.'

'Perhaps so. But is it possible to be a member of the Kenyan High Commission and of Mwakenya and the ANC all at the same time?'

He looked blank for a moment, then grinned broadly.

'You'd be surprised. But I assume you have been talking to your father.'

'Yes. And I passed on the papers you left.'

Again the blank look, but it didn't bother her. She was convinced Kanyagga had left the Bright scribblings and she wanted to know why.

'Which particular papers?' he asked.

Exasperated, she said, 'The Ugandan Commission on Human Rights evidence.'

'Ah, *those* papers. But just Mr Bright's notes, you say. Nothing else?'

Was this open admission or subtle denial?

Sairey said, 'Just the notes. What do you mean? You're not saying it wasn't you who stuck them in my book? It had to be you or Mr Archbell. There wasn't anyone else . . . well, there was Aunt Celia, but there'd be no reason . . .'

'And what reason would I have for leaving these mysterious notes with you, Miss Ellis?' he interrupted courteously.

'I don't know. Perhaps you thought that they might influence my father not to publish his memoirs.'

'And why should I want to do that?'

'Because, like you said, they may have stuff in them which would be very embarrassing to some highly placed Kenyans . . .' She had started triumphantly, but as she spoke, her voice slowed and finally tailed off into silence.

'That's right, Miss Ellis. Surely a member of Mwakenya would want to make sure anything calculated to embarrass the Kenyan establishment got published? And surely a supporter of ANC would want to find out all he could about the way covert support for white supremacy works in the UK? Odder still, though, surely a man wanting to embarrass his former employers would be eager to trade information with his enemies' enemies? Oh dear, why is it that every time we settle down to a nice cosy chat, we get interrupted?'

Sairey turned to follow his gaze. Two men were walking along the river bank towards them. One was tall, with broad shoulders flattening the corrugations of a corduroy bomber jacket, and muscular thighs stretching the seams of faded jeans. The other, shorter, slighter and darker, was rather incongruously dressed in a light-grey business suit.

As they drew level, the two men paused. They looked familiar.

'Good day, Mr Kirkman, Mr Cilliers,' said Kanyagga.

They did not reply nor even look at him, but the smaller of the two said courteously to Sairey, 'Excuse me, miss, but is this kaffir bothering you?'

His accent was impeccably English except for the word *kaffir*, which was pronounced with an intonation and a vehemence which had to be South African.

'No one's bothering me,' said Sairey indignantly, 'except, perhaps, you.'

'I'm sorry if I've offended you, but you can't be too

162

careful. These people are quite unpredictable. Don't worry. We'll be in earshot if you scream. Good day now.'

With a polite smile, he walked on. The bigger man looked Sairey up and down, shook his head slowly as if in disgust, then followed.

'Who are those awful men?' demanded Sairey.

'I hope you're not being indignant on my behalf, Miss Ellis,' said Kanyagga. 'I prefer gratuitous insult to gratuitous sympathy.'

'Don't worry. I'm too busy fighting my own battles to want to fight yours.'

'In that case, the big one is called Kirkman, the other Cilliers. I thought at first they might be friends of yours, but I begin to suspect I was wrong.'

'At first?' said Sairey, looking after the departing pair. 'I knew I'd seen them before! They were in that jeep that chased you along the beach at Camber. Why don't you call the police?'

'Why didn't *you* call the police that day?' enquired Kanyagga.

The two men had stopped a little further on to light cigarettes.

Sairey shrugged and said, 'I don't know. I thought about it.'

'Too busy fighting your own battles perhaps,' he said slyly.

'I suppose so. I think they're going to come back.'

The men had turned and were looking in their direction, as the wind made their cigarettes burn like fuses. It was a not imprecise image. Sairey had the feeling that an explosion might be close.

'In that case,' said Kanyagga rising, 'I take back what I said about fighting my own battles and welcome your protection.'

Rising and seizing her arm, he began to walk briskly back the way she'd come, along the river bank.

'Surely they wouldn't try to harm you out here in front of me?'

'Didn't stop them last time, did it? And your silence on the subject probably confirmed their belief that they were protecting you.'

'You're not saying those men have got anything to do with Daddy?' she demanded angrily. 'He hates South Africa.'

'You got the accent, then?' smiled Kanyagga. 'No, I admit they would be strange allies for Mr Ellis. Whereas you'd think that I would be the perfect ally, wouldn't you?'

'I suppose so.'

'I supposed so, too. Yet when I offered to trade off my information for his, he didn't act like a man about to startle the world with amazing revelation, Miss Ellis. He told me he'd think about it. And ever since then, I've been unable to get near him, except through you. And our two friends have kept on showing up, too. Now how do you explain this, Miss Ellis?'

'Perhaps . . .' began Sairey, but he put his finger to his lips and said, 'Rhetorical question. Whether these two mean me harm or not, I should like to shed their company. Would you be so kind, when we enter that copse, to run on a little way, then let out a good scream?'

The river bent ahead, and in its bow crowded a stand of birch, bright in the murky air. They passed among them, his hand touched her elbow. 'Now,' he murmured.

She ran, glancing back after half a dozen paces. He had vanished. She ran on, spotted a clump of alder by the river's edge, scrambled down behind it, and screamed.

Half a minute later, the two South Africans came

running up. Kirkman, the big one, was in the lead, his hand inside his bomber jacket. Cilliers was close behind.

'Hello,' said Sairey, without looking up. She was sitting on the bank, calmly contemplating the passing flood.

'What's up? Where is he?' demanded Kirkman.

'Who?' Now she glanced up. 'Oh, it's you.'

'Why did you scream, Miss Ellis?' asked Cilliers.

'Did I? Oh yes. There was a water rat. It frightened me. I don't much like rats, do you?'

It sounded rather clever and tough, the sort of thing they said in movies, but when she saw the responsive expression on Kirkman's face, she wished she'd kept silent.

'Come on,' said Cilliers. 'Let's head for the road.'

'What? No message for Daddy?' asked Sairey, forced by her own fear to persevere with toughness.

Cilliers squatted beside her as a teacher might do beside a small child's chair.

'It's not a game, Miss Ellis,' he said gently. 'Except if there's a game with only one rule, i.e. you can do anything you like except get caught doing it. Just tell Daddy you met us. Good day to you, now.'

He rose, and the two men loped off through the birch trees.

Sairey watched them out of sight. She found that, somehow, Cilliers' gentleness had been much more frightening than Kirkman's threatening scowl. Suddenly, this lonely river's bank seemed an unhealthy spot to be and she was not thinking of Aunt Celia's warnings about malaria.

She rose and hurried back towards Britt House.

16

Lunch was a more than usually hit-and-miss affair. Mrs Teal normally made sure there was something available in the fridge, but she'd gone down with flu and the shelves were bare. Vita seemed able to live permanently on her seed cake, supplemented by whatever fruit, vegetables or edible greenery she could lay her hands on. Sairey preferred bread and cheese, but, today, was indifferent to its absence. She'd tried to ring her father three times since her return, but there'd been no answer from Masham Square. Now she chewed her cake in silence, washing it down with decaffeinated coffee.

Vita made no enquiry about her unhappy mood, but Sairey felt those quiet eyes reading her, as a mariner reads the sky. The function of language is concealment almost as frequently as communication, Vita had told her once. But it takes a consummate actor to deceive physically.

So, let her see that something's bugging me, thought Sairey. She knows so much about me, why should I try to hide that?

But she almost wished that Vita would start questioning her. She had the knack of making you home in on the true source of your feelings, often many miles removed from the apparent source. However, all that the older woman said as she rose from the kitchen table was, 'No session tonight, Sairey. I have a meeting in town.'

Feeling absurdly piqued by this blunt statement, Sairey said, 'I see. So that's me relegated to my proper place in the scheme of things.'

At the sink, Vita paused in the quick rinsing of her cup, which was the nearest she came to domestic work.

'We can only be at the centre of our *own* existence *all* the time, Sairey,' she said. 'We are planets, not the sun.'

'Tell that to Ptolemy,' snapped Sairey.

This tickled Vita, who laughed out loud, a rare sound which encouraged Sairey to say, 'Couldn't we try a session before you go? Perhaps breaking the pattern will stimulate something.'

All I'm asking for is attention and reassurance, she told herself scornfully, as she spoke. But at the same time, with that keener self-scrutiny developed during her time at Britt House, she was aware that the pejorative motive was only part of the truth. Whatever was bugging her about this morning – vaguely appreciated as a seething discontent with being kept, like a child, in the dark, ignorant and afraid – had, in fact, brought her to the point where, consciously at least, she felt ready to follow the thread to the centre of the labyrinth.

Vita placed her cup on the draining-board.

'All right,' she said.

She came out of the trance with her clothes drenched in sweat, her limbs trembling. She forced her swimming gaze to focus on the school-room clock till the figures stopped circulating and their stillness confirmed she was back in real time again.

'Well?' she demanded.

Vita shook her head.

'Nothing,' she said. 'The same as before.'

'What?' cried Sairey, sick with disappointment. 'But the way I feel, there had to be something.'

'I'm sorry. Listen, if you like,' said Vita, pressing the rewind button. 'It's the sheer effort to break through that's leaving you like this. I got quite worried.'

Sairey rose and went to the window, opening it a little to let the cool air flow in. From here she could see across to the clump of birch where Kanyagga had done his disappearing act. She thought she glimpsed a movement among them now, then there was a flash, like light on glass. Then nothing.

The tape clicked to a halt. Vita pressed the start button. Her cool voice gave the date and time and tape number, then came the customary prolegomenon to the trance, then the questions, the nudgings, the suggestions. But all to no avail. Vita was right. There was nothing more here than had been on the three previous tapes.

'Shit,' said Sairey, as it finished. 'I'm going to take a shower. I feel as if I'd fought my way through a jungle.'

The shower refreshed her body and went some way to cooling her mind. Wrapping a towel around her, she returned to her bedroom, where she sat in front of her dressing table and began to dry her hair. Its spikes were long gone, and now, wet, her hair lay silkily close to her skull, and suddenly, with a shock which was physical, Sairey glimpsed herself in the mirror and realized she was looking at her mother.

Slowly, she let the towel slip to her shoulders. It wasn't quite her mother's face, the nose was a little longer, the brow a little broader, but her mother was there, and because her mother had been beautiful, beauty was there, also.

It was curious, she'd never thought of herself as other than vaguely plain. Childhood photos seemed to confirm this and perhaps she'd stopped really looking. From the age when she'd started to assume responsibility for her own appearance, she'd consciously tried to conform to whatever mode was approved by her peers, and unconsciously, so she now knew, to bury any resemblance to her mother.

168

She rose now and let the towel fall to the floor. The dressing-table mirror was too small so she moved to the full-length glass in her wardrobe. Given a choice, she would have preferred another inch or so on the leg, but, otherwise, there was no denying it – even with the absurdity of the white bikini effect left by her residual Spanish tan – she was OK; no, more than OK. She was beautiful.

A sharp knock on the door shattered her reverie like a stone in Narcissus's pool, and guiltily grabbing at her towel as if she had been caught in an act of indecency, she called, 'Yes?'

Vita, sensitive as always to the difference between a come-in yes and a stay-out yes, replied from outside. 'I'll have to be on my way shortly, else I'll miss my train. I just wanted to say, don't wait up. I'm not sure how late I'll be.'

'Hold on,' called Sairey, mind and body galvanized into action, 'I think I'll come with you.'

They caught the train with a few minutes to spare. Vita had expressed no curiosity about this sudden decision, which Sairey was glad of, as she had no ready explanation other than a need to see her father again and pin him down to some specifics.

The wind from the east had been tossing handfuls of rain around the station platform, but the train soon rattled them out of it into a more temperate zone of high, ragged cloud which pied the fields with evening sunlight, and eventually deposited them in the close muggy city, whose bronze air vibrated with the threat of thunder. It felt more like a journey halfway round the world than a trip of fifty miles.

They got a taxi at Liverpool Street. It was rush hour. The storm was breaking now and the lurid light made the people scurrying along the pavements look as if they were fleeing the Last Trump rather than the first raindrops. As they drove up Cheapside, a vein of lightning varicosed lazily across the sky beyond St Paul's dome, and the grumbling thunder at last exploded in anger. A few moments later, Vita rapped on the glass partition and said, 'I get off here.'

She got out, handed the driver some money, said to Sairey, 'I've paid all the way to Masham Square. See you in the morning, probably,' then started across the road. It was a typical Vita parting, swift and economical.

The taxi started to edge into the traffic again.

Sairey said, 'Wait.' She was into impulse time once more. She pushed open the door and stepped out. Three other people immediately converged on the cab and began to dispute the primacy, while Sairey dodged through the traffic across the road. She thought she'd lost Vita, then glimpsed her about fifty yards ahead, up a less crowded side street. Sairey followed, hugging the wall to avoid both detection and the rain. She needn't have worried about the first. Without the hint of a backward glance, Vita turned into a building and vanished from view. As Sairey approached, a taxi passed her, slowing down. It stopped about thirty feet ahead and a man got out. He was short-legged, bulky and apparently as indifferent to the rain as the animal he resembled. It was Archbell, and Sairey pressed into a doorway as if she were, indeed, a rambler who'd stumbled upon a bear unawares.

He paid the driver. Then a woman leaned out of the passenger window and addressed him. If Archbell were a bear, this was a gazelle. It was Fanny, her stepmother.

Sairey felt neither shock nor anger, and hardly even curiosity. She merely watched as Fanny handed Archbell a broad white envelope, which he stuffed negligently into

170

his jacket pocket before bending down to grip her chin in his pawlike hand and kiss her full on the lips, nuzzling deep as though he tasted honey.

Finished, he turned away and disappeared into the same building as Vita. The taxi moved on, taking the next turn left.

Sairey waited for a minute or more, trying to pretend it was from choice, but uncertain how much her legs would have obeyed her. Finally, she stepped out of the doorway and began to advance.

The building into which first Vita, then Archbell, had vanished was a four-storey office block, Victorian except for the door which gave every impression of being hi-tech, hi-security, with an entry code touch panel. A list of firms was set in the wall alongside. The first two floors were divided between two insurance companies, a domestic service agency and a firm of accountants, all of whose names sounded vaguely familiar. But the top two floors belonged to the Bureau for Economic Co-operation (Research Division) which she'd never heard of.

As to which of these bodies required the presence of both Vita and Archbell, she could not begin to guess.

She stepped back from the doorway to peer up, as though she hoped to spot one or the other leaning out of a window.

A hand touched her lightly on the shoulder. The touch was light, but so unexpected that she screamed and almost unbalanced as she span round.

Fanny, elegant in a powder-blue Gucci suit, stood there. Behind her, at the kerb, was a taxi.

Fanny said, 'I was sure that was you I spotted sheltering in a doorway further down. I wondered, can I offer you a lift home?'

Interview 21.7.81 Deputy Director/Nigel Ellis

DD: Nigel, you quite frightened my secretary when you rang. Is there a problem?

NE: A mistake. At least I hope it's a mistake because if it's not, then, yes, there's a hell of a problem.

DD: Oh dear. Tell me about it.

NE: It's this new assignment. What the hell's going on, Joe? It's a filing clerk's job in Registry.

DD: Come now. Rather more than that, I feel. You're virtually Collator of the East African section. Right up your street, I'd have thought, with your specialized knowledge.

NE: Specialized arseholes. Do you think I've come back to London to bury myself in that dusty warren?

DD: What did you think you had come back to London for, Nigel?

NE: To be briefed for Archie's job, that's what. When I heard you'd got the Deputy slot and Archie was coming back to the UK to take charge of Africa, I assumed . . . well, for Christ's sake, it's always been understood that when Archie finally moved on, I'd step in!

DD: Controller, East Africa. That's quite a step.

NE: Quite a step? It's the natural progression. I've got more experience out there than anyone. I know more about the situation out there than anyone.

DD: Even Archie? That's a little arrogant, isn't it?

NE: It's fact. Archie would be the first to admit that my experience at least matches his.

DD: Yes. Well, certainly, he gives you full credit for knowledge.

NE: Gives? So he has been consulted?

DD: Of course. You know how much importance we attach to a superior's report when we are considering a promotion – particularly when it's to the superior's job.

NE: Then Archie . . . but what . . .

DD: Archie feels that, while in terms of simple knowledge you are certainly qualified for the job, in terms of judgement he is less happy.

NE: Judgement? What the hell does he mean?

DD: He said, if I recall right, that your tendency to question policy decisions has always given some cause for concern. You have been spoken to about this at various stages throughout your career, I think you will agree? It's all on the record. Well, an enquiring spirit is always welcome in the Bureau, and many of your operational suggestions have proved extremely useful, no one's denying that. But when it comes to policy . . . well, that's water under the bridge. What concerned the appointing committee deeply, however, was Archie's feeling that the stress of the work, and of your own personal circumstances, has begun to cloud your field judgement.

NE: What? Oh, I'm beginning to get the picture . . . oh, you bastard, Archbell, you bastard.

DD: Steady on, Nigel. You mustn't get paranoiac. You really should be thanking Archie, not bad-mouthing him. He could easily have put you before a committee of enquiry on several occasions. In fact, at least once, I reckon he came pretty close to breaking the rules himself in not doing so.

NE: This gets worse. I can't believe any of this.

DD: Come on. Do you deny, for instance, that while acting as our closest and most trusted link with the Amin regime, you actually concealed a fugitive Obote supporter in your house in Kampala?'

NE: No. Yes. I mean it wasn't like that . . . it was a friend . . . the brother of a friend . . .

DD: It was an act of lunatic irresponsibility, both personally and professionally.

NE: Personally? What are you getting at, Joe?

DD: For Godsake, man, you had your family living with you! You knew as well as anyone what those bastards were capable of doing to their opponents. Yet you harboured a wanted man . . .

NE: Are you saying I should have let Juma Butabika and his madmen get their hands on him?

DD: Yes, if it meant keeping their hands off your own wife!

NE: Sarah? My God, Joe . . . Sarah . . . is this what this is all about? You think that Sarah died because . . . you're crazy. If Idi thought I was double-crossing him, he'd have had my balls off with a machete, like in his army days, no subtle warnings like killing my wife! For Christ's sake, Joe, those things you said when it happened, that was your grief talking, I understood that. But to let it fester . . . Joe, Sarah's death was dreadful, but it was a tragic accident, that was all . . .

DD: Accident? You call murder an accident? I suppose you'll say it was also accidental that you kept my granddaughter away from me as much as you could? It was my house she should have come to, not that eccentric spinster sister of yours . . .

NE: Joe, slander me as much as you like, but if you say another word against Celia, I'll push your teeth down your throat. As for Sairey, you had plenty of access till Celia realized what you were saying to her. My God, Joe, she was a little girl, needing to get over her mother's death, not have the grisly details rehearsed over her bed by a pathetic old man, stinking of brandy! Oh yes, we kept Sairey away from you all right, I approved, Celia enforced, but it was Sairey herself who wanted it. You frightened her, Joe. And if she hasn't let you get close as she's got older, it's because she can't forget that fear.

DD: I resent what you're saying, Nigel, but this isn't the time or place to discuss it. I assure you that decisions about your professional future are made on purely professional grounds. Accept them. You've had a stressful time out there, over many years. Relax and enjoy your leave with Sairey and . . . your wife . . .

NE: Fanny. They call her Fanny. Can't you bring yourself even to acknowledge her name? Did you expect me to stay in mourning for ever? What a tight little pair of conspirators you and Archie make, both hating me because I married Fanny. Oh, your reasons are different, but that's what it comes down to in the end . . . all right, all right, don't go puce, you'll have a seizure. If I'm not going to get Archbell's job, at least send me back there in some capacity. I'm useless to you in Registry, you know that. Let's put some distance between us, we'd both like that, wouldn't we? I'll swallow my pride if you'll dilute your revenge.

DD: For the last time, there is nothing personal in this. But an African posting's out of the question. Dicky Pepys, the new Controller . . .

NE: Pepys? You're sending Pepys out there? I don't believe this. He doesn't know his arse from an elephant!

DD: There's a feeling that Africa requires a fresh eye, Dicky is keen to start without prejudice. He doesn't want staff too tainted with the colonial past. In particular, Nigel, he doesn't want you. So I'm afraid, for the time being, it's either the Registry job, or . . .

NE: Or what?'

DD: Or early retirement. My secretary has the breakdown figures. I'm afraid they're rather meagre, but that's largely due to your own neglect of many opportunities to buy in the years before you came into the non-contributory scheme. You, doubtless, have made other arrangements . . .

NE: You, doubtless, know the ins and outs of my finances better than I do.

DD: Perhaps I do. So what's it to be, Nigel?

NE: Oh, you tricky bastard. It's not the nastiness, it's the slimy self-deceit that makes me want to puke. You want to know what I'm going to do with your job? You really want to know? I'm going to take it. You'll get so sick of me raising dust down among the files that in the end you'll be glad to ship me out again. But from now on, you and Archbell had better keep right out of my life, you understand that? Right out!

DD: Fine, Nigel. Goodbye, then. Try not to bang the . . . oh well. Interview terminates fifteen thirty-seven hours, Tuesday, June twenty-first, nineteen eighty-one. Transcripts: Ellis file; Director; Controller Medpsych. End.

GLOSS CO-OP 17/33/7
REGRET MEDPSYCH RECEIVED ONLY TRANSCRIPT NOT TAPE COPY. AUDIO ANALYSIS SHOWS ELLIS CLOSE TO REJECTING JOB. CONTROL EXERTED TO CHANGE DIRECTION. PLAYING FOR TIME? RECOGNITION OF POSSIBLE ADVANTAGE OF REGISTRY JOB? ON AUDIO BASIS MEDPSYCH WOULD NOT HAVE MAINTAINED ELLIS LEVEL OF CLEARANCE IN SENSITIVE AREA OF RECORDS.

17

Number 28 Masham Square echoed emptily as the door closed behind them. Sairey peered into the study to confirm that neither her father nor Allan was at home.

'Let's have a drink, shall we?' said Fanny, putting an arm round her shoulders and squeezing her gently as she urged her towards the lounge.

Sairey was taken aback. From their first encounter, Fanny had made it clear that physical contact beyond the purely social was not seen as part of her new duties. Sairey, keyed up to distrust and rebuff this unwanted stepmother, had instead found herself kept at such a polite arm's length that her passionate resolve seemed merely absurd. So the dimensions of their relationship had been set.

And now this. Because she feels guilty! And if she thinks a little togetherness can win me round, she's dimmer than she looks, thought Sairey unkindly.

Fanny poured two large glasses of white wine without further consultation and handed one to Sairey, who sat down, nursing the chilly goblet in both hands.

'You drank like that the first time I saw you,' said Fanny. 'Only it was orange juice and you dribbled a little.'

'What? At ten?' said Sairey indignantly.

'You were four.'

'You saw me in Africa? You never said.'

'I'd forgotten till now.' From anyone else it would have sounded like a lie, but not from Fanny. 'You were with your mother, she was having tea on the terrace at the

Norfolk. They made a great fuss of you and brought you orange juice. You held the glass in both hands and glowered at your own thoughts over the top of it.'

'You knew Mummy?'

'Only by sight. Someone pointed her out.'

'But if you and Daddy both worked for Mr Archbell . . .'

She found it hard to keep the distaste out of her voice.

'Yes, but I was only a secretary. Clerk-typist was my official designation, I recall.'

She smiled at the absurdity of anyone calling her a clerk-typist and Sairey smiled too, for it was absurd. Her mind was racing. She'd been armed for battle, but this unprecedented openness from Fanny was not to be ignored.

'You must have been very young.'

'About your age. Is that very young? It was my first job, my only job. Archie Archbell was an old friend of the family. I wasn't bright enough or well enough connected to make it to Oxbridge, and when he suggested Kenya, it sounded more my style than the University of Kent. Did you enjoy Karen Blixen's book, by the way?'

'It was all right. A bit old-fashioned in its attitudes, a bit condescending.'

This was meant to be sharp, but Fanny, even in confidential mood, was impervious to gnat bites.

'Yes, I read it years ago, before that feeble film. I got this idea of a place where life was never dull but where there was this intricate, almost invisible network of support. Like staying at Brown's and shopping at Harrods. Of course there was another reason why I went.'

She sipped her tea, replaced her cup.

'I was Archie Archbell's mistress,' she said.

Since the moment she had spotted them in the taxi, Sairey's mind had been skirting round the suspicion of an affair between Archbell and Fanny. But the idea of that cool beauty in the grasp of that hot brutishness was absurd, was obscene, was impossible. Yet here was Fanny, pre-empting whatever clumsy probing she might have screwed herself up to, with a simple confession.

'Don't look so shocked. Your father knew. Everyone in Nairobi did.'

'Why are you telling me this?' cried Sairey, flushing with embarrassment, not at the topic, but at her own feelings of inadequacy in dealing with it.

'You mean you weren't curious? I'm sorry. Perhaps I misread you.'

'All right. When I saw you with him . . . the way he kissed you . . . I wondered . . . are you still having an affair with him, Fanny?'

Her stepmother said, 'Now? Lord, no. Not since 1977, when I first went to bed with your father. There was, naturally, a slight overlap. One has to be certain. But not since. And, in case your schoolgirl curiosity takes you burrowing in the opposite direction, not before. If your father was ever unfaithful to your mother, it was not with me.'

Sairey looked at her, wanting to believe, but reluctant to trust.

'Sairey,' said Fanny, with gentle exasperation. 'Archie's taste is for young flesh. Ten years ago I was getting close to the end of my active life as far as he was concerned. Now, in his eyes, I am a well-hung pheasant to a man whose mouth is watering for spring lamb. You are prime meat as far as he is concerned. He's talked about you longingly. But I should advise against it. I'm sorry. That is impertinent of me. Your private life is your own affair. Forgive me.'

The brief moment of closeness was coming to an end. Fanny was steering them back to the bottom line of their relationship; courteous rejection on the one side, and on the other, a confusion of resentment and admiration and pain.

'Why don't you like me, Fanny?' Sairey burst out.

A look of surprise touched her stepmother's face.

'Don't I? I seem to recollect not much liking the look of that dribbling, glowering child all those years ago. But I really didn't connect her with you at all, till just now. So, no, I don't dislike you, Sairey. In fact, at times I think I get quite close to liking you, or at least thinking I shall like you when you . . . eventually. In any case, you mustn't set too much store on liking and disliking. Life *can* be like staying at Brown's and shopping at Harrods if you don't let likes and dislikes get too much in the way. I was lucky. I learned that early.'

Was there, momentarily, a hair crack through which pain showed? Sairey didn't believe it, or didn't want to believe it.

'How does Daddy fit into all this?' she asked.

It was meant to be an accusation, it came out as an appeal.

'Nigel? Perfectly, I'm glad to say.'

'You mean he just happened along when Archbell was beginning to hunt around for younger flesh, so you hopped off one gold card to another?'

Fanny began to laugh. It was a joyous, melodious sound, but Sairey responded neither to its mood nor its melody.

'And if you're not screwing Archbell, what *are* you doing with him? What was that paper you were giving him? Are you spying on Daddy? Why have you and that animal been talking about me? Where was he going? Why did he go into the same building as Vita? What the hell's going on?'

By the time she finished she was yelling and Fanny had

stopped laughing. Her stepmother rose and came towards her, her glassless hand outstretched.

'Sairey,' she said. 'I'm sorry, I've been insensitive, please, let's . . .'

'Don't touch me!' exclaimed Sairey, drawing back. 'Don't ever touch me. It's too late. It's far too late!'

She turned and ran out of the room, out of the house. Behind her, she heard Fanny calling but she did not pause till she was clinging to the park railings.

The rain had stopped, but scatters of drops were still being shaken from the trees by a rising wind, which sent dead leaves whispering across the glistening paths, like tiny crabs on the sea bed.

She thought of the last time she had run from the house to the doubtful haven of these stunted trees. Then she had encountered Allan Bright, her wounded boy.

Allan. She discovered in herself a burning need to see him, now. She didn't waste time analysing it – perhaps she was afraid to – but she ran across the park and out the far side. A stray taxi, rare in this area at this time of evening, confirmed that this was what fate meant for her.

'Where to?' enquired the driver.

A moment of blankness, the beginnings of panic. Allan had given her his address . . . somewhere in Victoria . . . she'd written it down but she couldn't recall what she'd done with . . . Then it popped into her mind, complete down to the post-code.

She did not doubt now that he would be at home. Nor did it matter that his expression as he opened the door had more of surprise than welcome in it. He seemed to think she'd come in anger, to demand an explanation for something, but she knew instinctively that there was no time for debate, either internal or external. She wanted him. She was going to use him. She put her arms round

181

his neck, drew his face to hers and kissed him passionately. She sensed a hesitation in him. Almost she, too, hesitated. Then into her mind strayed what Vita once said about her mother – for her, choice was never about judgement, it was always about commitment.

She redoubled her pressure on his lips, forcing her tongue deep into his mouth. Then she let one hand slide down his belly beneath his waistband.

He was silkily hard. Now, there was no more hesitation. And this time there was no interruption either.

18

'Well?'

'Well what?'

'Aren't you supposed to say, how was it for you?'

'All right, how was it for you?'

Sairey considered, then said, 'All things being equal, it was just about the best screw I've ever had.'

'So I noticed,' said Allan Bright.

'There are still a few of us about, you know. Eighteen-year-old virgins.'

'One less, now. Coffee?'

He rose from the narrow bed and went to switch his electric kettle on. He was totally unself-conscious about his nudity. His frame was too skinny for beauty, but the skin through which the shoulder bones and ribcage showed was like golden silk. Sairey tried to recall precisely what she had felt only a few minutes ago. Already, it was fading. There had been no ecstasy, that was for sure; some pain, but not enough to be a disincentive; and a strange feeling of invasion, which almost became union at the point where his body had arched like a golden bow, before going into spasm. At that moment he had ceased to be in control, so she was able at last to feel uncontrolled. It hadn't lasted long. She wasn't yet sure how much she liked it. But it had certainly left her feeling pleasantly relaxed.

She turned her head to look at the old-fashioned alarm clock on the rickety bedside table. She'd glimpsed it as they had first fallen rather awkwardly on to the bed. Only ten minutes had passed. Jesus, it felt much longer.

Something tweaked at her mind about another clock and another distorted time-span. Then Allan said, 'Here's your coffee,' and she had to struggle upright, making a conscious effort at unself-consciousness.

He didn't return to bed but flopped down in the room's only armchair. His expression was pensive, almost brooding.

She said, 'Allan. You don't seem as glad as I imagine a lot of men would be if a young woman came along and gave them her all.'

'Is that what I've had?' He tried to sound frivolous, but it didn't come off.

'So what's wrong?'

He drank his coffee, watching her over the mug's rim. The bedsitter was very small, but the chair and the bed seemed to be a gulf apart.

'I feel guilty,' he said.

'Guilty? You're not into Victorian standards, are you?'

'No. But I shouldn't have let it happen.'

'Don't flatter yourself,' said Sairey acidly. 'But, given that you had no choice, why would you have chosen to say no, if you had?'

'I think we may end up as enemies, Sairey,' he said, his gaze falling to his mug.

'Good Lord.' She rose from the bed and stood beside him, her unself-consciousness entirely unassumed now. 'Why? What's happened? Is it something to do with Daddy?'

'Why do you ask that?' he said.

'Because I can't imagine it's to do with me. I mean, you might not fancy me, but that's not going to make us enemies, is it?'

She saw he was regarding her with a compassion which irritated her vastly. No one who looked so young should look so understanding. What she wanted to see mirrored in his face was her own emotional chaos. People like Vita, Celia, her father, were proper materials for towers of strength. All she wanted from Allan Bright was a willow cabin to rest in for a while.

'What the hell is my father saying in this bloody book of his?' she demanded angrily. 'I can't get straight answers from anyone. But I know it's got everyone running around like the end of the world is nigh.'

Allan said, 'Haven't you asked your father?'

'My father thinks the best treatment for inquisitive daughters is to send them off to America without any supper.'

'He may be right. Sorry! Look, what he's threatening to expose is the extent to which the UK, with active support from Kenya, backed Amin, and kept on backing him, even after Entebbe. Also, he promises to throw in, for good measure, details of covert help in sanctions-breaking: oil to Rhodesia, arms to South Africa, that sort of thing. And as an appendix, he says he'll look at relations between Security and the ANC, which were improving recently in line with world trends, till a couple of ANC representatives got killed on their way to a secret meeting with the British.'

'You keep on saying he "threatens", or he "promises". Haven't you seen any of this stuff?'

'A bit, but he keeps things pretty close to his chest. I suspect that until his ex-employers can actually prove that he has (a) written and (b) intends to publish secret material, they can't actually set the law on him, which in any case is often worth a couple of million pounds of free publicity!'

'So what will they do?' she asked.

'Use other channels, I suppose.'

What did that mean? She didn't ask, but said, 'Does he ever mention my mother in these memoirs?'

He said slowly, 'Not much, that I've seen. But don't read anything into that. These are professional memoirs. It's the work that counts.'

'But he must mention in passing that his wife died, for God's sake!'

'Yes. He does that.'

He hesitated, then rose and went to the tiny wardrobe which prevented the door to the landing opening fully. From its top he took a battered briefcase. In it was a sheaf of typewritten sheets. He riffled through them, picked out four or five and handed them to Sairey.

'I've photocopied a few sections,' he said.

'Why? Does he know?'

The young man shrugged indifferently. Sairey's eyes dropped to the first line. 'In 1975 my wife died in tragic circumstances.' She immediately lost all sense of her surroundings or Allan's presence. When she finished reading, she found she was sitting on the bed with Allan beside her, his arm around her shoulders. She looked at him with eyes full of tears.

'It isn't much,' she said.

'I told you. It's not that kind of work. But he seems to have felt it deeply.'

His tone didn't ring true. She began to feel anger. It *wasn't* much, and to suggest that it was less, reduced it to zero.

She said, 'You don't believe that, do you? You think he's acting on paper.'

'I don't know what I think yet. Why are you so angry, Sairey? Because he hardly mentions you at all?'

She realized, instantly, how accurate this was, but it didn't make her any less angry.

'What the hell are you doing photocopying Daddy's writing anyway? Are you some kind of spy?'

186

'I'm just like you, Sairey, except that I lost my father as well as my mother,' he said undramatically.

'Oh God. Of course. I'm sorry.' Her emotional tunnel-vision had let her ignore that these pages were just as much about the death of Allan's parents. She put her arms around him and tried to pull him close but he resisted. She looked into his face then and suddenly saw things clear.

'Is this what you meant about us becoming enemies?' she said incredulously. 'You think my father was to blame for your mother's death?'

His eyes confirmed that she was right. She went on, urgently, 'Allan, that's stupid. Ocen would have had to leave some time, and it was surely better not to run the risk of him being found in Daddy's house. It was bad luck, terrible luck, that things happened as they did, but it wasn't anybody's fault.'

'It's always someone's fault,' he said harshly. Then his tense body relaxed a little and he added, 'But perhaps not necessarily your father's.'

It was a grudging withdrawal but she sensed it was the best she was going to get. She returned her attention to the printed sheets, reading with her full mind this time, not just the bit focused upon herself.

'There, he says it. What you were talking about before. "It wasn't till later that I was to discover the full extent of the covert aid to the Rhodesians and the South Africans and how far it went beyond oil and arms." He hasn't written about that yet, you say?'

'Not to my knowledge.'

'But it will make a lot of people very angry when he does?'

'What he's written so far is enough to make people angry,' said Allan.

'How angry? Enough to harm him?'

'Enough to want to stop him, certainly. But harm . . . I don't think so.'

Again that false note. He was trying to reassure her.

She said, 'Why not? They harmed you, didn't they?'

It was a wild, instinctive shot, but it struck home. He didn't even bother to attempt a rebuttal. She put her hand to the fading scar on his cheek and said, 'It wasn't an accident you were in the park that night, was it?'

'No,' he said. 'I was watching the house.'

'But why? You'd been in England for years without getting in touch. What happened to change things?'

He said, 'I got a letter. It said, "If you want to know who really killed your mother and your father and your uncle, check it out with Nigel Ellis." And it gave the Masham Square address. I wasn't lying when I said I'd no idea your father was living in London. I'd deliberately set about losing touch with him. I just couldn't bear anything which reminded me of my parents. He tried several times to see me when he came back to Nairobi after Amin fell, but I just refused, till finally he stopped. Now, I went looking for him. That night I had been at a party, that was true. And I was full of booze. So on my way home, when I realized how close I was to the Square, I diverted to have a look.'

'But it wasn't punks who beat you up.'

'No. It was two men. They just got out of a car and this big blond guy started into me. He kept on calling me a fucking kaffir . . .'

'And the other. Was he smaller, darker?'

'Yes. You know them? They're friends of yours?'

'Not of mine. I think they're called Kirkman and Cilliers and they sounded South African to me.'

'To me, too,' said Allan, with a reminiscent shudder. 'The smaller one . . .'

'. . . Cilliers . . .'

188

'. . . took my wallet and went through it and he found the note about my parents' death. Then he laughed and said, "This mulatto might be on our team, after all." The big guy stopped hitting me for a moment. I lashed out with my foot and, luckily, caught him in the crutch. I managed to pull free and dived over into the park. I got as far as the hut then collapsed. I heard a car pulling away . . .'

'What kind of car did they have? A red BMW?'

'No,' he said, looking at her curiously. 'It was a big black, jeep-type thing, Japanese, I think. Anyway, I hoped it was them but I wasn't taking chances. I stayed put. After a while, I found the tap and started to clean myself up. Then suddenly someone was running along the path towards me. I nearly died of terror! Then I heard a voice calling, "Sairey, Sairey," and I was back in Nairobi at your parents' bungalow and your mother was alive and my mother was alive and the sun was shining and we all had a life to look forward to . . .'

It was a good cue for them to weep on each other's shoulders, but Sairey was still thinking about cars and seeing the red BMW slowly cruising round the Square with Archbell peering out of the window, like a bear in a circus parade.

And then she saw Archbell peering into the window of another car, a taxi, and being handed a broad, A4-size envelope . . .

'You photocopied this on Daddy's copier?'

'Yes.' Allan sounded annoyed at this brusque diversion from nostalgic grief.

'Does Fanny ever use the copier?'

'I've heard her using it. Why?'

She stood up and began pulling on her clothes. Curiously, it was only when she was half dressed that any of the old self-consciousness returned, but she covered it by telling Allan about Fanny and Archbell.

He stopped looking annoyed and started looking interested.

'You think Fanny could be leaking the memoirs to your father's old employers?'

'Why not? Archbell used to be his boss, and presumably he's still working for the same people.'

'But why should she . . .?'

'I don't know,' she cried impatiently. 'I've never been able to understand why Fanny does anything. But I've got to see Daddy straightaway. He's got to be told, he might be in real danger.'

Allan regarded her with an expression which she could read quite clearly. He was wondering why, just because *she'd* managed to remain so unaware of what was going on, she should imagine everyone else had. But he didn't say anything, possibly gauging that it was going to make no difference if he did.

He, too, started to dress.

'You've been home and he wasn't there?' he asked as he wriggled his enviably slim thighs into his incredibly narrow jeans.

'That's right. But he's got to come back some time. What time did he go out? Did he say where he was going?'

He looked surprised, then said, 'Sorry, I should have said. I haven't been in today. He rang first thing and said he wouldn't be needing me.'

'Shit. Let's hope he's got back, then.'

She was assuming Allan would be going with her, she realized. And he was assuming the same. In fact, it turned out to be even better. In the street he steered her towards a battle-scarred Fiat 125 and said, 'Hop in.'

'Hop? I'd land on the other side.'

'Never mock a man's first car,' he said. 'Crawl in!'

Number 28 was empty. She felt it again, even as she unlocked the door. But she went right through the house to make sure. Fanny had got changed and gone out. Her powder-blue suit was hanging outside her wardrobe.

When she returned downstairs she found Allan in the study. He looked perplexed.

'What's up?' she asked.

'Look at it,' he said. 'Everything's gone.'

Sairey looked around. It seemed an exaggeration.

'All the memoirs stuff, I mean,' said Allan.

'He'd hardly leave it lying around, would he?'

'No. He kept it locked up,' said Allan. 'All safe and sound.'

As he spoke, he pulled open desk and filing cabinet drawers, bureau cupboards and finally the wall safe.

'Gone,' he repeated.

They stood and looked at each other and looked at the empty drawers and did not need to voice the question which was uppermost in both their minds. Who had emptied them? Nigel Ellis? Or . . .?

Sairey ran back upstairs to her father's bedroom. She checked his wardrobe, then went on to the bathroom and checked the shelves there.

'Well?' asked Allan Bright from the doorway.

'Nothing. He's taken nothing. I mean, I suppose I can't be absolutely sure about his clothes, but toothbrush, shaving gear, it's all here.'

She didn't realize how much despair was in her voice till Allan put his arms about her and started uttering words of comfort.

'It's nothing. He'll be back. Why should anyone want to harm him now? All they've got to do is stick the

Official Secrets Act on him and he's gagged, in this country, anyway.'

'Do you think that's it? Do you think he may have hopped abroad to get his book published?' she asked hopefully. 'But surely he'd have let me know? Or let Fanny know. Unless he suspects she's in league with Archbell. But she didn't seem at all worried when we came back and he wasn't there. But perhaps she knew . . .'

Her mind and her words were spiralling towards hysteria.

'Sairey, calm down!' ordered Allan. But she doubted if his simple pleas would have been enough. Then the telephone rang.

Allan got to it first.

'Yes?' he said. 'Yes, it is. Yes, she's here.'

He handed the receiver to Sairey.

'It's him,' he said. 'Your father.'

She grabbed the phone in both hands.

'Hello? Hello, Daddy,' she cried. 'Where are you? What . . .'

His voice cut across hers with authoritative ease.

'Sairey, what the hell are you doing there? Why aren't you in Essex?'

There was a sound in the background and a pause as Nigel Ellis obviously moved from the phone to close a door.

'Daddy, won't you please tell . . .'

'Get out of that house,' he ordered. 'Get back to Essex. I'll ring you there.'

'Daddy, but what's . . .'

The phone went dead.

'What's up? Has he rung off?' asked Allan.

'I don't know. I don't think so,' said Sairey. 'But it doesn't matter. I know where he is, Allan. I should have guessed. He's down at *Dunelands* with Aunt Celia. He's got some clothes and a toothbrush down there permanently, so he wouldn't need anything.'

'Are you sure?' asked the young man dubiously.

'Yes. I heard Mop barking. That's the Sealyham. I'd know his yap anywhere!'

'Why did he ring?'

'Because . . .' It was a good question. 'To tell me to get away from here, I think,' said Sairey slowly.

'But how did he know you might be here? No matter. Perhaps we'd better take his advice. I'll drive you home. To Maldon, I mean.'

'No, you won't,' said Sairey fiercely. 'You'll drive me to *Dunelands*. I'm tired of being pushed around like a parcel.'

She set off, without waiting for a response. And as she walked down the hallway to the front door, the doorbell rang.

'Sairey, wait!' whispered Allan urgently behind her.

But Sairey was not in the mood for waiting.

She flung open the door with a violence that made even Vita Gray look faintly surprised.

'Hello, Sairey. I thought I'd call on the off chance you were still here, so we could travel back together.' She glanced at the old wall clock in the hall. 'If we move quickly, we can catch the nine-fifteen.'

Sairey, too, glanced at the clock. For a moment, Vita's formidable presence had reduced all her fears to sick fantasies and herself to a neurotic post-adolescent. Then Allan came up behind her and she felt his hand touch her back. And she recalled that this was the woman she had seen going into the same building as Archie Archbell. And as she regarded the clock, the puzzlement which had stirred as she looked at the alarm clock by Allan's bed broke through to the surface.

It was a simple but devastating puzzle.

Her last hypnosis session had taken twenty minutes by the clock in the consulting room. Yet the tape she had listened to had taken no more than seven or eight.

The solution, too, had to be both simple and devastating.

She said, 'No. Why don't you come in, Vita, and play me the real tape of this afternoon's session? Then we'll discuss where we're going.'

This is session number twenty-two, at 1500 hours, October 21st. Do you feel comfortable, Sairey?

Yes.

You've been looking a bit tired lately. Are you sleeping all right?

I've not been dreaming, if that's what you mean.

I only ask what I mean, Sairey.

Yes. Sorry. Yes, I've been sleeping . . . well, no, I don't suppose I have. I wake up sometimes and think about things and it all goes round in my mind and I don't seem to be able to stop it . . .

Well, relax, and let's see if we can stop it now, shall we? Just relax. Try to catch up on some of that sleep you've been losing. Would you like that?

Yes, that would be nice.

All right. Just close your eyes. Think of somewhere soft and warm and cosy. Remember that big cushion in the swing seat on the verandah of your house in Kampala? You used to love snuggling down in that, didn't you? When you were little. When you were five years old. Do you remember? When you were five years old?

Yes. Five years old. I remember.

Uncle Ocen. Is he still in the house?

Yes, he's still there. But Mummy says I mustn't bother him.

But you do bother him, don't you?

Sometimes. But he says he doesn't mind, and he takes me in his arms and holds me in the air and says he is much, much better and soon he will have to go. And I say I don't want him to go. And he laughs and says no one wants him to go, but he has to.

And Auntie Apiyo, does she come to the house?

Sometimes. Daddy brings her sometimes in his car. I don't know she's in the car when he drives into the garage, but she is.

That's strange. Why do you think that is, Sairey?

I think she must be hiding in the car.

As a game, you mean?

That's right. As a game.

Do you play games like that, Sairey? Hiding, I mean.

Sometimes. Sometimes I do.

Who do you play with, Sairey?

Sometimes I play with Paula. And sometimes I play with Daddy.

And with Mummy? You play with Mummy?

Sairey, do you play games with Mummy?

No.

No? Never? You never play games with Mummy?

Never.

That's strange, Sairey. Don't you want to play games with Mummy?

Yes.

Then why don't you?

Because.

Because what, Sairey?

Because she's not there! Because she's not there!

Where is she, Sairey?

I don't know. She's gone. She's gone.

But she was there, Sairey, wasn't she? She was there last Christmas, wasn't she?

Yes.

And she was there when you moved to Kampala, wasn't she?

Yes.

Then where's she gone?

I don't know.

Let's try to find out, shall we? Where was she last time you saw her?

Sairey, I asked, where was Mummy last time you saw her? You do want to remember, don't you?

Yes.

Then where was she?

She was . . .

Yes?

She was . . . somewhere . . . I can't remember.

Sairey, you must remember. You can see her, can't you? I know you can see her. Where is she?

She's . . . she's in a box! She's lying in a long box!

Is she dead?

I don't know. I don't know what dead is.

What do you do?

I scream out. I struggle.

Is someone holding you?

Yes, it's Daddy. Daddy has me in his arms.

What does he do?

He hands me to Aunt Celia.

And what does Celia do?

She presses me to her breast. She carries me out of the room and down the corridor.

What do you see? What do you hear?

There's moonlight flooding through the windows and a smell of rotting flowers and a dog barking and it's very warm.

Where does Celia take you?

Up the stairs to my room. But I break free and she has to let me go and I run back downstairs and Daddy's standing there in the moonlight closing the long box and I won't let him and I look inside again and I can see . . . I can see . . . I can see . . . Mummy! Mummy! Mummy!

19

Sairey felt her head swimming as the tape ran silent. She felt herself being dragged from here and now into the world of her Dream. She gripped the desk in her father's study with all her strength, trying to anchor herself with its solidity. At the same time she forced her eyes to concentrate on the typewritten transcript. The same words, but black, plain, even – the concrete evidence that time had passed, that she had moved on from the horror of the trance and could now afford to sit back and view it calmly, if not safely.

The door burst open.

'Sairey, are you all right?'

It was Allan.

Vita had not disputed Sairey's request, but led her briskly into the study, set up the tape and presented her with the transcript. Allan had kept close to Sairey, but once she was seated at the desk, Vita had urged him out of the room. He had protested till Sairey said, 'Please, Allan.' Then, as Vita was about to close the door behind him, she added, 'Let's stick to the rules, Vita.'

The psychiatrist had said, 'Of course. And I have a phone call to make, if that's all right?' Then she too left.

Now she was back, right behind Allan, whose look of concern told Sairey how devastated she must appear.

'Yes, I'm fine,' she lied.

Vita said, 'Please, Mr Bright. We need a few moments.'

For the second time, reluctantly, he left.

Vita and Sairey regarded each other in silence. There

were a million questions to ask, a million accusations to hurl, but Sairey forced herself to be quiet. Yesterday, such an attempt to make the older woman speak first would have been little more than a childish game. Now it was a tactic in a deadly struggle, where the first thrust risked the first exposure.

Vita said, 'I didn't wake you straightaway, but kept you under till I'd faked one of the earlier abortive tapes with today's intro.'

This was typical of her. Not an opening, but an answer, as if Sairey had asked the question.

'I suppose you did it for my sake!' said Sairey with bitter mockery.

'To an extent,' said Vita.

'To spare me the shock of knowing you'd failed, was that it? Or to spare yourself the shame of admitting it?'

'Failed?' said Vita, as if faced with a neologism.

'What would you call it? The big idea behind all this psychiatric crap was for me to come to terms with the reality of Mummy's death, wasn't it? Then it would lose its power over my subconscious, right? OK, so you'd prefer to rephrase that in your usual prissy way, but I've got the gist, yes? All we've got to do is clear away the blockage, like with a landslide, remember that? Picture language for bird-brains! And as we got close, I threw up bigger and bigger blockages, wasn't that it? So now you've finally broken through these, and what do you find? The original blockage, absolutely untouched!'

'What blockage do you mean, Sairey?'

'Come on, Vita! Lose gracefully. You went for the reality and all you could dredge up was the Dream. I don't need hypnosis to get me there! I've always been able to manage that trip with no outside assistance.'

Vita, who up till now had been standing before the desk, pulled up a chair and sat down. She didn't speak for a moment, and for the first time ever, Sairey felt her silence derived from a need to control herself, not a situation.

Finally, she said, 'Sairey, this was never what I wanted to find, you must believe that.'

'Spoils your unbeaten record, is that it? But what I want to know is . . .'

A simple gesture of Vita's hand was enough to still Sairey's demand to know by what right and to what end Vita had taken the tape with her to this mysterious meeting. Or perhaps it wasn't the gesture; perhaps it was the expression of pity on the older woman's face, almost as rare as her smile.

'Sairey, hypnosis helps disentangle fantasies and symbols from reality. In some cases there may still be confusion. In your case, there has generally been nothing but the utmost clarity. In your trances, I have consistently stirred simple, often highly detailed memories, nothing more or less.'

'What the hell are you saying, Vita?' cried Sairey in alarm. 'That I've faked this or something?'

But she knew that this was not what Vita was saying. She knew that it was something infinitely more terrible.

And at last it was put into words.

'We've got to stop treating your Dream as fantasy, Sairey,' said Vita Gray. 'We've got to start looking at it as memory.'

'No!'

She thought she had only shrieked in her mind, but her mental cry must have masked her physical one. The study door burst open; suddenly, incomprehensibly, the room was full of people. Mrs Marsden was there, and her grandfather, Sir Joe, and behind them, the shambling bulk of Archie Archbell. But not Allan.

If Allan had been there she would have gone to him,

she was sure of that. But he wasn't, and in her need for someone to cling to and draw strength from, she turned to her grandfather.

He held her tight and made soothing noises which part of her mind, somehow contriving to stand back and view all this emotionalism with divine detachment, categorized as being more suitable for a retching baby or an injured dog than an adult human. But her need was still strong and she clung on till the detached segment took control.

'I'm sorry. I'm sorry, Grandad,' she said, pushing herself away from him. 'I'm sorry, everybody. I just had a shock, that was all. But I'm all right now.' She turned her gaze coldly on Vita. 'I'm not going to have any more shocks.'

Sir Joe said, 'Sairey, my dear, why don't you sit down? A glass of brandy. Mrs Marsden, I wonder . . .'

The little round-shouldered woman went off, with the resigned air of one long used to running errands for commanding males. Sairey went back round the desk and resumed her seat, facing them all. She took a deep breath, then another. Mrs Marsden returned with a decanter and a glass which she filled and handed to Sairey.

'Thanks,' she said. 'Where's Allan?'

She wanted Allan. Until she knew better, all those present were best regarded as enemies summoned by Vita. Except perhaps Mrs Marsden, whose presence must surely be coincidental.

Or perhaps not. It was this woman who spoke now and her voice, though soft, was not as self-effacing as her looks.

'He just left. I saw him go. He said, Tell Sairey I'm sorry.'

Sorry for what?

But that would have to wait till other times, other places.

She said, 'This tape, I presume you've all heard it? And all read this transcript?'

Everyone looked at Vita for a lead. She said, 'Yes.'

Sairey said, 'This blurb at the top. It's something to do with Daddy, isn't it? You're working against him. At least, three of you are. I'm not sure about you, Mrs Marsden.'

'I, too,' said the old woman, unhappily.

'It was nothing sinister, my dear,' said Sir Joe. 'Nothing personal. He was being a bit of a silly ass over these memoirs of his. Of course we could simply have set the law on him, but things have got so tangled the last couple of times that's been tried, that our political masters told us to gag him the best way we could. So a co-op was formed . . .'

'A co-op?' said Sairey, looking at the transcript. 'After the Bureau for Economic Co-operation?'

'Who's been sniffing at my porridge?' said Archbell mockingly. It was interesting to see that his self-image didn't exclude the ursine qualities others saw in him.

'A co-op is a non-standing committee, with unlimited powers of co-option,' explained Vita.

'. . . just to see what pressures might be brought to bear,' continued Lightoller, as though no one had interrupted.

'That sounds very friendly. Is that why you called it Operation Antenor? That sounds to me like you were trying to get him for something more than a bit of indiscretion. Didn't Antenor help the Greeks get into Troy?' said Sairey, sneeringly.

'Classics, is it now?' said Archbell. 'I'm getting out of my depth.'

'I was trying to be kind, Sairey,' said Lightoller,

sharply. 'By any definition, oathbreaking and the betrayal of secret information for personal gain are forms of treachery. It would have pleased me more than anything if your father could have been brought to see the error of his ways by simple persuasion. But it's too late for that now.'

'And what comes after persuasion? Blackmail? Threat? Violence? Even if you honestly believe he's wrong, is he wrong enough to merit that?' Sairey's voice was strong, assertive. She felt she was on top of this argument, but from the corner of her eye she could see that same compassionate expression on Vita's face and hated her for knowing that this was all so much procrastination.

It was, of course, Archbell who wrenched them back on course.

'Listen, my sweet,' he growled. 'This is all academic. Personally, I would have voted from the start for dropping your precious father down a hole and shovelling in the earth after him. But I can see how you might have argued against that. But now we've all heard the tape. And we've heard the expert's commentary on it. The case has altered. This isn't just a poor wimp, whingeing about his pension rights. I doubt if the law can touch him now for what happened to your mother, but in my book, anything we may do to him is only legal justice once removed!'

'For God's sake, man!' exclaimed Lightoller.

'Don't shower me with shit, Sir Joe,' said Archbell. 'Ever since it dawned on you what was being suggested, you've been mulling over four-and-twenty simultaneous ways of causing your son-in-law incredible pain.'

Lightoller turned away from Archbell, but he essayed no denial. Sairey looked desperately at Vita, who met her gaze, but made no response to her desperation.

'Vita, what's going on? You know this is absurd, the

204

Dream can't be true, they never brought Mummy's body home, and Aunt Celia, why should she . . .?'

Her voice trailed off, but Vita spoke as if the question had been completed.

'What would Celia do if she found your father in trouble?'

'Help him,' whispered Sairey.

'And how much would she help him?'

'To the extremes of her power.'

'No matter what he'd done?'

The answer was dragged from Sairey by an irresistible force.

'No matter what.'

'That disposes of Celia's part then.'

'But Daddy wouldn't . . . why should he . . .'

Sairey could feel her control slipping, could feel herself slipping back into childhood, where tears brought comforting and the promise of better times if you were a good girl.

She said, very quietly, because she needed to keep her voice on a very short leash, 'You're saying that Mummy may have died at home, that Daddy may have had something to do with it, that he and Aunt Celia conspired to remove the body from the house and fake a kondi attack on the road to Entebbe? All this on the evidence of my dream! You must be mad.'

They all looked at each other. Or rather, curiously, they all seemed to look at Mrs Marsden, who gave a minute nod.

Archbell said, 'There's something else, my sweet. You remember that stuff from the Ugandan Human Rights Commission you found in your book?'

'I knew it was you who put it there,' said Sairey.

'What? Not me, dearie! Why should I bother with something like that?'

He glanced at Vita and winked.

'*Vita*. You?'

Archbell laughed and said, 'Et tu, Brute. You see, I do have a smidgeon of classics, too. But what I was saying is, there's another instalment of evidence to that Commission which may interest you.'

He turned and went out of the room. Vita said to Mary Marsden, 'Is this necessary?'

'Don't get protective now,' snapped Sairey. 'Facing up to things is the name of your game, isn't it?'

'Where the hell's it gone?' fumed Archbell, coming back into the room. 'I had it, I know.'

He had an open briefcase in his hand, from which he shook papers all over the desk.

'It was definitely there.'

'You mean Gregory's evidence?' said Mrs Marsden.

'What else? It's gone. But how the hell . . .' Then he paused and said, 'That lad. Bright's son. Oh shit.'

Vita said, 'If he's read it . . .'

'But he doesn't know where Ellis is,' said Sir Joe.

'Yes, he does,' said Sairey, not understanding anything but their sudden concern for either Allan or her father. 'Daddy rang from . . . from where he is.'

'From *Dunelands*? Oh, it's all right, the call was intercepted and traced,' said Lightoller impatiently. 'And the boy has a car?'

'Yes.'

'Then I suggest we get down there after him, or we may find we've a real mess to clean up.'

They all began to move to the door, Sairey with them, still demanding explanation.

'What's happening?' she asked. 'What's the panic? Why should Allan rush off to *Dunelands* without saying anything?'

206

'He did say something,' Archbell reminded her. 'He said, Tell Sairey, I'm sorry.'

'Sorry for what?'

And Archbell over his shoulder growled, 'At a guess, for killing your father.'

Interrogation of Kakuba, Gregory, assistant guard in
prison block of Headquarters of Public Safety Unit at
Nagaru.
Day 3 (cont.)

Q. You handed the Commission some papers at the start
of your interrogation. (For the record, let it be noted that
these papers and their transcription now form Admission
835 of this investigation.) What was your motive in
producing these papers?
A. Sorry, boss?
Q. Why did you keep the papers?
A. Mr Bright say that when Idi Dada go and proper
gov'ment come, he tell everyone Gregory was good
guard, no cruelty, no torture, no stealing prisoners'
rations. But Mr Bright get killed in road accident . . .
Q. Do you believe that he was really killed in an accident?
A. Anyone can have accident with all these mad army
fellows driving up and down road to Jinja. Maybe he do
have accident, maybe not. But no accident while he is in
Gregory's care!
Q. Let's return to the papers. With Mr Bright's death, you
had no one to speak up for you, is that right?
A. Yes, boss.
Q. And you thought you would need someone to speak
up for you. Why?

A. Poor man has no voice of his own. Poor man needs someone to speak for him.

Q. So you thought if you couldn't get help from Mr Bright, you might get help from his papers?

A. Yes, boss. He always scribbling. I catch him but don't say anything. Like he would tell you, Gregory always kind to prisoners.

Q. Do you know what he wrote in these papers?

A. No, boss. Gregory can read big letters like on notice, but these little scribbly ones, like Mr Bright does, are out of sight.

Q. He wrote that he asked you to do a favour for him.

A. Yes, boss. I do lotta favours for Mr Bright. I help him when he first arrive in my cells. Mr Bright in bad way without Gregory's help.

Q. How was he in a bad way? Was he sick?

A. Sick? He was all smashed up, boss.

Q. You mean he'd been beaten?

A. Yes. Beaten bad. They say: feed him, make sure he get well. But unless I help, he cannot feed; unless I give lift, he cannot walk.

Q. So you helped him because those were your orders? Who gave those orders?

A. No! I help more than orders because here is a sick man who done me no harm and needs help.

Q. All right. But who gave the orders?

A. The bosses, boss. The ones with the big cars and the women, the ones who sit and laugh at the sledgehammer game.

Q. And who gave them their orders to stop torturing Mr Bright?

A. Don't know, boss. Only know who give my orders.

Q. So you helped Mr Bright. Did he make a good recovery?

A. Oh yes. He is very strong. Also very lucky. Nothing

209

broken, nothing important, only very little bones. He come along very nicely, thank you.

Q. And then he asked you to do this favour. Tell us what he wanted you to do.

A. Mr Bright always worried about his wife. You know his wife was Acholi? Bad to be Acholi in those times. Bad for Ugandan woman to be married to white man. I know nothing of this woman. Mr Bright wrote a message, asked me to take it and give it to this white man in Kampala so he could pass it to this Acholi woman.

Q. This message, what did it say?

A. I don't know. Like all the other papers, I cannot read.

Q. But you took it?

A. I worry what is best to do. If I get caught, there is big trouble. But Mr Bright is always asking, and day by day he is looking better, and perhaps soon he will look well enough to let him go and then Gregory has not done him the favour. Then there is holiday. Idi Dada has married again while all the big bosses are in Kampala talking big. I have to leave to go to Kampala to see my family. I have some beer and feel brave and think no one will notice if I take care. So I got to this house that Mr Bright has told me . . .

Q. Whose house was this?

A. White man called Ellis. This Ellis, friend of Idi Dada I find out later. If I knew that at first, I keep long way off from his house, no fear!

Q. How do you know this white man Ellis was a friend of Amin?

A. His wife gets killed soon after and everyone is very afraid because Idi Dada is very angry, asking who has done this, especially when all the big bosses are in Kampala. And PSU say it must be SRC and SRC say it must be PSU, but in the end both say it was kondis.

Q. So what do you do when you get to his house?

A. I go into garden. The beer has made me want to piss, but when I am done, I find I have pissed out my bravery with the beer. Now I wonder, is anyone else watching this white man's house? But then I think, no, tonight is big celebration night and all the big bosses will be filling themselves with whisky and chasing women, and all the little bosses, too. So I take a drink from this bottle I have brought with me, and soon I feel brave again. But before I can go up to the house, a car comes and a white man gets out and goes inside. I think this must be Mr Ellis and I think I am a fool because I do not shout and give him the message, then go fast away from there. But I am hiding in some bushes in the garden and I think that maybe if I shout from bushes, he would shoot me, thinking I was kondi. So now I take another drink. There are lights in the house and people moving, I can see this. Also, I hear a little girl crying. So I wait a little longer, take another drink. Then just when I am ready to deliver my message, a taxi stops in road and a woman comes hurrying up the little road to the house.

Q. A white woman?

A. Black. She look like Acholi woman and I think, ah, maybe this is wife to Mr Bright. Almost I call out, but then I think that woman even more than man will get scare of kondis in the bushes and scream, so I take another drink and wait. Time passes . . .

Q. How much time?

A. I don't know. Perhaps I sleep a little. Yes, I sleep, I think. When I wake it is because of the noise of cars.

Q. Cars? Arriving at the house?

A. No. Leaving the house.

Q. How many cars? What kind?

A. Two cars. One is the big car the white man who might be Ellis came in. The other is a little car. Little red car.

Q. Who is in the cars?

A. The white man drives the big one and the Acholi woman is driving the little red one.

Q. Is there any movement in the house?

A. There are some lights. Also, I still hear the child crying. But I see nothing. Now is the time for Gregory to go, I think. But my legs are not ready to go. I lie down to rest and get strength. Once more I wake by sound of car.

Q. Just one car?

A. Yes. The big one. White man and Acholi woman are both in it. They get out. He puts arm round her, she puts arm round him, they go into house. Now Gregory's legs work. I get up and go back to my family.

Q. And what about the message?

A. I put paper in my mouth and chew it up and spit it out. These things I do not understand.

Q. But this favour Mr Bright asked you to do, what did you tell him about that?

A. I tell him I cannot deliver message and I want to tell nothing else. But he asks questions all the time, and he gets angry and says I am lying because I was afraid to deliver message. Then I get angry and tell him what I see. I think he understand these things as less as me. He sits and thinks and thinks. Then two, three days later, patrol truck comes into yard. I see from my window. Two prisoners kicked out. One hit the ground and lie there. He looks like gone case to me. The other is a woman, hurt bad and face all smashed, but I think maybe I recognize her. Then I hear this great cry from Mr Bright's cell and woman look up and I know then she is Acholi woman he is married to. I run damn quick to his cell and drag him from window or else he be in trouble. But he in trouble anyway. They come for him soon after and he runs at them like madmen. But they just kick and beat him up bad and mock him, then take him away.

Q. When they mocked him, what did they say?

A. Things like, good fuck your woman, take three men at once, that sort of thing. Also, you got no friends. Even white friends don't want to know you. Fuck your woman then give her up to PSU, that's what your white friends do. Then they take him away. Come back one, two hours later. Teeth all broken, nails torn, things that do not mend. I know this time they don't plan he should go free.

Q. What happened to Mr Bright after that?

A. Nothing more. They leave him to me. I help how I can, but he is gone case. Last time I see him, he is in compound. They are making men play sledgehammer but he does not look, just sits. Then Towelli, big PSU boss, appear with white man. Mr Bright look up and see white man. Suddenly he find strength, or some of it. He jumps up, snatches sledgehammer from man and comes running at Towelli and white visitor. He is shouting, I cannot understand what, and he is swinging sledgehammer like he wants to kill someone.

Q. What happened then?

A. Someone trip him up. Then they start beating him. I go away. I have duties to do. Mr Bright does not come back to cells, and later I hear he is dead in car accident. I am very sorry for Mr Bright. I am his friend and I take his papers from where he hides them and keep them so that I can show how Gregory is not torturer like others but helps his prisoners and does them favours.

Q. The white man with Towelli, did you recognize him?

A. Oh yes, boss. He was Mr Ellis, white man whose house I visit in Kampala, friend of Idi Dada's.

Q. This session of the Commission's interrogation of this witness stands adjourned.

20

Sairey sat in the back of a green Volvo Estate and read the document with the help of a dull maplight. Mrs Marsden was driving, with Vita next to her. A car's length behind, Archbell was driving Lightoller in a red BMW. The frivolous thought flashed across her mind that security people showed their patriotism in strange ways, but she knew it was merely a lightning before death.

She leaned back in her seat and closed her eyes. Oblivion would be best, but when it wouldn't come, she found she had achieved an odd kind of relief through sheer satiety. How many impossible things was it really possible to stomach before breakfast? She menued them in her mind.

One: her father had been having an affair with his best friend's wife while his friend was in jail.

Two: accused of this by her mother, her father had killed her.

Three: aided and abetted by his sister and his mistress, Nigel Ellis had then dumped the body, burnt out her car, and waited to be told that she'd been murdered by kondis.

Four: he had then betrayed his mistress and her fugitive brother to the authorities.

Five: he had finally connived at the murder of his best friend.

There was a *Six*, which comprised what he had done to his only child. She merely toyed with this for fear that it should prove too easy to digest. But it was at *Seven*, superficially the least revolting dish on the menu, that she finally gagged.

Seven: in a fit of pique, he had started writing his memoirs, thus concentrating all the expert attention of his erstwhile colleagues on just those parts of his life which he must have prayed would remain buried for ever.

Funny; you couldn't be sure you knew someone well enough to affirm them incapable of murder and treachery, but you would stake your life they were too clever to do anything really stupid.

She found, after a very short while, she didn't have the talent for such detachment and sought diversion in anger. Reaching forward, she rapped Vita hard on the shoulder.

'How much are they paying you to get mixed up in this grisly job, Vita?' she demanded. 'Or have you always resented my father so much that you did it for free?'

Vita turned to look at her. 'I get paid what I've been paid for the past sixteen years,' she said calmly.

'How long?' said Sairey, taken aback.

'Sixteen years. Not full-time, of course. It was your grandfather who recommended me to the Co-op. He got to know me quite well as a friend of your mother's and felt I might be of use to their Medpsy Department.'

'So Daddy knew that . . .'

'No. Of course not. People only know their own sections. We don't have Christmas parties. I was . . . am . . . merely a consultant on interrogation psychology.'

'Is that grown-up language for torture?' said Sairey.

'No. It's concerned mainly with assessing how genuine defectors are. Also, how suitable prospective employees are. It has dovetailed nicely with my main areas of professional interest outside the Co-op.'

'Nice for you,' sneered Sairey. 'So what have I been, Vita? A footnote in a thesis? Or maybe even a monograph in a learned journal!'

Sairey yelled the last words so loud that Mrs Marsden jumped in her seat and the car lurched towards the kerb. Who the hell was Mrs Marsden, anyway? Sairey asked herself. The female equivalent of the stud chauffeur? Absurd!

Vita's voice was unchanged. Calm, patient, clear. The voice of a woman who has viewed all her works and seen that they were good. At that moment, Sairey hated her.

'When a co-op was set up to deal with your father's proposed illegal memoirs, I was seconded to it as the Medpsy representative. At first, I resisted on the grounds of my acquaintance with the family. I was persuaded by the argument that I would be able to ensure that proper justice was done.'

'And me? You wanted to do justice to me by ferrying intimate details of my treatment to all those grubby ears so they could sift through them, looking for crap to throw at Daddy? Christ, Vita, whatever professional list you're on, you ought to be struck off it with an iron bar!'

For the first time, she felt she had drawn blood. Vita turned her head away and took her time in replying. When she finally spoke, her voice hovered on the edge of uncertainty.

'Your father's memoirs and your problems are related, Sairey. More closely than I could have guessed, to start with. The very fact that he was writing them was probably one of many triggers that reactivated your trauma. When I heard that you were unwell . . .'

'Heard? How did you hear?' Sairey's mind must have been getting more finely attuned to the sub-texts of this shadowy world, for she provided her own answer almost instantly.

'Dr Varley! He was Mummy's family doctor, wasn't he? And someone with a job like Sir Joe's wasn't going to rely on the Hippocratic Oath when he could use the good old Official Secrets Act to gag his quack, was he? And it was Varley who suggested you!'

'I never told you that, Sairey,' mused Vita.

Sairey didn't even blush at this reminder of her eavesdropping, but she did accept this reminder of the sharpness of Vita's perceptions.

'So you agreed in advance to take me on as part of the job?' she accused. 'You can't even claim it happened by accident.'

'I took you on to protect you,' said Vita, with her old crispness. 'You are the daughter of the best friend I ever had, and I was determined no harm would come to you. I thought when I started that it was simply the trauma of your mother's death I was dealing with. It wasn't till the hypnosis sessions had got under way that I began to wonder if the trauma were not something much more massive than simple loss. And when I realized what was actually behind it, I felt I could not know how best to proceed without reference to the other facts as they were being collated by the Co-op.'

'Crap,' said Sairey. She didn't even shout. 'You've always hated Daddy ever since he took your best friend away by marrying her. It must have blown your mind when you realized what you might be able to pin on him. God, now I think of it, this unbiased committee of enquiry, I don't know who else is on it, but the ones I do know seem hand-picked because they've one thing in common: they all hate my father! There's you; there's Grandad, who always blamed Daddy for Mummy's death, even before you went running to him with my tape; and there's that animal Archbell, whose whore he stole!'

Vita said mildly, 'There *are* others on the Co-op, Sairey. And while normally it would have been chaired by our Deputy Director, that is to say, Sir Joe, it was decided that, in this case, his personal involvement made that inappropriate.'

'So, who *is* in charge?'

Vita replied, 'The Director.'

'And that guarantees fair play, does it? So where's this Director now when we need him? Because this doesn't feel like a posse galloping to protect my father, it feels like a lynch mob!'

'The Director will be there, never fear,' said Vita. 'Sairey, leave the debate about how right or wrong I've been till later. Try to look in on yourself and see how much of your aggression against the Co-op is merely a diversion of the aggressive feelings you now have towards your father. I was never happy with the story of your mother's death, nor with your father's reaction after it. But if we look at the new problems that . . .'

'Shut up!' screamed Sairey. 'Don't lecture me! You've got what you want, all of you. You started off after Daddy to stop him revealing the squalid truth about the way you fucked around and fucked up in Africa. But you knew that to most people, revealing all that crap would make him a hero. Now, you think you've got something on him which makes you feel good! Not that you're going to use it in the cause of justice. No, it just gives you something to blackmail him with. So, no more lectures. I'll decide what I feel about my own father. And I'll make up my own mind what to do. From now on, just keep out of my life and keep out of my mind and above all, keep quiet!'

She sank back in the seat, trembling with emotion. Were all declarations of independence like this? Screams of defiance on the cliff edge of despair? Outside, the rain had slackened to a damp haze which gave everything a luminous, insubstantial look. Houses, lamp-posts, hedges, trees, all went tumbling by like the furniture of a dream. A dream of darkness. What had her father really had in mind when he chose that title? She felt her mind like an ant in a wrecked anthill, scurrying from one piece of debris to another.

No one spoke. She closed her eyes for a while, then opened them again. Inside was worse than out. She let the pattern of approaching headlights sweep across her sight. It might have been hypnotic, except that she was done with hypnosis. She had lost track of time and space, but an instinct as old as both made her wind down the window, and in rushed the cold salty breath of the sea. It was not yet in sight, but the awareness of those surging cleansing waters so close filled her with a great longing to dive deep into their healing darkness.

Now they were among the dunes, moving slowly along the track which led to Aunt Celia's house. She felt a surge of distracting indignation as she thought of what the men in her family had done to Celia's life. Her girlhood had gone in keeping house for her father and bringing up her brother; then, just when it seemed that she might get a little mileage out of her maturity, the Mau Mau attack had condemned her to twenty years of nursing an invalid. A brief respite, then she found herself bringing up her brother's child.

And now, when it must at last have seemed that her life might be touched with a sunset serenity, her brother had tracked trouble into her home once more.

The Volvo came to a halt before the gate in the security fence. The BMW stopped behind them, Archbell got out, went up to the gate, and tried it. Then he came to the driver's window.

'Locked,' he said. 'What's the silly old bat keep in there? Monte Cristo's treasures?'

'No,' said Sairey. 'She just likes to keep bastards like you out here.'

'Not to worry,' said Archbell. 'She'll let *you* in.'

Sairey shook her head in disgust rather than denial, and said to Vita, 'So that's why you really came looking for me? Operation Antenor *would* need a Trojan Horse, wouldn't it?'

Vita said wearily, 'Sairey, you've got many more reasons for wanting to see your father than we have. Don't make a vice out of a necessity.'

'So we're into pragmatism now?' said Sairey. But she got out of the car and went up to the gate. Through the bars, she could see the house. There was no sign of any lights but she guessed this just meant the shutters were up. Was it her father or Celia who had felt the need to settle down to meet a siege? She pressed the bell button, long and hard, waited a few moments then spoke into the microphone grille.

'Aunt Celia, it's me, Sairey.'

'Sairey. Nigel, it's Sairey.'

A pause, then she heard her father's voice, at the same time anxious and angry.

'Sairey, what the hell are you doing here? I told you to go back to Essex.'

'I had to see you, Daddy. But I'm not alone.'

'Who's with you?'

'Grandad, Vita, Mr Archbell,' she said.

There was another pause in which she heard Mop and Polly barking distantly.

'And is that everyone?' he asked, with no detectable irony.

'Yes. Oh, I'm sorry. Vita's friend, Mrs Marsden, she's here, too.'

Suddenly Celia's voice spoke inaudibly and there followed a silence as Ellis switched off the mike. Then he came back on again.

'All right, I'm opening the gate. But be careful. Celia

220

says the dogs have heard some kind of noise outside the kitchen and she thinks someone may have got over the fence at the back.'

Allan.

Sairey spoke urgently.

'Daddy, be careful, if Allan shows up . . .'

'Allan? Is he coming too? What is this – open day?' Her father's voice sounded much more carefree. 'All right. I'm opening now.'

There was a click as the magnetic lock released itself.

Sairey began to push at the gate. Ahead, a line of light appeared in the dark square of the house, rapidly spreading to a rectangle as Ellis opened the front door to welcome them.

'Daddy, stay inside!' called Sairey. She could hear the dogs barking again and she trusted them more than her straining ears, which could hear nothing but the surges of the incoming tide.

But her father ignored her, advancing over the threshold till he stood silhouetted against the gold of the entrance hall light. Like a hero on a Grecian frieze. Or a target on a fairground stall.

'Daddy!' screamed Sairey, pushing through the gate and starting to run.

To her left, something moved. There was a sharp double crack and she saw her father spin round. Then, where he had been, there was only the untroubled light.

Behind her she heard the others spilling through the gate and there was another shot, but she had no attention to spare for anything but the crumpled figure on the hall floor. The light went out and she gasped in terror, thinking it must mean that Allan had got into the house, but as she reached the doorstep, she saw that it was Celia who had quick-wittedly switched it off, before stooping to minister to her brother.

He lay on his back. The heavy Norwegian sweater he was wearing had two holes burnt into it over the breast-bone. Smoke, and the sickly smell of burning wool were still rising from them. Miraculously, he was not yet dead. His limbs twitched and his eyes were open as Celia raised her head.

'He'll be all right, he'll be all right,' urged the old lady with what seemed a desperate optimism. Sairey knelt beside him. He recognized her and smiled. Her emotions were in a turmoil which made the confusion she had experienced in the car seem like flat calm. He might be dying, he must be dying, and all she wanted to know was whether he had really killed her mother. But how do you ask your father this as he lies in his death throes?

'Let me see.' It was Vita, urgently professional. She pushed Sairey aside and stooped over the recumbent man as if her expertise with the body matched that with the mind.

Her examination took hardly a second.

'Let's get him somewhere more comfortable and take a closer look,' she said. 'There'll probably be some nasty bruising.'

'Bruising . . .?' said Sairey.

Vita brushed the charred edges of the sweater holes with her fingers then widened them out, revealing, not pulverized flesh, but something like a section of burnt mattress.

'He was lucky they didn't aim for the head.'

Lightoller was in the hall, too. Celia had vanished up the stairs. He and Vita got Ellis to his feet and helped him towards the lounge. Sairey leaned against the wall, finding the resurrection even harder to assimilate than the death. He looked towards her. His face was grey but he tried to smile.

'Sairey, I'm sorry,' he said. 'You must have thought I

was a goner, eh? Get the girl a drink, someone. Get me one, too. By God, I need it.'

'No drink till we see how badly damaged you are,' ordered Vita, starting to drag his sweater over his head. Impatiently, he refused her help and with difficulty managed the task himself. But he let her unbuckle the bullet-proof vest.

Archbell came into the room, replacing an automatic in a shoulder holster. He stopped short when he saw Ellis, then came forward with a smile like a snarl.

'I might have known,' he said. 'Always a survivor, Nigel.'

'And how's the chap who did it? Surviving too?'

'Who knows? I took a shot at something but it could have been an insomniac rabbit. This looks like official issue. Confidential files weren't the only thing you purloined, then?'

He had picked up the discarded vest.

'Office perks, Archie. I thought you'd have understood all about them.'

Colour was coming back to Ellis's cheeks and colour into his chest, too, in the form of a cloudy bruising. Vita touched it and he flinched.

'No ribs cracked, I'd say. But a cold compress would help,' she said.

'I'll get it,' said Celia, who had reappeared in the doorway. She smiled wanly at Sairey, then went towards the kitchen.

Ellis said, 'Now can I have that drink, for God's sake? Then perhaps someone will explain what's happening. Why are you all here? And why should young Allan have taken a fancy to shooting me, if that's who it really was?'

'How many enemies have you got?' said Archbell.

'More than I care to count, I daresay, but I wouldn't have ranked Allan Bright among them,' said Ellis.

'Not even if he found out the truth about what you did to his parents and uncle?' said Sairey.

'And what would that truth be, my dear?' said her father.

'That you betrayed them. Like you've betrayed everyone and everything else in your life,' she said.

He started up from his chair, his face aged with bewilderment.

'Don't you dare speak to your father like that!'

It was Celia, coming back into the room with a basin and a cloth. Her expression was angrier than Sairey had ever known it and she felt herself cowed as no one else present could have cowed her.

'Nigel, sit yourself down. Let's sort this bruising out, then we can deal with this ungrateful child's delusions.'

She forced her brother back into his chair, took a plastic bag full of crushed ice from the basin, wrapped it in the cloth and pressed it to his chest.

'They're not delusions, Auntie,' said Sairey in a low voice.

'Oh yes, they are. You imagine your father's betraying his country and his colleagues by writing these memoirs, don't you? Well, let me tell you . . .'

'No!' exclaimed Sairey. 'OK, so he is breaking his word and maybe he's doing it more as a matter of pension than of principle, but that's not what I'm talking about. What do I care about all the shabby little secrets people like this crawl around under?'

Her gesture was inclusive.

'It's what he did to his friends, to me, to Mummy, that I'm talking about.'

'To your mother? What he did to your mother?'

Celia's face was wreathed in alarm.

'Yes. Didn't you know? Didn't you guess? Didn't you

224

even help him? First he betrayed her by sleeping with Apiyo Bright, then . . .'

She was prevented from the ultimate accusation by her aunt's response, a curious compound of scornful amusement and something which was not unlike relief.

'*He* betrayed *her*? You foolish child! It was quite the other way round. The same family, true . . .'

'Celia,' said Ellis, warningly, but she was not to be denied.

'It was Sarah who took a lover. Sarah who gave herself to that black man Nigel had risked his life to protect!'

'Ocen?' And across Sairey's mind moved a picture of startling clarity, in which she saw her mother removing Ocen's bandages and gently massaging his wasted flesh.

'Yes, *Ocen*,' said Celia triumphantly, but the triumph faded as she looked at her brother, who shook his head sadly and said, 'Oh, Celia.'

'Is this true, Ellis?' demanded Lightoller.

'What if it is? I neglected her, perhaps. It was the job. And they were thrown together. It was an unreal and distorting situation . . .'

He was missing the point, thought Sairey. Or perhaps he was being very clever. For it was not the degree of Sarah's culpability that was at issue, here. It was its effects on the previous, unconvincing scenario, which had Ellis as Apiyo's lover. Now, with him as the deceived rather than the deceiving husband, all the motives fell into place; for killing his wife, for betraying her lover to the authorities, for betraying Apiyo, too, though incidentally, and finally, because Bill Bright had learned from his torturers who was responsible for his wife's death, for conniving at his murder also.

'Oh, you bastard,' said Joe Lightoller. 'Then you did kill her? I always blamed you for taking her there, but never for . . . oh, you bastard.'

225

He moved forward as if to strike Ellis. Mrs Marsden grasped his arm, only lightly, but it was enough to stay him. And Ellis looked round the room with stricken eyes.

'Is this what you think? All of you? Sairey . . .?'

'No more play-acting,' said Vita Gray. 'It's more than what we think, it's what we know. We have a witness, two witnesses. Gregory Kakuba. And your own daughter.'

Her tone was not gloating. But its level matter-of-factness was far worse. It spoke of certainty confirmed rather than shocking revelation. And it held the conviction of justice rather than the promise of revenge.

'Sairey? What's she got to do with this? Sairey . . .?'

'I saw you, Daddy. I thought it was a dream, a nightmare, but all the time it was a memory. I saw you putting her in a box. I thought it was a coffin, but it was a trunk or a bedding chest. And you weren't taking her to bury her, you were taking her to dump her in the wild for the animals and birds to . . .'

Her voice, which had been as steady and even as Vita's, suddenly gave up on her. Then Celia came towards her, her face grey with grief, saying, 'Sairey, please listen,' and that gave her tongue again.

'No, Aunt Celia, I owe you more than I can say, but when it comes to Daddy, you're not to be trusted. You were there. You got there just in time to see what he had done and all you did was help him. Perhaps my mother wasn't dead then, perhaps she needed help too, perhaps . . . but all you could see to do was what you were used to doing – sweep up the mess after your precious menfolk. I'll never forgive you for that. Never.'

'Sairey . . .' the old woman cried, looking for the first time older than her years. Then, after a despairing glance at her brother, she turned and rushed from the room.

Ellis cried after her, 'Celia!' Then, strangely, he turned

to Mrs Marsden and said, 'It wasn't meant to be like this.' And she replied, 'I'm sorry, Nigel. I can't help you now.'

'When could you?' he cried bitterly. 'When could any of you help anyone but yourselves?'

Archbell and Lightoller and even Vita were standing, rapt, like spectators at a riveting drama. And that was what it felt like, thought Sairey. A play, the latest melodrama, which might not get the critics' applause, but, by God, it would pack in the coach trippers for decades! This was her way to survival – to find some spot in her mind where she could relax like a tripper, and know that no matter how violently each *coup de théâtre* hammered her heart, eventually the curtain would fall and ordinary, everyday life would carry on. So, enjoy the final act, she told herself hysterically. It's been bloody marvellous so far, but can the playwright keep the shocks and tension going through to the end? It needs something new here, a dramatic entrance perhaps . . .

On cue, the door opened and Allan Bright stepped into the room.

Archbell's hand went inside his jacket and Sairey screamed, not knowing if she were screaming a warning to her father or to Allan. She didn't have to find out. The barrel of a gun appeared, resting on Allan's left shoulder and a voice said, 'Easy, Mr Archbell, and no one else need get hurt.'

Then Peter Kanyagga was in the room, too, his pistol shepherding them all into a loose, easily targetable group around the seated Ellis.

'That's fine,' he said. And his eyes met Sairey's and he smiled as though he'd read her recent thoughts and he said, 'So here we all are, just like in those cosy detective

227

plays they used to write before the war, all lounging around the library waiting for the final solution. Well, they got it and so shall we. Now, let me see, who shall begin?'

21

'No volunteers?' said Kanyagga after a little pause. 'Then let me set the ball rolling. My name's not Kanyagga, of course, but it will do. And I am a supporter of Mwakenya, but that's not the big thing in my life. Kenya will sort itself out sooner or later, but there are other problems, much more pressing, which need concerted action in Africa and world-wide.'

'You're ANC,' said Vita Gray.

'Indeed I am. I was sent to England to further the cause, not as a public face but behind the scenes, raising funds and public consciousness, that sort of thing. Shortly after I arrived, I was told that Mr Ellis here was writing some memoirs which might be of interest to me, first because they blew the lid off British and Kenyan support for Amin in the seventies, but also because they were going to reveal the degree to which there has always been unofficial official British connivance with white regimes in Africa, sanctions-busting in Smith's Rhodesia, for instance. And all kinds of covert support for South Africa.'

'What about covert support for the ANC?' sneered Archbell. 'Were you as interested in having that published?'

'It exists,' admitted Kanyagga. 'Naturally, we don't wish to embarrass our friends. But we had pressing reasons to be interested in an ex-security man's revelations. Just over a year ago, approaches were made from what we identified as British security sources, offering to trade advice and assistance for access to our intelligence networks in South Africa. We were interested. A meeting was set up in Botswana. Driving there, our two representatives were forced off the road and killed. After that, we lost interest in deals with Britain, but we never lost interest in who was responsible.'

'So you went to see my father,' said Sairey.

'Who was strangely reluctant to admit common cause with me,' said Kanyagga, looking at Ellis, who had shown little reaction to this latest interruption. From time to time he looked up at the ceiling as if trying to penetrate it to his sister. His face was pallid and his expression withdrawn and distant. Kanyagga paused courteously as if offering him the right of reply, then went on.

'Not so strange, perhaps, was that soon after I made contact with him, I found I had company, two gentlemen called Cilliers and Kirkman. Colonel Cilliers and Lieutenant Kirkman, as I discovered they were later. You recall them, I'm sure, Miss Ellis. They were so keen to save you from the importunity of the nasty kaffir.'

'Yes, I remember them,' said Sairey. So far, she felt completely indifferent to what Kanyagga was saying. No new drama this, merely an interlude in which she might gather her thoughts and see if there were any future where she could hope to survive with the knowledge that her unloving father had murdered her adulterous mother.

'They would like to see me dead, I am sure. But BOSS treads very warily in Britain, now. There have been too many scandals in recent years and their political masters are reluctant to risk alienating a country that is still their best friend in the West. So, on the whole, they contented themselves with trying to scare me off till a nice accident could be arranged. Mr Ellis, too, they hoped to scare into silence, and in this they looked for aid, or at least non-interference, from his former colleagues in the Co-op. But, despite the fact that every man's hand seemed

230

turned against him, and every woman's too, he showed a dogged persistence that eventually got his enemies panicking. Isn't that right, Mr Ellis?'

'This has gone far enough,' said Ellis. 'This is no longer important.'

He was looking at Sairey and there was an anguish on his face which almost made her sorry for him. Almost.

She said, 'Important? Do tell, Daddy. What is it that you *do* find important?'

Kanyagga said gently, 'Please, just a little longer, Miss Ellis. I may be able to help.'

'Help? A plea in mitigation, you mean? So that he'll just get off with probation for killing his wife and betraying his friends?'

Kanyagga frowned and said, 'As for your mother's death, I'm sorry. I know nothing of that. But for the rest . . . please listen. They decided that the only way to guarantee your father's silence was to have him killed. But it had to be a killing with no strings. Mr Bright here presented himself as the ideal candidate. Already suspicious of your father's role in his parents' death, it would take just a little piece of hard evidence to trigger him off. He got that tonight with Gregory Kakuba's submission to the Commission on Human Rights. He had it on him when we . . . met. I read it with great interest. The thing is, I was present at Kakuba's examination, as an observer. Mwakenya has many friends in Uganda. It was a closed session, so someone must have paid a lot of cash for a transcript. And it was a most accurate transcript. Except for the end.' He paused and looked at the assembled faces. Just like the detective in an old-fashioned play, thought Sairey; inviting the culprit to make a break for it through the library window, where PC Plod is waiting. She felt a fit of hysterical giggling build up in her throat.

Then Kanyagga resumed, speaking with great emphasis.

'In my recollection, when Kakuba was asked if he recognized the white man whom Bill Bright tried to attack in the PSU compound, he said, no, he'd never seen him before. So it wasn't your father, Miss Ellis. Whatever else he might have done, he did not connive at Mr Bright's death, nor, by implication, did he betray this boy's mother and uncle to the authorities. You know that now, don't you, Allan?'

'Yes,' said the young man, speaking for the first time. He looked weary, vulnerable and, as always in this condition, appeared little more than sixteen years old.

Sairey, regarding him steadily, no longer felt any urge to giggle. She wasn't yet ready to deal with this partial exoneration of her father, so she concentrated on her golden boy instead. How would I have felt about him if he *had* succeeded in killing Daddy, she asked herself? How do I feel about him anyway? I don't know him. The boy I imagined I knew wouldn't have been capable of shooting a defenceless man in cold blood, even if he hadn't made love to that man's daughter so soon before.

Nigel Ellis seemed to make a conscious effort to bring his thoughts back into the room, as though he might find some distraction here.

He asked with more of curiosity than passion, 'Allan, how could you decide to kill me, just like that? Surely there was enough of the past . . . enough of the present, too, in our knowledge of each other, to make me worth a doubt?'

'Yes,' said Allan. 'I'm sorry . . . but I didn't . . . I couldn't . . .'

'What he means is, it wasn't him, Mr Ellis,' said Kanyagga. 'You don't think they would leave something as important as your death in the hands of an untutored youngster?'

'No,' said Allan. 'It wasn't me. They were waiting for me when I got out of the car. But I might have done it. I was so certain, see, and I might have done it . . .'

He was talking to her, Sairey realized. He was refusing the total way out because he wanted no half-truths between them. She felt a surge of love for him but she dealt with it as easily as with the giggles. Where she stood now she wanted no one to lean on, and she felt she might collapse if anyone tried to lean on her.

She said, '*They* . . .?'

'The men who beat me up in the Square . . .'

'Kirkman and Cilliers,' said Kanyagga. 'They were expecting him, I think. And the idea was, when you all arrived they would blow Mr Ellis away, shots would be fired after them into the dark and later the boy's body would be found in the dunes, a gun by his hand, a bullet in his back. So Mr Ellis's death would be tidied away with much relief all round, a vendetta killing, no BOSS or Co-op involvement. Only two things went wrong. Mr Ellis seemed very well prepared. And I happened to be taking a walk among the dunes when I came across our Springbok friends about to turn young Mr Bright into a piece of evidence.'

He suddenly smiled broadly, as if pleased at his euphemism.

Sir Joe said, 'So, now we know where we are, perhaps you wouldn't mind putting that gun away, Mr Kanyagga.'

'Not just yet. There are still a lot of mysteries to be explained.'

He was right. Sairey's head was full of them, but she felt little urgency to seek their resolution. No matter how much light was shed, it could never touch the darkness in her heart.

But her father was still in search of distraction.

'So who altered the Ugandan transcript?' he asked.

'And who went blazing away with his gun when we arrived?' said Vita Gray. It was a typical Vita question, pointing the way to answers far beyond its apparently simple scope.

'No,' said Archbell. Then as if realizing the full extent of the accusation being levelled against him, 'No!' he bellowed.

His hand went inside his jacket, but before it could emerge, Kanyagga had taken one smooth stride forward and brought the barrel of his gun crashing down on the side of his head. His body slid to the floor. The Kenyan reached under his jacket and plucked out a pistol. Archbell tried to push himself upright but the black man pressed the muzzle of his gun to the other's forehead and he went still. Only his eyes moved, focusing on Mrs Marsden.

'Now, don't be silly, Archie,' she said, speaking in the tones of a kindly schoolmistress whose patience is wearing slightly thin. 'We can work something out, you know that. We always can.'

'Hold on!' commanded Kanyagga. 'What's happening here? I don't know who you are, lady, but if what I'm thinking is right and this is the man who got my ANC brothers killed, then no one's going to work anything out but me.'

Mrs Marsden was suddenly no longer a vague middle-aged lady, nor even a kindly school-marm. Her face was set and cold, she had all the self-assurance of Vita Gray, but while the psychiatrist's came from clarity of thought, hers derived from certainty of power. The truth of her ambiguous presence struck Sairey, then, with all the force of the obvious.

She said, 'You're the Director!' but no one paid her any attention as the woman spoke.

'I assured your masters we would put our house in order,' she said chillingly. 'But it is *our* house and it will be *our* order. If it's simple revenge you're after, you should have joined the Mafia. Check with your masters if you must, but check before you act, or this could be your last official action.'

'Is that a threat?'

'The price of ANC co-operation with the Co-op was that we put our house in order. That would also be our price for dealing with them. In my book, emotional operatives make for a disorderly house.'

'You should know,' said Kanyagga. 'So, you're the boss of this pathetic outfit. Look at you! A geriatric, a psychopath, a traitor and a butch headshrinker, all ruled over by a little old lady. If this is Security, what do the people you're meant to be protecting look like? Don't talk to me about putting houses in order. If someone was threatening us, like Mr Ellis there, we wouldn't have needed to form a committee to deal with him, I promise you!'

'For Christ's sake, shut up,' said Ellis wearily. 'Mary, this is all going wrong. You said nothing would come out about . . .'

'Stop whingeing, man,' said Mrs Marsden crisply. 'It's better out. And as for going wrong, it all looks to have gone entirely to plan to me. We've got what we were looking for.'

It was all getting too confused for Sairey's tight-stretched mind. Words were being spoken which made sense and nonsense simultaneously. She felt the same dislocation that reading *Alice Through The Looking Glass* had caused her as a child. She opened her mouth

235

to scream in protest, in appeal, in anger, in terror, in she-did-not-know-what. But before the sound could come out, the voice of pure reason spoke.

'I take it this Co-op has all been a set-up,' said Vita Gray calmly. 'And its function was not to find ways of stopping Nigel, but to flush out quite another Antenor, with Mr Archbell here as the prime candidate.'

'Yes. Vita, I'm sorry, but you see how impossible it was to let anyone else know. The Co-op had to perform its stated function with complete naturalness. Archie was not the only suspect, you understand.'

Mrs Marsden had reverted to her former self in addressing Vita. Her tone was conciliatory, apologetic. Perhaps, after all, truth was stronger than blind power, thought Sairey.

'I understand that I could hardly be a suspect,' said Vita Gray. 'I also understood that when, for the sake of the Co-op, I extended medical confidence to include you, I could expect total reciprocity.'

'Please, Vita, don't ride such a high horse. And ask yourself if your motives in pursuing Nigel were quite so Simon-pure as you'd like to believe!'

The woman had resumed something of her directorial tone. It was a mistake.

Vita Gray said indifferently, 'I'll send you my written resignation. Or you may prefer to forge it.'

She made for the door, passing Sairey without a glance. Curiously, that hurt, and when, only a few seconds after going through the doorway, she reappeared, Sairey felt her heart leap at the certainty that Vita had returned to speak to her. Then the woman was hurled into the room with such force that she fell over the kneeling Kenyan, and now the doorway was filled with the large form of Lieutenant Kirkman. Kanyagga had lost his gun in the collision with Vita. He dived desperately towards it, but the big South African moved forward and drove his foot into Kanyagga's face.

'You stay down there, kaffir,' he said, scooping up the gun. 'Man who can't even tie a good knot deserves to crawl on his belly, wouldn't you say?'

Cilliers was behind him. He looked pale and there was blood drying round an abrasion on his brow.

'Colonel Cilliers, this is a mistake,' said Mrs Marsden sharply. 'So far it's only an irritation. Don't turn it into an incident. BOSS used to be very professional. When an operation failed, you aborted and got out.'

'Was that in the good old days when we were all friends?' sneered Kirkman. 'Before even the Tories went soft on commie kaffirs?'

Cilliers said, 'Shut it, Dave. Mrs Marsden, there's going to be no incident. I agree, the operation's failed. What we *are* going to do is relieve you of the burden of our black friend here. No one will miss him. After all, I doubt if he really exists. Also I'm sure he will find your little ways with naughty boys in the Co-op hard to understand. They don't believe in wrist slapping, not when you've got an old tyre and a can of petrol. Better all round if we relieve you of this embarrassment and call it quits.'

To her horror, Sairey could see Mrs Marsden considering this. Or perhaps she was merely looking for some way round the dilemma. But Kirkman was not ready to wait for a mere woman's decision.

He said, 'Let's just take the bastard. No one can complain if there are no witnesses. You, Ellis, you should by rights be dead already, so why don't we start with you?'

It was probably heavy-handed joking, but they never found out. As he laid his gun barrel along Nigel Ellis's jaw, there was an explosion from the doorway. Kirkman let go of his weapon and grabbed at his shoulder. His hand found blood. He looked at it in amazement. Pain and shock were draining colour from his face and it looked as if some strange osmosis was sucking it all to his fingers. Suddenly he groaned, and fell like a tree. Sairey looked towards the doorway.

Fanny was standing there with a small automatic held in both hands. Her face wore its customary expression of untroubled beauty. It was impossible to tell if her accuracy had been a matter of luck. Cilliers found out. Turning, he cried, 'You crazy bitch!' and took a step towards her. She shot him in the thigh and he fell, screaming, with blood pumping from the wound. Then she tossed the weapon into a corner and, delicately stepping over the wounded South Africans, she knelt beside her husband.

It seemed to Sairey that now everyone had a function except herself. She was an underage spectator at an adults-only movie. She lost all sense of time. Was this what they called shock? If so, it was comfortably anaesthetizing, removing you for a time, at least, out of the world of blood and shots and betrayal. Vita moved swiftly among the injured, ministering first to the South Africans, before tending the lesser damage to Kanyagga and Archbell. Ellis and his wife were having the deepest conversation Sairey had ever observed them in. Perhaps, she thought almost lightly, Fanny was trying to explain her relationship with Archbell. Mrs Marsden was in the hall, talking rapidly, incisively, into the phone. Sir Joe had subsided into a chair, and lit a cigarette as if he, too, were resigned to a spectator's role, but his gaze, as it flickered from one face to another, was not the gaze of a spectator. His eyes met Sairey's for a moment and seemed to register nothing except her presence, her

238

position. Then recognition came, and he smiled at her fondly, but the smile died quickly as the gaze moved on.

Only Allan Bright seemed as totally detached from all this as Sairey felt. He stood close by her side, their hands touching but not holding.

He said in a low voice, 'What will you do?'

It was not a question that concerned her.

She said, 'Does it matter? And you?'

'The same.'

'Nice to have something in common.'

'Like murdered parents.'

'But at least not the same murderer.'

She looked at him now. Why it should be important that her father, who'd killed his own wife, should not have been responsible for the death of Apiyo and Bill Bright, she could not say. But it was important.

'No. I believe that now. It never seemed possible, not really.'

'But killing my mother did?'

'A crime of passion. We're all capable. But betrayal to death takes a special kind of coldness.'

There was an interruption. Newcomers arrived, quiet young men in casual clothes, who obeyed Mrs Marsden's commands like well-trained sheepdogs. Cilliers was carried out, presumably to a car. Kirkman, semi-conscious, was providing a problem. Kanyagga and Archbell, both still groggy, had managed to get to their feet. They made an odd couple, thought Sairey. The Kenyan paused at the door and looked at her.

'It's OK not to fight,' he said, 'as long as you do something worthwhile. Don't let them turn you into a watcher.'

He went through the door. Archbell said, 'The wisdom of Africa. We taught 'em to read and they got hooked on calendar mottoes. Mary, a word.'

239

His little animal eyes flickered towards Allan.

Mrs Marsden said, 'You, young man, make yourself useful. Could you give that pair of weaklings a hand?'

Two of her young men were still struggling with the huge frame of Kirkman. Vita Gray was trying to help. Allan, blank-faced, went forward and took a leg. Archbell waited till the four of them had negotiated the South African into the hallway, then, in a voice meant only for Mrs Marsden, but which Sairey caught quite clearly, he said, 'You know why I altered that transcript, Mary.'

'Do I?'

'That prison guard didn't know the man he saw, but he gave a very good description.'

'Yes, I read it.'

'Read it?' Archbell grinned his humourless, animal grin. 'So you did know?'

'That it was you who turned Mrs Bright and her brother in and had to make sure Mr Bright didn't come out to look for you? Of course I knew.'

'I did it to protect that fool Ellis from his own idiocy. We needed him in station.'

'Excellent motives. You never put them in a report.'

'Some things are better not put in reports. You'd know that if you'd had much field experience.'

It was a commonplace gibe against the Director, Sairey guessed. What was she? An administrator appointed to control the wild men? More than that. There was steel there, too.

'Field decisions are one thing,' Mrs Marsden said equably. 'Fighting our masters' policies by betraying secrets to another intelligence organization is another.'

'Not even when you're ordered to, like in Rhodesia?' he sneered.

'That was another world, another age. We must change or die, Archie.'

'Perhaps. But you know so much that you must know by now, whatever else I did, it isn't me who's been feeding information to BOSS.'

He spoke with a persuasive vehemence.

Mrs Marsden replied, 'Perhaps I do, Archie. What I certainly know is that you're not the kind of operative we want in the Co-op of the nineties. Enjoy your retirement, Archie. And please, don't even think of writing your memoirs.'

The helper tugged at Archbell's arm and he let himself be led away without resistance, in the end as pathetic as a dancing bear on a chain.

Mrs Marsden glanced at Sairey.

'I daresay you heard most of that? I shouldn't speak of it to young Mr Bright. His near-miss might have got revenge out of his system. It would be a shame to reinfect him.'

In this slow-motion world she was inhabiting, Sairey found that her mind was working at incredible speed, at least, relatively so. She had all the time in the world to work out problems or to study responses. Now she found the appropriate one.

'You make me sick, all of you,' she said.

'That's what surgery usually does to the layman,' said Mrs Marsden. 'Joe, I'd better go off with the convoy to make sure that everything's sorted out with minimum fuss. I'll leave you here in the bosom of your family to tie up loose ends, shall I? Then, tomorrow, we must have a long talk to make sure this kind of debacle can never happen again. I'll look forward to working closely with you on that, Joe.'

In that moment, Sairey's new computer-paced thought processes confirmed what she had half guessed as Archbell defended himself. It was Sir Joseph Lightoller, Deputy Director, who was the Co-op's Antenor, Joe

241

whose pro-white priorities, as he established the post-colonial African networks, had not been able to adapt to new situations, new thinking. And Mrs Marsden knew too, perhaps had known for some time, but she didn't intend to drive him out, let alone hand him over to the law. No, she was going to use him as she had clearly used Sairey's father when she got wind of his proposed memoirs. She had spoken to him, flattered him, convinced him that he was still valued, could still serve. And serve he had, but at what a price. And his reward . . .?

Mrs Marsden gave it.

'Nigel, thanks for your co-operation. Yours too, Mrs Ellis. It's all worked out reasonably well, apart from . . . well, never mind. I think in the circumstances, though, it might be inappropriate for you to return to active service. I'll have a word with Finance about an enhanced pension. They'll be in touch. And by the way, all your memoir material, notes, drafts, everything, don't worry about returning it. I've arranged for it to be collected.'

Nigel Ellis looked at her indifferently, as if not understanding, or not caring, what she said, but Fanny said, in the tone of amused puzzlement she reserved for servants who needed to be told twice, 'He's to have Africa, that was the arrangement.'

'Africa's not for wild colonial boys these days, Mrs Ellis. Besides, I think he's got other things on his mind.'

'After this, haven't we all?'

'Most of us will shed them, but your husband's going to carry his burden a bit longer, I think. Also, his judgement's flawed. You should know that, Mrs Ellis. Why should I trust a continent to a man who can't do what's best for his own family? That child should have known the truth long ago.'

She went through the door, passing Sairey, who wanted to scream, 'Don't talk about my father and me as if we're not here! We are here!' But she wasn't certain if it were strictly true.

Lightoller was standing, looking down at his son-in-law. His face was that perfect blank which gives away seething passions almost as much as their natural expression. My mother: his daughter: how are we both to deal with her killer? She watched almost dispassionately, as though looking for tips.

Fanny said, 'Joe, I'd like a word with you. In private, please.'

'What? Oh yes, of course.'

It was like watching a man given an excuse to step back off a ledge. Allan was right. Killing people had to be done fast; slow took a special kind of coldness. As he passed her, Sir Joe took her hand and pressed it. This was the hand that had caressed her mother when she first came into the world. This was also the hand which had passed on the information which had sent the two ANC men into that gully in Botswana. And God knows what other treacheries had started at this hand.

Perhaps he felt her reaction. He let go her hand without speaking and left the room.

Fanny said, 'Talk to your father.'

Suddenly, Sairey didn't want to be left alone with him. She said, '*Were* you having an affair with Archbell?'

Fanny said, 'Your father asked me to pass him passages from his memoirs for the Co-op to see. It was all part of the plan.'

'But how far did the plan take you, Fanny? How convincing did you have to be?'

'Does it matter, Sairey? Intention, action, what's the difference? In the end we're always what we pretend to be. Growing up is when you stop pretending about the pretence.'

'I don't understand you, Fanny. I've never understood you.'

'What's to understand? Talk to your father. Try listening, too.'

'Fanny . . .'

But there was to be no further putting off. Her stepmother had slipped out of the door and quietly but firmly pulled it shut behind her.

Slowly, Sairey turned to her father.

22

It was Nigel Ellis who spoke first.

He said, 'I'm sorry to have got you involved in this mess.'

Sairey needed a shocked moment to realize it was the Co-op plot he was talking about, not what had happened in Kampala, that night all those years ago.

This was a delaying tactic, at best a long road in, but she found herself accepting it with gratitude.

'It doesn't matter. You did try to get me to America.'

'Yes, when I realized how dirty it might get. I didn't know about Vita, by the way. I'd no idea that she was involved in the Co-op. All these years . . . but I should have guessed about Varley. They've made a fool of me, haven't they? I'm an easy man to deceive.'

His voice broke. Having accepted the slow approach to the darkness, Sairey was terrified by this threat of a headlong plunge.

She said urgently, 'Daddy, why did you let them talk you into it? Why didn't you just go ahead and publish your memoirs?'

He said, 'They would have stopped me, or tried so hard, my . . . our lives would have become a misery. I'm not sure if my motives would have stood up to the kind of public hammering they would have received. Mary Marsden's a clever woman. She probably guessed what I was up to among the files, long before I put pen to paper. I'd started writing when she came to see me. She said she agreed with much of what I wanted to say, she, too, was dedicated to change. But, she went on, effective change would come only from within, not from public exposure. I was persuaded. I *wanted* to be persuaded. This way, instead of saying my life's work was crap, I would be doing something to preserve the good in it. Also . . .' he laughed bitterly, '. . . she hinted that I would be taken back into the fold, that my voice in African operations would be a potent one. Principle and profit, who could resist? My twin excuses for writing the bloody memoirs in the first place!'

'You thought, all for the best,' urged Sairey. She found herself on the point of kneeling beside him to comfort him, then remembered what lay at the heart of this confrontation. Not reconciliation, but revenge; not a desire to understand, but a need to punish.

It was time for the headlong plunge before the long roundabout approach took her so far from the goal, that she lost sight of it.

She said, 'Why did you kill Mummy? Whatever she was doing, however angry you were, how could you do that to her?'

He tried to meet her gaze, failed.

'It was an accident,' he said wretchedly.

'An accident?' she echoed, with stern disbelief. 'You mean, like you pushed her downstairs, not meaning to do more than break a few limbs? Or you hit her on the head, only intending a slight fracture of the skull? What kind of accident, Daddy? What kind of bloody accident?'

Her voice rose to a scream.

'I don't know.'

'What?'

'I don't know. Not precisely.'

She stared at him in incredulous anger.

'You mean you can't remember? But you can remember it was an accident? Now that's a very convenient memory you've got there!'

In the full flow of her rage, she would have wagered there was nothing he could say to stem the tidal wave of contemptuous condemnation she was about to send rolling over him. But she would have lost.

'I can't remember, because I wasn't there!' he cried.

'Not there . . .?' Her mind, till now so clear, reeled drunkenly. All the anger and bitterness which she had looked to spit out, and suspected she would be spitting out for the rest of her life, began to melt and change and become something else which tasted, in part, of fear.

'You weren't there? Then who . . . Ocen? . . . Apiyo? . . . what are you saying, Daddy?'

The door burst open.

'Sorry to interrupt, Nigel,' said Fanny. 'But it's Celia. I thought she must have shut herself in upstairs during all the excitement, but I can't find her anywhere.'

'Celia? Oh, Christ,' said Ellis, rising from his chair. He looked at Sairey and said helplessly, 'I'm sorry.'

What was he sorry for? Not for killing her mother, the words were inadequate for that. He brushed past her and she heard him running up the stairs.

'Sorry for what?' she demanded of Fanny.

'Sorry for all the crap life hurls. He wanted to shield you, but he's got no talent for it. That's why we get along. I've got my own shields.'

'Why's he so worried about Aunt Celia?'

'Because truth-time is here, and all his shields have failed.'

Now Sairey was out of the room and running upstairs after her father. She found him in Celia's bedroom looking around as though he thought his sister was hiding somewhere.

'What the hell's she playing at?' he demanded angrily, but Sairey could see it was the angry despair of love.

247

Fanny said, 'I think she may have gone. She left this on her bed.'

She held out an envelope. Ellis reached for it, but Fanny said, 'It's addressed to Sairey.'

They watched her as she opened it. No doubt they would have given her privacy if she'd asked, but it made no difference and she had a sense that time was all-important.

There were two sheets, covered in Celia's strong, old-fashioned hand. There was a date, back in September, back when she'd been staying at *Dunelands*, Sairey recalled. Towards the end of her visit, she thought. After she'd met Kanyagga on the beach, about the time that Vita came . . .

The opening sentence confirmed it.

My dear Sairey,

I've just been talking to Vita Gray and something she has said, plus something you asked me today, has filled me with the most terrible fear. I was brought up to believe that the proper way to deal with trials and tragedies was to tuck them away, and not talk about them, and get on with life. To burden a child like yourself with past horror and future care seemed absurd. But I should have known from my own experience that such a burden is not so easily avoided or shed. And now this dreadful suspicion is on me that, far from compensating you (though I know how impossible compensation is, believe me) with protective love all these years, all that my silence has done is permit a darkness in you to fester and grow. I pray God I may be wrong. But if I'm not, and because I doubt your father will ever reveal the truth unless constrained, I shall write it down now. At my age the call may come swiftly and without warning and I might not then have time to tell you what happened.

First, there's something you must know about me which no other soul but your father knows. On that dreadful day in 1952 when those murderous terrorists attacked our farm, I did not hide unscathed in the barn, as all accounts said. They found me there and they violated me, many of them, six, a dozen, I cannot recollect how many. After they had gone, I crawled out and was able to help my father till assistance came. I told no one of my own ordeal till Nigel arrived, and even him I could only tell because he knew me too well to keep such horror hidden. He took me to a doctor who helped me physically and confirmed there was neither disease nor impregnation, but I neither sought, nor felt I needed, any help for the mind. It seemed simply natural to me that I should want to get back to a country of white men as soon as possible, and, happily, my father felt the same after his experience. It was not my intention, then, ever to return to Africa, but when some property business came up which could be most easily dealt with by my presence in Nairobi, and as this would also give me a chance to visit my brother and my niece, it seemed foolish not to go.

I soon discovered my mistake. In Nairobi, alone, with all my old acquaintance dead or departed since Independence, I found myself uneasy and unhappy. Black waiters, black shopkeepers, black drivers, all filled me with unease, and if I found myself in a room with nothing but blacks, I could feel panic rising in me. So I brought my business to a close with great haste and wired to my brother that I would be arriving several days earlier.

They never got my wire. Things were very uncertain at that time. So when I reached Entebbe and found no one to meet me, I hired a cab.

When I reached the house in Kampala, it was in darkness. I discovered later there was a power cut. The doorbell didn't work. But when I tried the door I found it was open. I went in and called. No one answered, but somewhere I could hear the sound of running water. I went towards it. There was a downstairs shower room. I pushed open the door and peeped inside.

It was dark, you understand. Perhaps anyone would have interpreted what I saw as I did. Perhaps not. But what I thought I saw was your mother under the shower, being attacked by a naked black man. I rushed forward and grabbed him by the head, and pulled him back. I think I had hold of one of his ears. He screamed and turned towards me, but as he did, he slipped down to his knees. I started to beat his head with my fists. I doubt if I'd have done him much harm, but to my amazement, I was now seized from behind in my turn, by your mother.

'What are you doing?' she cried in a furious voice.

'Ring the police,' I commanded, thinking she was merely hysterical.

'What the hell for?'

'To arrest this animal who was trying to kill you.'

Then she began to laugh.

'Celia, don't be so naïve,' she said. 'He wasn't killing me, he was . . .' I can't write what she said. It took a second for it to sink in. And then I was filled with such disgust and such rage that I hit her. All I could think of was that this was Nigel's wife, in Nigel's home, and I slapped her across the mouth with all my strength. That, in itself, was not enough to knock her down. But she stepped back and in stepping, lost her footing on the slippery tiles. As she fell, her head hit the brass shower regulator set into the wall.

I think she died instantly. I didn't see her move after she fell, but I didn't stay to look closely. I left the shower room and went down the corridor into what I think was the lounge. I felt sick and faint and had to sit down. I felt as if I was back in the barn on the farm at Nyeri, full of pain and shock and disgust. I am not trying to excuse what I did, but I want you to know what I felt. Suddenly the lights came on and I realized the black man was standing in the doorway. He had a robe round his body and he said, 'I think you have killed her, old lady.' I wasn't so old then, but I felt, and must have looked, antique. I went with him. I wasn't afraid of him any more. I still hated him, but not as a black rapist. He was simply the man who had brought shame on my brother.

I couldn't believe it when I saw he was telling the truth. I sat with Sarah's head on my lap and started to cry. The black man said something about getting in touch with his sister. It didn't make sense then, but I realize now that as a fugitive he must have been terrified at what might happen when Nigel came home. I heard him using the telephone but I didn't pay much heed. I don't know how long I sat there but when I looked up, Nigel was with me.

I told him as best as I could what had happened. He didn't say much. I can see now what a tremendous shock it must have been for him. A wife dead, that was enough. But to realize she had been killed by his own sister who'd found her in the embrace of the wanted man he had been harbouring . . . Of course, all I wanted to do then was explain and, if possible, atone. I said he must ring the police. I would tell them what

250

had happened and take full responsibility. It was then he told me not to be stupid, the first time in our lives he had ever spoken so sharply to me. Then he explained why this was impossible. He said we must take Sarah away from the house. He went in to talk to the black man whose name I now gathered was Ocen. What they said to each other I do not know, but soon after, they came back together and carried Sarah into the dining room. Nigel got some of her clothes and I dressed her. It was grisly but I was desperate to be doing something. Then Nigel brought in a long bedding box and he and the man, Ocen, lifted Sarah into it.

At this point Ocen's sister, Apiyo, arrived. It was clear from every point of view that Ocen would have to leave the house. We all went into the lounge to talk about it. I felt as if I were in a trance. If once I stopped, I would collapse. Then we heard a noise from the dining room. Nigel rushed through and found that you had come downstairs. You were still half asleep, but unfortunately, as Nigel snatched you up, you glimpsed your mother lying in the box. He gave you to me and told me to take you upstairs. But at some point, you wriggled out of my arms and went running back into the dining room.

I finally got you to bed and nursed you back to sleep, telling you you'd had a nightmare, a dark dream, that was all. Nigel and the woman, Apiyo, went off, he with the box in the Land Rover and she driving Sarah's little car behind. When they came back, Ocen was ready to leave, and he and his sister went off together. I could see the man was genuinely upset but I could feel little sympathy for him. All my feeling was reserved for Nigel and for you.

That is all my story. I took to bed and lay quite ill for several days. It was put down to reaction to the tragedy I suppose. You used to come in to see me. I could hardly look you in the face with the knowledge of what I'd done. Then Nigel told me I must take you home. I refused at first. It would be like living with a constant accusation. But he told me it was my duty, and our lives had to go on, and that I was the best hope for you to have a normal life, a decent upbringing.

So that's what I did. To start with, I did it for my conscience's sake and for my brother's sake. But soon I knew I was doing it for the sake of my love for you.

I am still so much of a coward that I pray you will never have to read this, though my heart tells me that one day you must.

Vita will, I hope, and I fear, take you to the truth. She is a woman of great strength. I hope she has great compassion to go with it.

Perhaps if I'd seen someone like Vita after the farm was attacked, after I was attacked, much of this would not have happened. Odd, isn't it, that my greatest joy, which was bringing you up, could not have happened without my greatest cause of grief and guilt?

I can say nothing to mitigate the harm I have done you. That it was an accident is scarcely the shadow of an excuse, knowing as I do that the 'accident' had its roots in my own deficient psyche. All I can say is that my care of you might have started in guilt, but it ended in love. Whatever else you think of me, never doubt that.

You will find that the house and the dogs are yours. Take care of them, the dogs I mean, and they will reward you with unstinting affection. As for the house, I pray that its memories will not be so tainted you can never stay there. You told me recently it felt more like home than anywhere else. So now I give it to you, a home.

Finally, forgive your father. He is a good kind man but he has always lived in a world of action and plotting and this has left him woefully deficient in understanding and insight. He has always needed someone to take care of him. Rather to my surprise, I am coming to believe that Fanny is the right person for him. She fears the world so much that she has to keep it at a distance, but she sees things very clearly from this detached viewpoint. And her attitude to you, which you seem to feel as indifference, might, with a little adjustment, be seen as respect.

But what right do I have to offer you advice? All I should be doing is asking forgiveness, not just for what happened but for concealing it for so long.

Forgive me. At least, try not to think too harshly of me.

With all my love,

Aunt Celia.

Was there nothing but pain, wondered Sairey. Would it ever be possible to read anything again without the anticipation of pain? Everything she touched these days seemed electric with it. She re-read the letter, ignoring the almost tangible impatience of her father. This time, she saw something beyond the pain, and it came to her like a blow that this was not just a confession and a plea for forgiveness, but a farewell.

She pushed past her father and Fanny and began flinging open doors, then downstairs to continue what she knew was a vain search. Seated round the dining-room table like the remnants of a failed dinner party she found Vita, Allan and her grandfather. They looked up in alarm, but she did not stay to offer any explanation.

'She's not in the house,' said Fanny, behind her. 'I've looked already.'

They were in the kitchen. Sairey found herself staring at the huge empty basket by the stove.

'The dogs. Have you seen or heard the dogs?' she demanded.

'I thought I heard a barking from the beach before, when we came back from the track after Mrs Marsden and the cars had gone.'

It was Allan. He and the others had followed to see what the excitement was about.

She pulled open the kitchen door to let in a rectangle of turbulent sky.

Her father said, 'Sairey, wait. Tell us . . .'

She turned round and thrust the letter into his hands and screamed, 'No one is to come after me. No one! Understand?'

At another moment it might have made her feel a twinge of triumph that her vehemence brought a look of alarm and surprise into the untroublable eyes of even Vita and Fanny. But there was no time now for such irrelevancies.

She ran over the garden and through the open gate into the dunes, climbing, climbing, till at last she reached the crest and began descending towards the level gleam of the tide-swept beach. On she ran, with no slackening of speed, not lightly, as when a child, but with will and muscle straining to their limits as each successive stride seemed to plough deeper into the sodden sand. Ahead, against the phosphorescent glow of the receding surf, she could see figures moving and for one beat her pounding heart contracted with hope. Then the figures were racing towards her, barking a welcome, and behind them the line of surf was unbroken.

Now she slowed down, her hands automatically fondling the eager heads of Mop and Polly as they gambolled around her. Before her, on the dark sand, she could see a darker patch, and her hope finally faded when she found herself looking down at the old tartan beach robe. She stooped and picked it up. The dogs woofed enquiringly. Then she put it round her shoulders and sat down on the sand and looked out to the sounding, surging, receding sea. Polly and Mop resumed their game of chasing each other along the water's edge, but after a few moments they came and sat beside her, one on either side, pressing close against the warmth of the old robe, and watched with her a while before falling asleep. But Sairey did not sleep.

Dawn, when it finally came, was the pinched grey of her mother's face as she lay in . . . not her coffin; in a container, it didn't matter what. This was simple memory now, and she could pick it over at her leisure or leave it alone for ever.

Now, the grey began to flush with pink and gold and the sea's wraiths eddied and curled above the living waves. Sairey stood up and stretched. Instantly awake, the dogs rose with her. She turned inland and started to walk away. Polly and Mop hesitated. The terrier ran to the water's edge and barked. The setter took a few hesitant steps after him, looked round at Sairey, made up his mind and went galloping in her wake.

Seconds later the little dog was there, too.

As she clambered up the dunes towards the house, she became aware of figures on the crest looking down at her. Her father, Fanny, Vita, Allan, her grandfather. They were standing slightly apart, as if to force her into an unambiguous choice of who she went to. She came to a halt a couple of yards away from them.

She made no effort to control her voice, but let it come out as it wanted, and it came out strong and even.

She said, 'She was the best of all of you. The only harm she ever did was by accident. The only motive she ever had was love. She was the best of all of you. The best of all of us.'

No one spoke. She saw them, oddly, as stall-holders in a market, each offering their special ware: love, respect, insight, passion, security. But she herself was no longer coming empty-handed to the market place. Now she, too, had things to offer.

'If you care to come inside, I'll see if I can find you some breakfast,' she said.

And walking past them, with the dogs at her heels, she went into her home.

there are complications –
and then there are just
unridables

Patrick Ruell is the pseudonym of Reginald Hill, novelist and award-winning crime writer. Born in County Durham, he was educated in Carlisle and at Oxford. Author of some twenty-six books, he is married and lives in South Yorkshire.

By the same author

The Long Kill
Death of a Dormouse